If you like one of our books you will probably
like them all!

Write for our free 20 page booklet of extracts from early books
- surely the most erotic feebie yet - and, if you wish to be on
our confidential mailing list, from forthcoming monthly titles
as they are published:-

Silver Moon Reader Services
109A Roundhay Road
Leeds
LS8 5AJ
United Kingdom

http://www.adultbookshops.com

or leave details on our 24hr UK answerphone
08700 10 90 60
International acces code then +44 08700 10 90 60

New authors welcome
Please send submissions to
Silver Moon Books Ltd.
PO Box 5663
Nottingham
NG3 6PJ
or
editor@electronicbookshops.com

Slaves of the Girlspell first published 2001, copyright William Avon
The right of William Avon to be identified as the author of this book has been asserted in accordance with Section
77 and 78 of the Copyrights and Patents Act 1988

SLAVES OF THE GIRLSPELL
by
William Avon

Also by William Avon in Silver Moon:
The Girlspell

1: Melanie

Melanie Kingston strained against the imprisoning straps of the riding machine, forcing the device to its maximum extension. As sprung rods thrust her backwards the Major's cock slid up the cleft of her coffee-brown buttocks, penetrated the rubbery oiled-ring of her anus and buried itself to the root in her rectum.

She groaned in mingled dismay and delight at the intimate intrusion, her breath rasping about the bit clenched between her teeth.

The Major's riding crop flicked across her sweat-streaked thigh and he hunched over her, clutching her swaying naked breasts. "Last furlong, girl!" he said huskily. "Give it your best!"

She thrust herself forward with all the strength of her legs, rebounding from the springs with greater force, impaling herself again and again on his hard rod of flesh.

She felt hot sperm spout within her.

Melanie woke with a start, blinking in the grey light of dawn as it filtered through the door bars of her kennel. Her fingers were thrust into the sticky cleft of her groin. It had been a dream! The Major hadn't ridden her last night. All the pack girls had been allowed to rest - because today was Hunt Day!

The realization banished the last of the sleep from Melanie's mind even as she felt warm slickness welling up afresh between her engorged public lips in anticipation. She was lubricating like a bitch on heat. But then that was exactly what she was - a bitch of the Markham Hall girlpack; a collared bondslave destined to be the sexual prize of whoever could catch her.

The thought should have inspired disgust and horror, but instead it only made her excitement grow more intense. She ran her finger deeper into her cleft and felt her nipples prick up and harden. Once again she was astonished at the transformation she had undergone.

Just a few days before she had been a constable in the

Hoakam district police force. Determined to prove that a black woman police officer was as good as anybody else, she had tracked down an ingenious cat-burglar named Amber Jones; catching her in the act of adding to her secret stash deep in Hoakam Woods.

But Jones had resisted arrest. In the struggle that followed a stolen oriental-styled black lacquer box Jones was carrying had burst open, revealing a curious keyboard-like panel within its lid and three ivory phalluses. Both women had immediately felt an inexplicable but overwhelming desire to use the phalluses on themselves. Jones had briefly escaped with the box but its influence had drawn Melanie after it. When she found the box, one phallus was missing and Jones' jeans and pants were lying discarded beside it, but there was no sign of Jones herself.

Unable to resist the lure of the box, Melanie had used one of the remaining phalluses on herself, stimulating an orgasm more intense than anything before. When she recovered she found herself in woods different from those she had been in only moments before. There was no sign of the mystery box, only the inexplicable feeling that she had travelled a tremendous distance in some unknown direction.

She soon found out how strange this new land was when she was captured by the owner of the woodland estate, Major Havercotte-Gore, and his niece, Arabella Westlake. Recognising Melanie as an 'outsider', she had been forcibly stripped naked and whipped, then given a stark choice. She could either be prosecuted for trespass and vagrancy, the punishment for which was public auction and degradation as a bondslave; or else she could volunteer for a year's service in the Major's girlpack. This meant, by the customs of this alternate version of England, that she would be worked like an animal, given to guests as a sexual plaything and hunted for sport.

Melanie chose the pack as the lesser of two evils.

She had been put into bondage, been intimately and hu-

6

miliatingly tested and examined, treated like a dog, run on a track naked, forced to make love to another packgirl and sodomized by the Major on his riding machine. But, against all reason, she found herself enjoying her subjugation. She became the First Girl of the pack and the Major's favourite, and his honest pleasure in her exertions, both sporting and sexual, made her feel more valued and more alive than she ever had before...

A key rattled in the outer door of the kennel room, interrupting Melanie's thoughts. The door opened and the lights came on.

"Time to get up, girls," came the cheery voice of Alison Chalmers, the kennelmaid. "We've lots to do before the hunt."

There were stirrings from the other cells as the rest of the pack awoke. With a clank of bolts Alison released the master lock of the tiered kennels. Melanie pushed her door open and crawled out onto the coconut matting that covered the floor. In a few moments there were twenty-two naked young women standing with her; stretching, rubbing their eyes and brushing back their hair. On the glossy black collars locked about their necks was a metal strip embossed with the words: 'PROPERTY OF THE MARKHAM HALL HUNT PACK', and a number. Melanie was number 9. The same number was imprinted in indelible ink on the coffee-brown upper curve of her right buttock, framed by a pattern of chain links and the Markham Hall crest.

Melanie felt the brush of silky naked limbs against her flanks and exchanged happy, anxious smiles with her sisters in bondage. She saw her own tremulous anticipation mirrored in their faces. Nipples of all sizes and hues were swelling and hardening at the thought of what was to come, and the air filled with scent of barely contained female excitement.

Alison's long switch flicked across rounded buttocks.

"Get along to the ablutions sharply, girls," she said. "Then straight outside for morning exercise. No dilly-dallying now."

In a chattering file the packgirls were herded towards the toilets. The prospect of the hunt was overwhelming. Thoughts of duty and speculations about the whereabouts of Amber Jones melted from Melanie's mind.

2: Amber

Amber Jones was roused by the toe of a boot prodding her side.

"Wake up, girl. I've brought you breakfast."

Amber squinted through bleary eyes. Narrow slots of low morning sunlight slipped past the sacking hung over the windows of the old loft, illuminating the disused three-sided planking storage bin she was lying in. Standing over her was a well-scrubbed and freckle-faced young man carrying a covered bowl.

Still half asleep, she mumbled: "Go away, Nigel. I'ss too early... You know I had a busy time last night."

Nigel Gosset prodded her again, this time less gently.

"You do what we tell you, girl. That was the agreement."

Amber came to her senses with a start, remembering where and what she was. Hastily throwing back her blankets she rolled onto her hands and knees and bowed her head over the young man's feet. The heavy chain padlocked around her left ankle jingled.

"Sorry, master," she said. "Your slave was not thinking - she really did have a busy night. Please forgive her."

She felt his eyes pass over her naked body, perhaps lingering on her buttocks which bore the crimson stripes of a recent caning. Gosset had helped put some of those stripes on her flesh. He was also responsible, together with four of his friends, for the well-used soreness of her vagina. She shivered at the memory even as a familiar tingle began to grow in her lower stomach.

"Sit up," he commanded.

Amber obeyed, sitting back on her heels and automatically clasping her hands behind her neck. The posture thrust out her neat, shapely breasts, which were also criss-crossed with cane marks. More stripes decorated her stomach and upper thighs. She felt the blood pulsing into her nipples, causing them to smart even more fiercely. Gosset watched her teats harden with open fascination, then reached down and squeezed a hot breast.

Amber bit her lip.

"Does that hurt?" Gosset asked.

"A bit, master - but in a nice way. Don't stop."

"You like what we're doing to you, don't you?"

"Most of it," she admitted. "More than I thought I would."

"You really wanted the cane last night."

Amber blushed but could not help replying frankly. "I know. I don't normally go out of my way looking for pain. But when it's mixed in with sex... well, it's different. It makes the pleasure more intense somehow - even if it is pretty exhausting."

Gosset put the bowl down and took off the lid to reveal a steaming helping of porridge. "You'd better keep your strength up then - because we're planning a lot more of both for you later."

With a fluttering stomach Amber ate. Gosset watched her with frank interest, as befitted the young master of an attractive sex-slave. She felt a warm slickness growing between her love lips.

How had she got herself into such an incredible situation, she wondered? But then who could have guessed what the puzzle box would contain. And it had been sheer bad luck that PC Kingston had turned up just when she'd discovered the box's concealed lock. What power within it had compelled her to use one of the phalluses contained inside when she should have been making her getaway? Of course she had got away, but rather further than she had planned! Using the phallus had somehow shifted her into a parallel England where outsiders had no rights and were considered fair game by one and all. Soon after

9

arriving she'd been captured and gang-banged by three of Gosset's friends. Escaping from them she'd run straight into the arms of Constable Bailey, who proved only too adept at dealing with young female lawbreakers. Convicted as a vagrant and illegal alien, she'd been sentenced to public flogging and pillory in the police yard, then sale as a bondslave.

Amber finished her porridge. Taking a deep breath she shuffled over to her waste bucket and squatted over it. She didn't try to hide anything and kept her splayed legs facing Gosset, who watched intently as the pee spouted from her cleft. A bulge began to grow in the front of his trousers.

Gosset, together with the others who had first waylaid her, had sneaked into the police yard one night with the lockpicks they had found in her bag. They offered to give her the tools to break out of her cell if she agreed to be their sex-slave. Amber had accepted, thinking she had more chance of escaping from them than official captivity. Besides, they had the phallus which might hold the key to returning home.

Amber finished wiping herself with the crackling, school-issue toilet paper and began to wash. She saw Gosset was getting impatient, but she knew she had to keep him waiting just a little longer. Part of their agreement was that she should be housed in reasonable conditions and be allowed to keep herself clean and tidy. This old disused stable loft was dry and reasonably warm, and she had food and basic toilet facilities. However, the rest of her scheme hadn't gone quite to plan. She'd thought she could play along with them, putting up with their demands while gradually turning their adolescent lust to her advantage. But an unexpected development had occurred - she was beginning to enjoy being their slave!

Gosset's eyes were locked onto her every movement as she quickly soaped herself over, causing the pliant globes of her breasts to glisten, working lather into the cleft of her buttocks and the silky hair-rimmed furrow of her love mouth. A hot bath would be delicious, but all she had was a flannel soaked in a pail of cold water. She shivered as she rinsed herself down, causing her nipples to crinkle and harden once again, then began vigorously towelling off. Gosset's breath rasped in his throat. He pulled off the old jersey he was wearing and ran a finger around his collar.

Amber had dabbled in a little S&M back home, a world away. But here slavery was an accepted part of everyday life. And her captors, though rank beginners, were learning fast.

The five young men had turned out to be senior pupils at Cranborough House, a local minor pubic school. At the moment the boys were alone in the school apart from Sister Newcombe, the school matron, having had their Easter holidays curtailed as part of the punishment for an offence for which they believed Arabella Westlake had framed them. Amber had already suffered an uncomfortable encounter with Arabella while she was in the police yard pillory, and the desire for revenge on that cruel and spoilt young woman was something she and the boys held in common. Amber had planned a means of achieving this and securing her own early release, but it was getting harder to keep focused on her objective. The boys were each having her individually two or three times a day, when they could slip away from the odd-jobs they were doing round the school which Sister Newcombe was overseeing. Then at night they were sneaking out for an enthusiastic gangbang, sustained by raw lust and the recuperative powers of vigorous youth. It seemed that however many times they emptied their balls into her they kept coming back with more.

Amber finished combing through her short-cropped hair and turned to Gosset. The poor boy was half bent over, shuffling his feet awkwardly and looking distinctly uncomfortable.

"There, I'm nice and clean and fresh for you," she said with a smile, knowing what was to come. "Now, how do you want me?"

With a grunt of barely contained need, Gosset took her by the shoulders and pushed her backwards onto the pile of blan-

11

kets and sacking that formed her makeshift bed. He straddled her chest, making Amber gasp as his weight drove the breath from her.

The sides of the stall were studded with metal rings and hooks, from which hung lengths of rope with ready-looped ends. With their aid Gosset quickly secured Amber's wrists so that her arms were drawn out from her body. Extra tugs pulled them taut until Amber winced. Only then did Gosset loop the rope ends about their securing hooks, opening up the hollows under her arms to his gaze.

For a moment their eyes locked and Gosset bent over and kissed her fiercely, as she had encouraged all the boys to do, probing her mouth with his tongue, allowing her to savour the fresh cleanliness of his hot breath. Then he sat back and, grinning maliciously, pinched her sore nipples so that she yelped in pain.

But it was all right.

She would take almost anything from them once they had kissed her; as long as there was that moment of true intimacy that reminded them she was a person. Now she was happy to be used casually, even selfishly.

He stood up again, the bulge in his trousers like a tent pole, and kicked her thighs.

"Spread yourself... no, wider than that."

Amber strained to obey, splaying her legs until they made a right angle. More loops of rope went about her ankles, leaving her heavy ankle chain in place. The boys were determined she would not escape from them a second time. Gosset hauled on the rope ends, pulling her tighter and wider until the big tendons on her inner thighs stood out.

Now she was ready for him, bound in the most basic and blatant position of sexual display and availability a woman could be made to assume, her crinkled pink cunt lips glistening and gaping so that the dark mouth of her vagina was exposed to his view. Amber thrilled as her instinctive feeling of helpless out-

12

rage clashed gloriously with her sexual arousal.

Gosset drank in her spread-eagled naked form for a second, then feverishly stripped off his trousers and underpants. She had a brief glimpse of purple-tipped penis standing out so hard and firm that it almost seemed to touch his stomach, then he fell upon her.

His silky-skinned iron-hard young cock penetrated her waiting hole and slid up into the slick ribbed passage beyond until his full length was lodged within her. Amber gasped as she was perfectly filled, then Gosset's pale buttocks lifted as he withdrew. He lunged into her again, rapidly building up a frantic rhythm, ramming in and out of her like a piston, his eyes screwed up, using her without any thought for her pleasure; his only concern to release the aching pressure in his balls.

As always with the boys it was over too soon.

With a shiver and shudder Gosset spermed inside her. He managed a couple more reflex thrusts, then collapsed over her bound body, head resting between her breasts, his hot breath tickling her swollen nipples, leaving her internal muscles contracting desperately around his shrinking cock as she tried to draw the last particle of pleasure from it.

After a minute Gosset recovered. He withdrew from her clinging cunt, climbed off her and reached for his discarded clothes.

"Please finish me off!" she begged him. "Just rub your fingers up and down my slit!"

Gosset shook his head. "Jackson said we should leave you wanting more. He thinks it'll make you more ready to please later."

Amber groaned and tugged futilely at her bonds. "Aren't you going to untie me?"

"But then you'd only bring yourself off. We know girls can do that just like boys. Don't worry, we won't leave you very long. Harris will be along soon. He's next on the rota."

"The rota?"

13

Gosset finished dressing and pulled a piece of paper from his pocket. Unfolding it he pinned it to a post of her stall. It was a list of her five joint masters' names with periods of the day set against them. "This is to make sure we all have you the same number of times," he explained. "And we can put down marks for how well you pleased us."

I'm on a fucking list! Amber thought. With marks out of ten!

But she had to ask: "Er... how well did I do just now?"

Gosset wrote a figure in a column with the stub of a pencil then grinned at her. "I'm giving you a minus."

"'A minus!"

He stepped between her splayed legs and slid one foot forward. The toe of his boot nuzzled into the split pouch of flesh at the junction of her thighs from which a sticky trickle of fluid was seeping. Amber immediately dipped her hips and squirmed desperately on her bottom, kissing the tip of his boot with her cunt lips as though trying to suck the leather into her so it might bring relief to her hardened love bud.

Suddenly Gosset pulled his foot away, leaving her rubbing on empty air.

"You got a minus because you kept me waiting too long," he said.

With a whimper Amber dropped her head back onto her blankets. She heard Gosset climb down the trap door and pull it shut, then his steps faded away on the ladder below.

This is what I've been reduced to she told herself bitterly, trying to ignore the terrible ache in her loins - being left so frustrated I'm ready to work myself off on a shoe! And she'd been worried at first that the boys' apparently insatiable intentions would wear her out! She'd happily take a caning again rather than be left feeling like this. But then that was the idea. And tonight, no doubt, caning was exactly what she would get. Did all boys in this world have such a natural talent for torture?

Miserably Amber tried to distract herself by thinking of her revenge on Arabella. Yes, that would be sweet. As long as they could find the girl from her own version of England that she had deduced Arabella was keeping captive somewhere. The girl must have found and used the last phallus in the puzzle box. Amber wondered dryly if she was having as much fun as she was.

3: Sue

Sunlight glowed around the dusty, faded curtains of the tiny window as Sue Drake woke in pain. Her whole body seemed to ache. Certain places were worse than others.

She was bound face down on the underframe of a narrow bed, wrists and ankles chained to the bed posts, her body resting on a lattice of canvass webbing. The heavy pale bells of her breasts had been forced through gaps in the fabric so that they ballooned outward again under the bed; hanging like fruit ready for picking. The scattered morning light revealed them to be scored by criss-cross welts and abrasions. Even the pendant nipples were reddened beyond their normal colour.

A little way down from her abused breasts a length of broom handle emerged at an angle from the webbing. Its lower end rested on the floor beyond the foot of the bed, held fast by cords tied to the bed legs. The upper end was lodged deep inside Sue's plump-lipped cunt, its shaft darkened by the female juices its presence had stimulated. It was another degradation, another step in her training to become the perfect slave, which seemed to be Sue's predestined role in life.

Yesterday, her Mistress had hired two men to abuse Sue for her amusement. They had handled her cruelly and used her for their pleasure in every way imaginable. Yet, after it was over, Sue had begged for more - and had been granted her wish. Despite still being sore and bruised from that encounter, twice during the seemingly interminable night Sue had succumbed to the temptation the broom handle had offered - even though she was allowed no pleasure without pain.

Rising from between the soft white hemispheres of her upward-facing buttocks was a thick sprig of holly. Its trimmed stalk, too slender for her to expel, was embedded in her anus. Every time she tried to pleasure herself on the broom handle, the movement caused the holly to do its worst. The inner cheeks of her buttocks and the soft swell of her upper thighs were ringed by scratches and pinpoints of dried blood.

Pain and pleasure. The distinctions were becoming blurred in Sue's mind, along with so much else.

She had no idea where she was or how she got there. She'd been on a cycling holiday. Passing through Hoakam woods she'd come across a strange black box with its irresistibly alluring phallus. After using it she had fallen somehow. There was a bruise on her head. She must have been unconscious. When she woke she found she was already a prisoner - a sex-slave. It all seemed too incredible. Perhaps she was lying in some hospital bed dreaming it all? No, it was real - more real than anything else she had known.

Down below her a key turned in a lock. Sue caught her breath. Footsteps clattered on the wooden stairs. It was the sound Sue both longed for and dreaded. The door of the tiny bedroom opened and Arabella Westlake walked in.

Sue's stomach knotted as she twisted her head round to look up at her mistress. Arabella was dressed in culottes, riding jacket and boots. In her hand she carried a horse crop. A smile twitched the corners of Arabella's fine lips as she took in Sue's prostrate form. She sat on the edge of the bed and ran her fingers down the hollow of Sue's spine. Reaching her bottom she pried apart the fleshy buttock cheeks and examined the damage the holly sprig had done. Sue whimpered as the movement drove more spines into her skin. Arabella smiled and turned to the foot of the bed. Untying the cords that secured the end of the broom handle, she drew it out of Sue with soft sucking pop.

16

"I see you were excited last night," she said, examining the glistening darkly stained head of the broom handle.

"Yes, Mistress," Sue said in a tiny voice.

"Did it hurt when you tried to pleasure yourself?"

"Yes, Mistress."

Arabella sniffed the stained handle, then flicked out a pink tongue tip and licked it delicately, savouring Sue's intimate honeydew. "Good," she said. "Did you come?"

"Twice, Mistress."

"Indeed. Despite the pain it entailed?"

"Yes, Mistress."

"Would you like me to remove the holly now?"

"Only if it pleases you, Mistress."

Arabella reached up into the humid haven between Sue's thighs and carefully plucked the holly sprig out of her slave's anus. Sue gave a shudder. "Thank you, Mistress."

Arabella took the dog leash which had been hanging over the end of the bed and clipped it to Sue's collar. Then she unlocked the padlocks that secured Sue's chains. Sue almost fell off the bed as she tried to move her numbed and stiffened limbs. Her breasts were ringed by white and purple weals where the webbing of the bed had cut into them. On her hands and knees she crawled awkwardly after Arabella as she was led down the narrow stairs.

In the low beamed sitting room below, food and water had been set out in two tin bowls. Sue drank and ate hunched over her simple meal, picking up her food with lips and teeth and making no attempt to use her hands. Her sore nipples brushed the floor. In one corner of the room her bike and cycle packs rested against the wall; a reminder of the world she had come from. Would she ever return?

When she was finished, Arabella led her through the back door and into a small overgrown garden, surrounded by a tall thick hedge. The sun was still low and there was dew on the grass, but the day promised to be a warm one. From outside it was apparent that the house was really a slightly reduced model of a half-timbered thatched cottage. In fact it was an elaborate children's playhouse fallen into neglect.

As she had been taught, Sue scraped a hole in earth of one of the flower beds and squatted over it like a dog. When it was filled with her wastes she wiped herself clean with handfuls of long grass, then carefully covered the hole in again. Shuffling back to Arabella she bent and kissed the tops of her riding boots, then looked up at her mistress with wide eyes full of fear and helpless adoration.

Arabella ruffled Sue's thick mane of shaggy blonde hair as one would pet a dog, admiring the curves of the girl's full, hour-glass figure, noting how her pale skin highlighted the marks of her various punishments. But Sue's face was the greatest delight; so innocent and open, so easily made to contort in distress or pleasure. Blue eyes that ran so readily with tears. She was a creature made to be moulded and mastered.

For a moment Sue thought she saw in Arabella's gaze the unreserved approval she sought with all her heart. To know that Arabella accepted the gift of her submission and loved her for it was all Sue wanted. She would live happily under her heel if she was granted that one gift. But then the look was gone and cool composure returned to Arabella's features.

"I shall be busy for much of today and won't be able to attend to you personally," Arabella told her. "But I have ensured that your training will not be interrupted. The girls have their instructions. I have something rather special in mind for you..."

And she showed Sue the new torment she had planed for her.

Outrage and disgust flickered briefly within Sue as she learned what was to come, even as she admitted with helpless resignation that it was entirely appropriate.

Sue said meekly: "If my suffering will please you, Mistress..."

4: Vixens

Long chains had been slung from the wrought iron angle brackets that projected at regular intervals from the inner walls of the girlpack yard. Onto these chains all twenty-two packgirls had been fastened. Their arms were held over their heads by snaplinks clipped to the rings built into the wrists of their thumbless, thickly padded, elbow-length black rubber mittens, which were known as 'paws'. Their flat-soled knee boots were of the same material. In between was naked flesh waiting to be decorated.

Alison Chalmers and George Platt, the head keeper, worked their way along the line of girls, each carrying a pot of body paint and a broad brush. Alison painted a red-brown oval on the girls' backs, extending from their shoulders to the upper slopes of their buttocks. Two additional brush strokes coloured the outer curves of their thighs. Platt in his turn put an oval of pure white on their stomachs, from the top of their pubic deltas to the undercurve of their breasts, then added smaller dabs on their sternums and throats. Two more strokes picked out the lines of their inner thighs.

Painting completed, Alison and Platt went back into the storeroom and the girls were left to dry for a few minutes.

From beyond the walls of their yard they could hear the excited barking of dogs from the kennels next to theirs. These were the animals that would be used to hunt them down. The noise made the girls squirm, clenching their thighs in an attempt to squeeze lovelips itching with nervous anticipation.

Melanie tried to steady her breathing. "Is it always like this before a hunt?" she whispered to Una, who was tethered beside her.

Una had short dark hair and a wonderfully lean and strong body with neat, high-set, pointed breasts. She'd been First Girl of the pack before Melanie had beaten her in a fight. Her initial resentment had been muted by Melanie's determination not to

19

let there be any bad blood between them, and now she seemed to have accepted her change in status.

Una gave a thin smile. "Yeah," she admitted softly. "You never get used to it. Some of the girls'll be wetting themselves soon. But you've just got to remember to run as fast as you can for as long as you can. Don't be frightened of the dogs; they might give you a few scratches but nothing worse. And anytime you're out of sight of them you can..." She hesitated.

"Yes?" Melanie said.

"Pee up against a tree, then double back on your tracks. If you can find a fallen branch or suchlike that you can rub in your slot that's also good. Confuses the hounds and makes the riders think they've treed you."

"Thanks for telling me," Melanie said as warmly as she could.

"That's so clever. Can... I try that as well?" Gillian asked tentatively.

Gillian was a slender blonde tethered on the other side of Melanie. She'd been persecuted by Una before Melanie came because of her upper class roots and for failing to please guests, so letting the pack down. Melanie had done what she could to improve relations between them.

Una looked at Gillian uncertainly for a moment, then smiled. "Sure. You just give them the best run you can."

"I will. I promise I'll make the Major proud of me."

Platt and Alison came back out into the yard with a box of masks and began putting them on the girls. These were very light shells of painted papier machÈ that went on their heads like caps, merging with their own tied-back hair, and were held in place by rubber chin straps. They had fox-like pointed ears and protruding snouts, cutaway on the underside so that their breathing would not be impaired. Melanie blinked through the eyeholes at her transformed companions. The fox-masks curiously complemented their naked flesh, producing a theatrical yet at the same time surprisingly convincing effect.

20

Platt emerged from the storeroom again with a smaller box containing some curiously shaped objects and stepped up to the first girl on the chain. Melanie watched him work his way along the line towards her with tremulous fascination, even though she knew what he was doing. As the Major had explained to her yesterday, the hunt would be a race against the clock so they had to know when each girl was captured. This was the most convenient method when any part of their anatomy could be made to serve some practical purpose.

Platt reached Una. From the box he took a small rubber ball studded with soft prongs. A six-inch length of fine chain trailed from it with a numbered metal tag on the end. Platt checked it against Una's collar number, then loaded the ball into the end of a smooth slim tube so that the chain hung within it. Una spread her legs and pushed her hips forward. Platt slid the tube up into her front passage with practised ease, then withdrew it leaving the ball inside her and the tag hanging beneath her pudenda.

Then it was Melanie's turn.

She gulped and spread her legs obediently. The applicator tube slid up into her moist hole easily, but she gave a little gasp as she felt the rubber prongs spring out inside her. Reflex caused her vaginal muscles to contract about the curious object. The radiating prongs did not hurt, but she was very aware of their presence, as she was of the chain and dangling metal tag shining brightly under her dark cleft of flesh.

As Platt continued along the line, Alison carried a wooden trestle into the yard, followed by a box brimming with lengths of brown fur. Then she began releasing the girls who were already tagged. As each was freed they quickly ran over and knelt beside the trestle.

When half a dozen girls were waiting, Alison returned to the box by the trestle and gestured to the first girl in line. She immediately laid herself over the trestle, resting her gloved hands on the far side and spreading her legs wide, so the cleft of her

21

buttocks and the dark crinkled pit of her anus pointed skyward.

Alison took one of the furry objects from the box and smoothed it out. It was an artificial foxtail almost two feet long. She stood between the packgirl's spread legs and slid the plug-end of the tail into her oiled anus. When it was in place, Alison took a long key from her pocket and inserted it into the hollow metal shaft of the tail and twisted several times. She tested the tail, pulling hard to check it was secure, then patted the girl on the rump. She got off the trestle and the next girl took her place.

Platt finished inserting the tags and released the rest of the pack, who joined the queue by the trestle.

In turn, Melanie laid herself across the trestle and looked back over her shoulder as Alison picked up another foxtail. Its mount was more complex than the simple rubber plugs that held packgirls' normal smaller false tails in place. Extending from the end of the mounting pin was a short length of soft rubber tube with a nut set into its tip. Alison bent over Melanie's rear and Melanie tried to relax her sphincter as the tube slid deep inside her.

When it was fully inserted, Melanie felt the key slide into the hollow shaft. Alison began turning. The key fitted the head of a screw bolt enclosed by the pin and which engaged with the nut. Turning the bolt pulled the nut closer and so caused the tube to bunch outwards. Melanie felt it swell up on the inner side of her narrow anal passage, intrusive yet darkly exciting. The rest of the springy metal mount ran up the cleft of her buttocks until it reached the small of her back where the fur of the tail itself blossomed in an outward curve. Alison removed the key and gave the tail a firm tug. It did not move. For the first time Melanie was truly plugged; her rear passage closed off to all other functions except for providing a mount for her new tail until somebody removed it for her.

Alison slapped her rump and Melanie got off the trestle and joined the other newly-tailed girls. The soft mass of bushy fur hung down over her thighs as she crouched on all fours,

22

teasing her bottom with its whisper-soft touch.

In a few minutes the whole pack had been similarly fitted out. Neatly marshalled into three ranks they all crouched on their hands and knees as Platt inspected them.

He nodded in quiet satisfaction. The transformation from human to animal was complete. Their black boots and gloves resembled the black 'socks' of a fox, with their human fingers concealed and constrained by their paws. Their tongues were silenced by obedience and training while the nipples on their dangling breasts were swollen and hard with anticipation. Every movement reminded them of the foreign devices lodged inside their tender orifices. Half-veiled by bushy tails, swollen nether lips pouted glistening from between sturdy thighs. The air thickened with the musky scent of helpless female arousal. The Markham Hall bitches had become vixens ready for the hunt.

"Very good," Platt said finally, standing before them. "You girls who have run before know what's expected of you. For those that haven't, just remember this. You belong to the Markham Hunt, the finest in the South. You will run fast and you will run hard. You don't stop while you can still put one foot in front of the other. Today you're wild animals, so you don't give up even if you're cornered. Those ladies and gentlemen out there expect good sport not easy trophies, and that's what they're going to get. I'll be checking your times, and I'll have the skin off any of you caught inside ten minutes of the riders' start!" In the silence that followed, Melanie heard water splattering onto the cobbles as fear or excitement loosened some poor girl's control over her bladder. She didn't look round to see who it was. Platt consulted his pocket watch. "Right, it's time. Make me proud of you."

He picked up a long switch. Alison opened the inner gate of the yard and together they herded the girls through the covered passage beyond in a press of naked limbs and bobbing tails. On hands and feet with their bottoms high, the pack surged out into the stone-flagged stable court. The barks and yaps of the hounds got louder. Melanie's heart was thudding. In a tight group they were driven through the arches that opened onto the great oval of gravel that lay before the Hall itself.

And there were their hunters waiting for them.

There were thirty five or forty riders, both men and women. All were immaculately turned out either in red or black, but with narrow coloured sashes slung across their shoulders. Major Havercotte-Gore alone amongst them was wearing a distinctive pink jacket. Most were already mounted and stirrup cups were being handed round. A cheer went up as the pack appeared and silver goblets were raised in ironic toast to them.

Melanie felt their eyes upon her and her stomach knotted afresh. The cosy confines of the pack yard seemed a long way away. Suddenly she was horribly aware of her nakedness and was desperately grateful for the small degree of anonymity her mask offered.

The pack was brought to a halt before the riders. Platt's switch flicked out over their bent backs. "Make a line!" he commanded, and they scampered to obey him, spreading out until they formed a single row facing the hunters, kneeling almost shoulder to shoulder.

"Show!" Platt said.

With the rest, Melanie sat back on her heels with her back straight and knees spread wide, folding her pawed hands behind her neck. The hard chocolate cones of her nipples were standing up from the heavy domes of her out-thrust breasts. The metal tag hanging under her mound of Venus twinkled for all to see.

The hunters walked their mounts up and down the line of twenty two vixens, examining them with interest, commenting freely on their bodies and likely speed and agility in a chase. Melanie, as the only black girl, received particular attention. Under their gaze she felt her self-control weakening and began to tremble. The thought of what these people intended for her was too much to bear. A wave of sickness rose up within her...

Then she saw the Major beaming down encouragingly at her. Immediately Melanie felt a lifting of her spirits as a warm glow replaced the terrible cramping fear within her. The Major's honest appreciation of her body and delight in her physical prowess was something she had never experienced before, but it thrilled her more than she could say. She remembered that she had promised she would run her best for him. Well so she would!

Then she realised Arabella also had her eyes on her and shivered. Melanie could have coped with straightforward lesbian lust, but there was also an unpleasant cruel streak in the young woman. She vowed silently that whatever happened she would not let Arabella catch her.

The barking of hounds suddenly swelled in volume.

"Submit and lift tails!" Platt commanded.

The packgirls bent forward with heads down, flattening their breasts on the gravel and thrusting their bottoms up into the air. Reaching behind them they scooped their tails up so that they fell down the length of their backs.

Straining at their leashes, the pack of hounds entered the courtyard, dragging half a dozen handlers in their wake. Their excited yelps rose in frantic chorus as they saw the line of prostrate girls with their exposed hindquarters facing them. The dogs surged forward until they were trampling over the girls' booted legs, nuzzling and sniffing at the aromatic row of split flesh-peaches so conveniently displayed for them. Gasps and moans and a few helpless giggles rose up from the line of human vixens.

Melanie felt cold noses at her slit and discovered a new low of degradation. Yet at the same time came the stirrings of the dark tantalizing excitement that she had only known in these last strange days. In her confusion her mind veered from disgust at such treatment to the thought that this was perfectly natural. The hounds would be tracking them down, so what better way to learn their most intimate and personal scent?

After what seemed an eternity the dogs were pulled off them and they were ordered to assume the sejant position, crouching at the alert. The Major's voice rang out, echoing back over the gravel from the imposing facade of the Hall.

"We're ready to send the vixens off," he told the riders. "They'll have the usual ten minute start. Is everybody wearing their team colours?" There was an affirmative chorus. "Time-keepers: have you got your tag clocks ready?" Devices like bulky pocket watches slung on lanyards were held aloft. "Good." The Major consulted his own gold hunter. "Ready the pack," he told Platt.

Platt's switch flicked across the girls' backs and they lifted their bottoms like sprinters on the starting blocks. Melanie's heart was racing, desperate for the waiting to end so that she could be in her own element once more. Her surroundings seemed to fade into the background as she focused all her attention on the Major's next word.

"Go!" he shouted.

The girls sprinted off across the gravel, buttocks twinkling and tails streaming out behind them, accompanied by the cheers of the hunters. As the pack pounded through the wide orna-mental gateway they fanned out, heading out over the open ground towards the woods.

And suddenly Melanie was on her own in the open field; the quarry, the naked prey, with only her own strength and wits separating her from capture and the fate that entailed. But in-stead of dismay she felt exhilaration. For the first time she truly knew herself. She laughed as she lengthened her stride, revel-ling in the play of her muscles, flying across the rough grass and feeling the air rush over her naked body and the heavy bounce of her unrestrained breasts.

She was a bondslave yet she was free to run, to experience the true thrill of the chase. And in that moment she found per-fect happiness.

5: The Book

Miss Newcombe paced slowly up and down the stone-flagged terrace at the back of Cranborough House, examining the ground with critical eyes. Standing by a barrow full of weeds, mopping their brows with the backs of grimy hands, were Nigel Gosset and his four fellow students. They were watching Miss Newcombe intently, hoping she would find the results of their morning's labours acceptable.

Of course, they would have watched their nurse and School Matron closely in any circumstances. Sister Newcombe was an attractive thirtyish woman, with her dark hair tied up in a neat bun and keen, smoky blue eyes shining out from behind small, round steel-rimmed spectacles. Her dark blue nursing uniform revealed her trim waistline, emphasising the more than adequate curves of her bust and hips. Despite their recent acquisition of Amber, Miss Newcombe was still a favourite subject of their nightly fantasies. In fact they did not need to speculate as to what lay beneath the correct layers of her uniform. A while ago they had contrived a way up to the school roof from their dormitory. This gave them access to the skylight serving the small bedroom which Miss Newcombe used when her duties required her to stay the night on the school premises. Memories of what they had seen during those expeditions had been the cause of many youthful nocturnal emissions.

Miss Newcombe finished her inspection. "Yes, a job well done," she said, to their great relief. "I'll find something else for you this afternoon, but meanwhile you can amuse yourselves until lunch time."

"Thanks, Sister," they chorused.

Their overseer's fine brow creased for a moment, as though lost in some inner debate. Then she held out a brown paper-wrapped package she had been carrying.

"I think you might be interested in this," she said, as Jackson, their natural leader, took it uncertainly from her.

He pulled back a fold of paper to reveal a thick hardback book. On the cover was the title: 'THE CARE AND TRAINING OF BONDSLAVES.'

For a few seconds their faces were frozen in masks of stunned shock, accompanied by gurgles of horrified amazement. Fortunately Miss Newcombe did not seem to read anything deeper into their reactions than natural surprise.

"It's the standard reference work on the subject," she continued. "After we talked about sex and female bondslavery the other day I thought you should be presented with the facts in an orderly fashion. You're all old enough, and I think this matter falls within my remit to care for your general health and well-being. The interest you've already shown is a normal part of physical and emotional development. And of course when you're older, you may very well have bondslaves of your own. But you mustn't let unbridled curiosity get the better of common sense. Remember it was spying on Arabella's foolish young friends that got you here in the first place."

The boys nodded solemnly, eyes still riveted on the book, still too surprised to speak.

"Well, read it through, then talk to me again if there's anything you're still not sure of," Miss Newcombe said. "But clean yourselves up first. It wouldn't do to get dirty fingermarks all over it."

Jackson managed to gulp faintly: "No, Sister... thank you, Sister."

The boys had never washed and changed so quickly. Inside ten minutes they were in their dormitory clustered round the precious volume, turning pages with a mixture of reverence and impatience.

There were descriptions and charts and diagrams and photographs. There was advice on feeding, sanitation, training, restraint and punishment. They saw what could be done with straps and chains and special appliances, and they realised how

28

unimaginative they had been in the treatment of their secret slave. Every unsuspected detail of feminine anatomy and function was laid out before them, leaving them amazed at the uses to which a female body could be put and the service and pleasure it could provide.

Eventually Jackson tore his eyes away from the page to glance at his watch, then firmly shut the book ignoring the protests of his friends.

"We've got to get started with lunch now," he reminded them. "We can look at it again later."

"Fancy Sister giving us this," Gosset exclaimed, still not recovered from the surprise.

"She's a really good sort, she is," said Harris emphatically.

"But could you look her in the eye and talk over some of those things?" Parsons wondered, jabbing a finger at the incredible book. Harris blushed.

Bickley had been frowning intently. Now he spoke up: "I wonder if Amber knows about this stuff - all the ways you can use women, I mean."

There was a thoughtful silence which Jackson broke. "You think she deliberately hasn't said anything so she'll have an easier time of it?"

"Maybe."

"She must have known," Gosset said. "Girls always know more about these things than boys."

"Then she should have told us," Harris exclaimed, bristling with righteous indignation. "She is our slave after all. It's her duty to please us."

"We'll find out this afternoon," Jackson said decisively. "If she's been holding back, we'll make her regret it!"

6: The Butt

"The hunt's away," Belinda Jenkins said as she squeezed back through the overgrown and sagging garden gate of the playhouse and tugged it closed behind her. In the far distance they could hear the baying of hounds and the sound of horns.

"I wish we could ride with them," said Penelope Hazeldine wistfully. "I wonder what it would feel like, hunting bondslaves down? I bet they squeal and cry a lot."

"Our parents would never let us," Ernestine Chadwick pointed out. "They say we're still too young."

Belinda took her seat with the others. "Well I'm going to ride in a girl hunt just as soon as I can," she said firmly. "If Arabella can arrange it my parents won't need to know."

"You wouldn't dare," said Penelope.

"Yes I would," Belinda said indignantly. "I've watched Arabella. I can ride as well as she can and I know how to handle bondslaves."

"Your pony wouldn't be able to keep up."

"Arabella could lend me a horse."

Ernestine stretched back in her chair, shaking out her auburn ringlets. "I think it's too warm for riding today anyway. They'll get terribly hot. Much nicer to lounge around like this."

The four girls had taken a table and some chairs out of the playhouse and set them out on the lawn under the shade of a small cherry tree. They all had lunch baskets with them and the table already bore a plate of biscuits, glasses and pitchers of fruit juice.

Jemima Moncrief, the last and quietest of the group, said hesitantly: "You don't suppose any of the girls they're hunting will try to hide in here?"

"Why?" Ernestine asked.

"Because then the hunters would follow and they might find her. Her eyes flicked anxiously in the direction of the playhouse.

"Arabella said packgirls aren't allowed to hide inside buildings," Belinda said. "They've got to keep to the woods and fields."

"If one did," Penelope said mischievously, "then we could capture her and hide her away like the other one."

"Only if it's the new brown girl," Ernestine added. "That's the one Arabella really wants for herself."

"I wish you wouldn't say things like that," Jemima said, looking alarmed. "Isn't keeping one outsider in secret enough?"

"You're such a wet hen, Jem," Belinda scolded. "Don't you think helping to train our own private slave is exciting?"

"But it's... rather cruel."

"You have to be strict with bondslaves," Belinda said. "Arabella explained that's how they learn. You can see she's taking to it, so it can't be that bad. Anyway, if it bothers you so much, why do you keep staring at her with that silly look on your face?"

Jemima suddenly looked defensive. "What do you mean?"

"It's true, Jem," Penelope said. "You go all wide-eyed and dreamy."

"And your mouth drops open," Ernestine added. "It's very lower class, gaping and gawping. Makes you look like a fish."

"Are you secretly thinking of what you'd like to do with her yourself?" Belinda teased.

Jemima blushed. "No! I don't do any such thing! I mean I wouldn't..."

But the others were laughing at her embarrassment too loudly to listen to her protests, and Jemima was forced into sullen silence.

"Whose turn is it next, anyway?" Belinda asked at length, looking at her watch.

"Jem's," Penelope said with a grin.

"Oh..." Jemima started. "I don't think I can, not just now."

"Yes you can," Penelope said. "You've had as much as the rest of us. You're just being silly."

31

"Must I do it?" Jemima said miserably. "It's so dirty and... rude!"

"It doesn't count as rude with bondslaves," Ernestine replied. "It's just teaching them their place."

"Go on, Jem," said Belinda sternly. "Or else we'll tell Arabella you wouldn't do your bit. You don't want her to get angry with you, do you?"

Glumly, Jemima got up from the table and walked with dragging steps over to the old garden pump. Working the squeaking handle she filled a bucket with water.

"And make sure she says everything just as she's supposed to," Belinda called out after her as Jemima carried the bucket off, trying not to slop water over her frock.

Around the corner of the playhouse was a narrow passageway a few feet wide formed by the side wall of the house and the overgrown garden hedge. In this rested a large rainwater butt with rusting hoops and mouldering staves, closed at the top with a heavy lid. An old wooden box had been placed beside it to serve as a step.

Jemima put her bucket down and stared at the butt. Her heart thumped and she felt a sense of disbelief creeping over her. With a deep breath she hitched up the skirt of her frock and tied it round her waist, revealing virginal white cotton panties trimmed with lace. Hooking her thumbs through the waistband she pulled her panties down and stepped out of them, baring her pale and prettily rounded bottom and full brown bush of pubic hair to the world. Even as she peered anxiously about to reassure herself she could not be seen, Jemima shivered as a delightfully guilty thrill coursed through her at the feel of the air playing over her newly exposed flesh.

Jemima lifted the lid off the water butt, then stepped up onto the box and peered anxiously inside. Framed by a bedraggled halo of golden hair, Sue's woebegone face looked back up at her from the dank interior.

Sue sat naked in the bottom of the butt in a few inches of

dirty water. Her arms were tied behind her back and her legs were splayed apart and bent at the knees. Her ankles and calves were crossed and bound so she could neither stand nor bring her knees together.

For a few seconds Jemima could only stare at Sue in dumb fascination. The damp chill of the butt made her look paler than ever. The nipples of her heavy breasts were shrunken and crinkled, but by contrast the purple and scarlet lash marks criss-crossing the tender flesh around them seemed even more livid. She was so horribly, wonderfully, helpless; so shamefully, thrill-ingly degraded.

Unconsciously Jemima's fingers stole down to her pubic bush and into her warm cleft.

Could the girl actually become used to it? Jemima wondered. Would she even come to like being treated that way? What would it feel like to be bound like that, to endure the punishments Arabella had heaped upon her?

Jemima felt herself blushing at the thought. Then she realised her fingers were rubbing the nub of flesh normally hidden be-tween her nether lips, which had become strangely moist. She jerked her hand away guiltily and rubbed her sticky fingertips on her rolled skirt. She had secretly played with herself before now, but always under her bedclothes or in the bath. This time a curious warm tightness remained in her loins.

Resolutely Jemima clambered onto the rim of the butt and sat down with her legs splayed and feet dangling over the sides. The rough rotted tops of the butt staves pressed against her bare bottom.

Now Sue was looking up through the 'V' of Jemima's spread thighs, up at her 'cunny', as the other girls called it. What must she look like from that angle? Jemima wondered with a guilty thrill. Nobody had ever seen her like that before. Could Sue see every fold of her private parts? What would it look like if their positions were reversed...

Jemima clutched the rim of the butt for support, suddenly

coming over light-headed. She was feeling very strange. Her heart was pounding and a hot tingling knot seemed to be tying itself somewhere below her stomach. She must just do what she had to as quickly as possible.

"I'm sorry," she whispered to Sue. "Arabella says we have to do this."

"I am your slave, Miss Jemima," Sue replied mechanically. "I am here to be shamed. Please use me as your toilet."

Closing her eyes, Jemima took a deep breath... and nothing happened.

Jemima reached down with two fingers and spread her vaginal lips so that her pee hole was exposed. Still nothing happened. She groaned and bit her lip. Her bladder was full of fruit juice and she really felt the need to release it now, but she was too tense inside. She opened her eyes and stared almost apologetically at Sue's expectant, upturned face. Her gaze wandered down to the girl's poor abused breasts and the damp golden tangle between her spread thighs...

Jemima's fingers moved deeper into her slit. A hardness was growing between the soft petals of flesh as the bud of her clitoris filled. She'd felt a little like this the previous day when she had watched Arabella torment Sally Potts in the police yard. She knew it must be wicked and unnatural, but she couldn't help herself. She hated to see bondgirls suffering like that, yet at the same time she could not help being excited, wondering what it would feel like.

Sue was still looking patiently up at her. To her horror Jemima realised she was playing with herself right in front of her eyes - and she couldn't stop! The aching bulb of pleasure between her legs had suddenly become the focus of her world. Nothing else mattered. Her vagina seemed to be growing enormous, it was burning hot and dripping wet. She smelt a musky aroma and realised it was the perfume of her own secretions. Surely she must burst under the pressure as her sex pulsed against the sweetly tormenting tautness of her bladder.

Jemima's fingers became a frantic blur.

Her loins seemed to squeeze to a pinpoint and then erupted, sending a wave of pure pleasure through her body. She gasped aloud as a starburst of raw ecstasy exploded in her brain.

With the joy of release came what felt like a damburst. Her pent-up water gushed from her in a hard stream and splashed over Sue's face and breasts, spurting fitfully as she spasmed, thrilling Jemima as never before as it left her body through her engorged and ultra-sensitive sex, piling sensation on sensation, filling her with undreamed of delight.

Then her eyes rolled up and she collapsed forward, sprawling limply over the top of the water butt. For a minute she lay still except for the unsteady rise and fall of her chest. The pale moons of her bottom were exposed to the sky. The last droplets fell from her pubic hair.

Jemima had had her first orgasm.

From within the butt, Sue said: "Thank you for teaching me my place, Miss Jemima."

For a moment Jemima hugged the butt to her, wishing she was inside. Then, slowly, she slithered off to the ground. Her legs still felt very weak. She couldn't quite believe what had happened, but she knew instinctively that it was an important milestone in her life.

She put her pants back on and smoothed down her skirt, then nervously peered down at Sue; the girl she had just peed over... the girl who had seen her masturbate!

"Please don't tell the others," she begged.

"It's not my place, Miss Jemima," Sue said, lowering her eyes.

On a sudden impulse, Jemima reached into the butt and stroked Sue's sodden hair. "I'm so sorry for you," she whispered.

"Don't be," Sue said in a tiny voice. "I think I was born to be a slave."

"But you don't have to be treated like this. Arabella's so

cruel sometimes!"

"I'll survive. We can't choose who masters us."

Jemima picked up the bucket of water and poured it over Sue, washing her down. Immediately the water began seeping out the bottom of the butt from between the ill-fitting staves.

Sue shook the droplets form her hair. "Thank you... Miss Jemima."

Jemima picked up the lid, but before she could put it back on the butt, Sue said quietly: "I thought you looked lovely when you played with yourself."

Jemima gulped. "I was looking at you... thinking what you must be feeling."

Sue lifted her eyes to hers. "I'm pleased if I gave you pleasure."

Breathing tremulously, Jemima leant over the rim of the butt and kissed Sue; first on the forehead, then, almost overbalancing, on the lips. Sue's skin was cold but her lips were warm. Jemima's own lips parted. The tips of their tongues touched...

"Jemima! What's taking you so long?" It was Belinda's voice.

Jemima started in sudden dismay. She slammed the lid back on the butt, snatched up the empty bucket and ran back to the others.

7: Hunted

The woods and fields of the Markham Estate echoed with the sounds of the hunt. Hooves pounded and harness jingled. Riders called to each other. Hunting horns trumpeted. Dogs yapped excitedly as they followed scent trails. The first squeals of cornered vixens began to ring out.

A naked packgirl darted through a copse with three hounds snapping at her heels.

One of the hounds closed its jaws upon her fluttering foxtail and dug its paws into the ground. The anal plug held fast and the sudden jerk made the girl stumble, breaking her stride. In a second the other two hounds were upon her and she crashed to the ground under their weight.

The hounds snarled, fighting over possession of the tail. They trod the squirming girl under them, marking her with their own muddy paw prints. The anal plug twisted inside her as the dog tugged to and fro, but it remained in place. The packgirl struggled to her hands and knees and tried to crawl away but the hounds bore her down again. Curious snouts began to probe between her thighs, snuffling at the source of the scent they had been trained to follow.

With triumphant shouts three riders wearing red and yellow striped sashes appeared, galloping hard towards the struggling group. As they drew up, one of the riders blew three sharp blasts on a small horn, then tossed a handful of chocolate drops from his pocket onto the ground. A second rider slid from his saddle and ran towards the melee. At the sound of the horn, the hounds released their hold on the foxtail and scampered over to the scattered sweets, their prey forgotten as they enjoyed their reward.

The packgirl staggered to her feet even as the second rider made a grab for her hair. True to Platt's instructions she nimbly dodged his grasp and sprinted off again, outpacing her would-be captor. The dismounted rider cursed loudly as he and his companions spurred their mounts after their elusive prey.

They overtook her before she reached the thicker trees, swinging their long handled sticks with their flat rubber-paddle ends. The girl yelped as the stinging blows rained down, beating her to the ground where she rolled up into a ball so that only her smooth back showed.

The dismounted rider pounded up and threw himself onto the girl, grabbing her wrists and dragging her arms behind her back as he hauled her upright out of her huddle.

"Get her tag!" he shouted, as the girl jerked and twisted in his grasp.

They dropped from their saddles and caught hold of her. Even for the three of them it was no easy task. The girl kicked and struggled fiercely, exciting them with her futile resistance and forcing them to handle her naked flesh harshly, letting them know the strength of the wild thing they had captured.

Finally they managed to wrench her legs apart, exposing the silvery metal tag that danced and twinkled under her pouting pubic pouch. One of the hunters snatched at it and tore the securing ball out of her, bringing forth a gasp from the girl as it grazed her tender passage. The hunter pushed the chain into the slot of the recording clock he was carrying and twisted a key. The chain locked into place and the clock stopped.

As the click of the lock sounded the girl's struggled ceased. Her masked head dropped forward and except for the heaving of her chest she hung limp and still in their grasp.

The three hunters checked the time on the clock.

"Not bad," one said. "In the first five, I should think."

"She ran well though," said the second, pulling off the girl's fox mask so that they could admire her flushed but pretty face. Their hands weighed her warm, plump breasts and stroked her smooth thighs. Stiff fingers were thrust into her slit and the sticky heat within told them of her state of arousal. Grinning, they tied her gloved hands behind her back with a team sash and threw her to the ground. Unbidden, she spread her legs wide as the first rider began unbuttoning his flies.

She had run hard and fast that day, but she had not finished providing her masters with good sport.

While he waited his turn, one of the hunters walked a few yards off and drove the spiked end of a flare into the ground and lit the touchpaper. In a few seconds a plume of orange smoke was rising over the trees.

When they had each done with her, wrenching an orgasm from her well-used body and leaving their coats and britches smudged with her body paint, the first rider drew out his penknife and extended a blade. The girl caught her breath and held very still as the rider pinched together a sprig of her pubic hair and cut it off at the root. The girl's eyes watered as her tender flesh was stretched by the blade.

And so each rider took a cutting from her pubic bush - a memento of a fine day's sport and the prize they had won.

Guided by the flare, George Platt and a groom rode up. Hitched to the rear of the groom's saddle was a lightweight bamboo 'A' frame, which bumped along behind his mount on two wire-spoked wheels.

"How are we placed, Platt?" the first rider demanded as soon as the keeper was in earshot.

"We'll have to check the tag clocks, but you're just the second capture I've attended, sir," Platt said.

"That looks promising," said the first rider.

"I hope she ran well for you, gentlemen?" Platt asked deferentially as he dismounted and unstrapped his camera.

"Oh, she was a very lively little vixen,' the second rider said, affectionately prodding the girl who sprawled limply on the ground with the toe of his boot. "A credit to your training."

"Most kind of you to say so, sir," Platt said, setting up his tripod. "Now if you gentlemen would like to take up your positions..."

The traditional hunter's picture was taken with the three standing shoulder. The packgirl was rolled onto her side facing the camera and laid along their feet, so that the each rider could stand with a foot resting on her head, waist or hip.

When they were done the team's timekeeper handed over the tag clock to Platt.

"Have we time to try for a brace of vixens?" one of his companions wondered.

"Why not?" said his friend.

"Back to the Hall for another clock, then. Tally Ho!"

They mounted their horses and set off at a gallop.

Platt packed away his camera, then helped the groom haul

the exhausted packgirl onto the net slung across the wheeled frame, stretching out her arms and legs so they could clip straps onto her wrist and ankle rings. When she was secure, Platt lifted her head and gave her a drink from a canteen of water, which she gulped down.

"I ran well, didn't I, Mr Platt?" she asked anxiously.

Platt checked the time on her tag clock.

"Fair enough, Molly. The gentlemen were pleased with you, that's the main thing. Just you make sure you serve them well tonight."

"Oh, I will, Mr Platt," Molly promised.

Panting, Melanie crouched down in the shelter of a thin belt of trees.

It was midday. In the preceding hours she had run as she never had before. She was scratched, streaked with sweat, splattered with mud and weed from hiding in ditches. Her legs ached, her chest burned. But she felt wonderful. Twice she had been spotted by riders, but each time she had managed to lose them before they could close on her. She had heard hounds baying in the distance several times, but by backtracking and plunging through streams she had thrown them off her scent.

By making a great half-circle about the perimeter of the estate she had now arrived where she hoped she would be least expected; opposite the back of the Hall itself.

She could see its roofs through a gap in the trees. Stealthily she crept forward until she could survey all of the house and its immediate grounds. There were tiny figures of riders moving in the fields about the front courts, but there was no sign of life at the back. All attention was focused on the main drive where riders and captured vixens would return. Even the servants would be there, those not helping with the hunt watching from windows.

A ring of fallow fields and paddocks separated the woodland from the orchards and ornamental gardens surrounding the House. If she could get inside that ring and find some place to hide she should be safe for a while. Of course she would be caught eventually when the rest of the grounds had been scoured, but the thought did not trouble her. The inevitability of her capture was simply the natural conclusion to the hunt, and part of her yearned for the consummation to come.

She had discovered the pure delight and strange thrill of being a naked hunted prey. Yes, thrill was the word. She had run in a constant state of sexual arousal. The stimulation of the hard plug of her tail mount and the tag ball lodged so intimately within her ensured that. When they caught her she would be ready, but she wanted to be the last captured to please the Major.

The realization dawned on her that nothing she had done for days had been without the Major's approval. She could not cover her nakedness, use her hands properly, void her wastes in private or choose when or how she had sex. She was an absolute slave. The knowledge should have appalled her, but instead it brought a strange sense of comfort.

Melanie edged her way along the fringe of the wood until she was opposite the end of a hedgerow: thick and high with several small trees growing out of it at intervals. As long as she kept in its shadow she should go unobserved. Much of the white bodypaint on her stomach and thighs had been worn off or obliterated by a coating of mud and dried duck weed. That combined with her dark skin and hair made for a pretty good job of camouflage. Pity a pale-skinned blonde trying to do this, she thought.

Melanie took a deep breath and darted out of the wood into the shelter of the hedgerow, crouching down immediately in the shelter of a clump of cow parsley. All was still and quiet, save for a horn sounding faintly in the woods on the far side of the grounds. She worked her way along the hedgerow in a stooping run.

She was half-way across when it happened.

Melanie never saw where the riders came from, but suddenly there were two of them on the far side of the field. Instantly she dropped flat into the long grass and peered between the stalks. If she just held still enough maybe they would miss her.

The pair showed no sign of haste. They cantered across the field side by side not quite towards her. As they approached she saw they were a middle-aged man and woman, both turned out in immaculate riding gear and wearing purple team sashes.

Thirty yards from her the pair suddenly divided, one turning up the field, the other down, and riding parallel with the hedge. Melanie's eyes darted from side to side as she tried to keep both in sight without moving her head. Where were they going?

Abruptly both riders turned back on themselves, this time in the very shadow of the hedge. And suddenly they were not cantering but galloping straight for Melanie swinging their paddle sticks - she had been neatly cornered!

Melanie sprang to her feet and sprinted out into the field, even though she knew it was futile. They had known she was there all along and had cleverly forced her out into the open where they had the advantage. They would not let her reach shelter again.

They caught her before she had covered fifty yards, despite her desperate weaving run. Suddenly they were flanking her and she was walled in by horseflesh. Their paddles lashed out, the woman forehand across her rolling buttocks, the man backhand across the top of her breasts. There were two sharp cracks as the rubber paddle blades met her skin and Melanie cried out at the burning, stinging, shock of the blows. A second swing from the man caught the snout of her mask and knocked it down over her eyes.

Blinded, gasping and reeling, Melanie skidded to a halt. She tore her mask off and turned back the way she had come.

The riders checked their mounts, gouging ruts in the grass,

wheeled about expertly and bore down on her again.

Crack, crack! The blows fell this time on her shoulders. Instinctively flinging up her arms to protect her now exposed face, Melanie opened herself to two backhand blows that caught her bouncing breasts full on. With a shriek of pain she doubled over, stumbled and fell.

They were back on her in seconds.

Before she could get to her feet they were circling about her, raining down blows with full swings of their paddles. They were not letting her rise or giving her any chance to crawl between them. Round and round they went, beating every square inch of her huddled body.

Dazedly Melanie realized there was only one paddle striking her. But before she could move, a booted foot descended on her ponytail of hair where it lay on the grass and trod it into the earth. She shrieked as it tugged her scalp and tried to pull free or push the foot away, but she could get no grip or leverage. However she squirmed or twisted her head was pinned down on its side and she couldn't raise it. More paddle blows stung her. She could only roll up into a ball and hug her knees to her chest, knowing she was quite helpless in the hands of experts at incapacitating a bondslave.

A hand reached between her thighs to the tag dangling from her pouting split peach and jerked it out of her, the soft rubber prongs teasing the flesh ribs of her passage.

The key of a tag clock clicked.

The paddling stopped.

Trembling, Melanie opened her eyes and looked up at her captors.

They were a middle-aged couple, rosy-cheeked from their exertions. He had an old fashioned military-style moustache, she was blonde and slightly plump. She would never have given them a second glance back home. Who would have guessed what they were capable of? Melanie noticed for the first time that the man had a pair of binoculars slung around his neck.

They must have been watching her from the moment she started out across the field.

"You were right, Sam," the woman said heartily, eyeing Melanie with satisfaction. "There's always one in the pack who tries this trick."

"Well, my dear, we're getting a bit too old to race around half the countryside. Leave that to the young'uns. Softly, softly, I always say."

"But we're not too old to enjoy ourselves, Sam," she chided gently.

"Never that, my dear." He looked around. "No need to signal for the keeper. We can lead her in ourselves and have our picture taken in front of the Hall."

The woman looked at the tag clock then at Melanie. "It won't be the fastest capture today, but I'm sure it'll be the sweetest reward."

The man chuckled and prodded Melanie's fleshy buttock with the toe of his boot.

"James's prize brown vixen. We're going to have some fun with you tonight, girl."

They led Melanie back to the Hall in style.

Her hands were tied behind her back with one of their team sashes, while the other was twisted in a figure-of-eight about her breasts, squeezing them out proudly. She held a riding crop clenched between her teeth, forcing her lips back in a grin. A tether was tied to the handle thong of a second crop, the end of which was buried in her dripping vagina so that its supple shaft bent and jutted out before her, wagging from side to side as she walked. Melanie held it tightly in place, knowing she must not let it pull free, even as she knew the degrading spectacle she made.

Every little tug on the tether worked the shaft of the crop deliciously round inside her; a sample of what was to come. She had no doubt she would give her captors pleasure that night. She had no choice; now all choices were made for her. All she had to do was obey.

44

8: By the Book

Amber was sitting up very straight with her back against one of the loft's stout timber posts. She had no choice. Her hands were tied behind her and ropes crossed over her chest between her breasts. Her splayed legs were tied at the ankles to a length of two by four, making it impossible to bring them together.

She looked down at the pouting, hair-fringed cleft of her love lips. Rising from it she could still smell the lingering, almost chemical tang of the boy's sperm, mingling with her own musky exudation. It was a hungry little mouth that had been well fed but wanted more. But bound as she was there was no way that she could satisfy its deep, needy ache; which was obviously how the boys wanted it to be.

At least they'd allowed her a folded-up blanket to sit on.

Amber knew she was losing her influence over the boys. They were still living up to the letter of their agreement, but they were treating her much more strictly. They'd discovered the simple fact that they could take what they liked from her as and when they chose. What was worse, they now knew that she quite liked to be treated harshly. It was her own fault. Hadn't she virtually begged for the cane the previous night?

She should have recognised the signs earlier. When she'd been in the stocks in the police yard - stark naked and a target for all the pillory shot people cared to throw at her - she'd begun to get turned on by the experience. Even in the agony of Arabella's sexual torture she'd succumbed to an orgasm. Had this latent masochistic streak always been in her, or was it due to something in the air here?

Whatever the reason, she'd surrendered to the urge without thinking of the consequences. She had to focus. She had to manoeuvre the boys into stealing from Arabella the outsider girl Amber had deduced she was secretly holding. Then perhaps she could also talk them into enjoying the charms of her ex-cellmate Sally Potts, when she got out of jail.

They'd soon learn that keeping a harem entailed a lot of responsibility and, hopefully, give up the idea. Otherwise Amber would be kept here for however long their school summer term lasted - assuming she wasn't discovered by somebody in authority before then and returned to jail to serve out her sentence.

But she was losing the initiative. At lunch, when Jackson had spoon-fed her without releasing her hands, he'd looked at her almost resentfully, as though she'd displeased him in some way. When she'd tried to talk he'd said nothing.

Once again she heard the sound of hammering from the old tack room below her. It must be the boys. They'd cleared and sorted a lot of material there as part of their penitential odd-job work. But what were they up to now?

Finally she heard footsteps on the ladder and the trapdoor opened. The boys climbed up through it into the loft, dragging something behind them. Amber's frustrated desire was replaced by a terrible sinking sensation as they set it out before her.

A length of thick planking about nine inches wide had been nailed to the top of an old wooden trestle, so that it ran along its length and overhung the ends a little. Fixed transversely to the underside of one end of the trestle was a four-foot wooden beam. Dangling ominously from the beam ends were two old brass pulley blocks threaded through with rope. Beside the device they placed a galvanised bucket with a coil of hosepipe showing over its rim.

Amber said, in a slightly strained voice: "That all looks interesting. I suppose it's for me."

Jackson looked at her coldly. "That's right. We found the design in this."

He held out a book for her to see, showing her the cover so she could read the title: 'THE CARE AND TRAINING OF BONDSLAVES'. He opened it at a marked page. It held line drawings of several strange devices, including the blueprint for the thing before her.

46

It was labelled: 'Training Horse'.

"But I bet you know all about that sort of thing," Jackson continued. He fanned the pages of the book in front of her eyes, giving her flickering glimpses of every kind of sexual position, restraint and posture.

"I don't know what you mean," Amber said, utterly bewildered but trying not to sound too concerned. "You don't need that thing to enjoy me. Why not put me back on my bed again, nice and tightly stretched out?"

Bickley said ominously: "You're going on here and we're going to ask you some questions."

Amber shivered. "Just tell me what's wrong, boys... I mean, Masters. Your slave wants to know how she has offended you. She's done everything you asked, she's given you pleasure whenever you wanted it..." She was sounding desperate now. "How can she do more?"

"You could have done lot's more," Harris said accusingly.

"But you didn't tell us," Parsons added.

"You wanted it easy for yourself," said Gosset.

"You agreed that we could do anything we wanted with you," Jackson reminded her. "Now you've displeased us we're entitled to punish you."

They untied her from the post, freed her legs from the spreader bar and lifted her onto the training horse. Amber struggled futilely as they laid her on her back on the plank, her buttocks resting above the transverse beam, and an old leather strap was buckled over her waist. Her arms were pulled downward and drawn straight and the wrists tied to ropes running up from the feet of the trestle. Leather straps fitted with dangling metal rings were buckled about her mid thighs and ropes from the pulley blocks were fed through the rings and then tied about her ankles. The boys hauled on the pulley ends of the ropes. The blocks rattled and squeaked while Amber's legs were wrenched apart and bent double. Her ankles were inexorably drawn up under her thighs, while the thighs themselves were pulled in opposite directions towards the pulley blocks. Inch by inch she was pulled apart until the sinews on her inner thighs stood out on either side of her splayed sex.

"No!" Amber gasped. "Masters, please stop... that's too far!"

But they continued hauling on the ropes.

Her pubic mound was standing out from thighs that were being pulled flat on either side of it. The stretching skin was drawing her outer lips apart. Never had she been exposed to such a degree before. Her supple body was being bent to its limits. Amber thought they were going to snap her like a wishbone. A shriek of pain erupted from her only to be stifled by a balled handkerchief stuffed into her mouth.

Just when the strain was becoming unendurable they tied the rope ends off.

Amber vibrated in her bonds as taut as a bowstring.

The pressure on her legs was sliding her body up along the plank top, while her straining arms anchored her in place. Between the two forces her back arched as far as her waist strap allowed, lifting her firm breasts up in the air, her nipples perversely hard and pointed.

She rolled her head from side to side and gazed imploringly at the boys, but they were just staring at her trembling, contorted body in fascination. The glistening pink grotto of her labia was open so wide that the mouth of her vaginal passage showed as an almost perfect circle. Below it the taut skin of her buttocks caused the pucker of her anus to gape, revealing the dark tunnel beyond.

Jackson took the cane they had used last night down from its hook and took up a position to deliver a backhand blow.

Swish - crack! A red line appeared on Amber's flesh, crossing from one thigh to the other and kissing the parted lips between them.

Amber's eyes bulged as her shriek of pain was muffled by her gag. Her soft inner thighs, the tender mound of her sex, her clitoris under its inadequate hood of flesh were exposed to the

48

full force of the cane as never before.

The shock on top of the agony she was already suffering was too much for her self-control. Her bladder cut loose and a stream of pee jetted four feet across the loft floor.

"We've made her wet herself!" Harris exclaimed.

As they laughed at her enforced display of incontinence, Gosset impatiently snatched the cane away from Jackson and swung his own blow. Amber jerked wildly as another line was blazed in her flesh. On her drum-tight immobile thigh skin it felt like a line of fire. Another explosive discharge of urine was forced from her, then the flow slowed to a dribble.

Harris took the cane from Gosset and raised his arm...

By the time the cane had gone round a second time, the flesh of Amber's inner thighs and pubis was crimson and she was lost in a haze of pain: her head lolling on its side, her eyes closed and her cheeks tear-streaked.

Jackson grasped her hair and pulled her face round towards him, wrenched out her gag and slapped her cheeks until her eyes flickered open. Again he held up the book accusingly.

"Why didn't you tell us about all these other ways we could have had you?" he demanded. "You must know about them."

"What are you talking about?" Amber sobbed, her voice shrill with pain and real fear. "I don't know what you know. You want to have me up my bum? Do it! I'll suck all of you off if you want. I'll do anything, but for God's sake loosen the ropes! They're cutting off my circulation. I can't feel my hands anymore. You want to give me gangrene? Your bloody book doesn't say do that, does it? Does it!"

Blinking though her tears she saw the onset of doubt in their expressions as they took in her obvious distress. Bickley said hesitantly: "Maybe this is a bit mean on her."

"But she's got to remember who's in charge," Jackson persisted.

"Look at me!" Amber almost shouted. "I'm your slave... but I'm not a fucking mind reader! You could have shown me the book first. You promised you'd treat me responsibly..." Her hands and feet had gone quite numb and she groped desperately for some further lever. "This is the way Arabella Westlake would treat a slave!"

The accusation struck home. The last person they wanted to be compared to was Arabella.

"All right. Loosen the ropes," Jackson said.

Amber gasped as her body unbent. Harris stooped down and examined her hands. "They do look dead," he admitted. "And they're rather cold..."

Hurriedly they untied her and Amber rolled grotesquely to the floor, her legs still locked in their splayed position, the skin between her thighs scorching. They carried her over to her makeshift bed and began massaging her hands and feet. Amber groaned as the blood began to flow back to her extremities. Harris took out a pot of petroleum jelly from the bucket they had brought and began rubbing some into Amber's thighs and reddened pubic flesh. While the others worked on her Bickley took the book from Jackson and flicked through to the index. After a minute he said:

"It does say if you're using a restraining device, the slave should be secured with leather or rubber cuffs. If you use rope, it mustn't be too thin, and the skin should be protected with strips of cloth." He looked down at Amber. "We didn't see this. Sorry."

Amber groaned again, but her mind was racing as the boys massaged the life back into her. They must never realise how close they had been to breaking her spirit. She must turn the situation to her advantage and regain the initiative. Time to be magnanimous and win herself a few brownie points.

She wriggled gently and sighed with obvious relief.

"Oh... that's so much better. Do keep rubbing... yes, especially there."

"Look, we really are sorry," Jackson said.

"I know you didn't mean to really hurt me," Amber said

nobly. "It was just a misunderstanding. Keeping a slave must be as new to you as being one is to me. I've never been on a device like that before."

"Maybe we shouldn't have made it," Bickley said.

"Oh no!" Amber said quickly. "It was clever of you to make one so well. It's a really ingenious device. I'll be just at the right height and position for two of you to have me at the same time."

"You mean... you'd go on it again?" Harris asked hesitantly.

"Of course," Amber said. "I'm your slave. I can't stop you doing whatever you want with me. That is what you find exciting, isn't it? But try to ease up a little. I can please you a lot better if you're not trying to tear my arms off or split me in two at the same time!"

The boys laughed, looking more cheerful again.

"While I'm getting over that first session, why don't you take a look amongst the junk downstairs?" Amber suggested. "There's bound to be some leather strapping on those old harnesses that you can make into cuffs."

The boys obeyed eagerly.

Some broad strips of leather were found. As the boys worked on them, cutting and piercing holes for ropes with the collection of old tools they assembled, Amber said: "I'd be interested to read that book of yours to find out what else you have in store for me. To avoid any more misunderstandings."

They looked slightly shocked at the idea.

"You'd really like to read it?" Jackson said.

"Why not? I might be surprised at some things, but I doubt if I'll be shocked. For instance, I saw a rubber hose in that bucket and Martin nicely used some vaseline on me. I guess you were planning to have anal sex with me, right?"

They blushed. Harris said: "The book said it was different from the normal kind..."

"Vaginal sex," Amber prompted gently. "Yes, you'll find my bottom's hotter and tighter that my cunt. Men often like that. I'm sure you will."

Amber felt the familiar stirrings beginning within her loins as she spoke. These strange naive yet intimate conversations with the boys seemed to have that effect on her. It was probably best that she started to warm up anyway, knowing what was to come.

"You've done this anal sex before?" Jackson asked

"A few times. I didn't know you hadn't heard of it until now." They suddenly looked embarrassed and ashamed. "But you're learning now," Amber said quickly. "What are you going to use as a douche bag to clean me out first?"

Bickley took a hot water bottle from the bucket.

"How clever!" Amber said. "Has it got warm water in it already? Good."

The improvised cuffs were ready, and Amber meekly extended her wrists and ankles for them to be fitted. The cuffs were tight, but the leather was pliant enough not to cut and broad enough to spread the pressure on her skin. Amber took a deep breath and said brightly: "Right, I'm ready now."

They helped her up, two boys holding an arm each, half supporting, half controlling her. Bizarrely it felt almost as though they were escorting royalty. She was a slave to be used and abused, yet also a valuable prize to be guarded. A sex princess?

They fastened her to the training horse and pulled on the ropes until she was splayed and stretched wide enough for their purposes but not to the ligament-tearing extent they had before. It gave Amber a tolerably degree of discomfort and a terrific sense of helpless exposure. She felt her slit growing slick and sticky.

"We also made this," Parsons said, holding up a length of rope about fourteen inches long, it was already tied in a loop and knotted at each end to hold on two rubber washers that had been threaded onto it. Amber blinked at it in incomprehension.

"It's for when we do this," said Harris, reaching under the head end of the training horse and drawing back a bolt that had been fastened lengthwise to the underside of the plank. The end of the plank hinged downward some 45 degrees, tilting Amber's head back with it. Suddenly she was in the ideal position for oral penetration.

Amber fought to maintain her composure even though everything was suddenly upside-down. "Of course, the rope is a teeth-spreader, isn't it? It wouldn't do for me to accidentally bite you. But please remember you've got to pull out every few seconds to allow me to breathe."

They nodded distractedly. As the growing bulges in their trousers showed, urgent need was overcoming them. They would not be denied their relief a second time. In a moment she would be silenced; reduced to a living sex toy for as long as they cared to use her. Parsons bent over her to insert the spreader.

"I expect a lot of tit-squeezing when you're using my mouth," Amber said quickly. "And whoever's up my bottom must play with my cunt - gnhhh!"

Parsons pushed the washers into the sides of her mouth so that the rope passed between her teeth, and pulled the loop over her head, drawing back her lips into a rictus of a smile and baring her teeth. For a moment it felt as though it would tear her flesh, then the loop passed over to the back of her neck and the strain eased slightly, leaving her mouth gaping invitingly open.

Jackson had vaselined the rubber hose and now he slipped it into her bottom. Amber shivered as a foot of tube slid into her entrails. Bickley held up the water bottle with the hose end screwed into it and tipped it over and squeezed.

Amber gurgled and rolled her eyes as her stomach swelled with the water being forced through her, which then gushed out into the bucket placed between her legs. The flow ceased and the tube was withdrawn. She had been flushed out for her masters' use. A finger replaced the tube and teased and tickled as it lubricated her orifice ready for penetration.

About her, trousers were dropping and hard young cocks were springing up to attention. The boys crowded close until

53

all she saw were their erect organs. Which of her holes would be used by which boy?

Hands grasped her spread thighs and a cockhead nuzzled against her anus even as somebody clasped her chin. Her tongue lapped eagerly at the purple plum driving between her lips and towards her throat. A hairy ball sac brushed her nose. With a thrust from below her anal ring was stretched wide and her rectum entered. Urged on by her sucking lips, the shaft in her mouth slid down her throat.

Pistons of flesh were driving into her from both ends and she was ascending to heaven.

Her breasts were being slapped and wrenched in time with the thrusts into her gullet. Prying fingers had found her hardened clitoris and were rolling and pinching it just a little short of cruelly.

It was perfect.

With grunts of delight the first two boys spent themselves liberally within her. Her bottom received the gift of sperm with desperate clenchings, while her lips drank thirstily as of a rare nectar.

The training horse had become her throne of sacrifice and reward. Its worst excesses were now safely reserved for somebody who would appreciate them.

9: Pack Love

It was early afternoon by the time Melanie crawled though the small packgirl door into the pound at the back of their kennels.

Most of the pack seemed to be there, sprawled out on the grass or sitting under the small shade trees. Some were curled up in exhausted asleep, others chattering excitedly in small groups. As Melanie appeared they hurried over to greet her, moving on their hands and knees in the rapid but graceful shuffle that set their hanging breasts bouncing and swinging in fluid motion. Like Melanie they once again wore their regular tails and boots with the wedge soles that made walking impossible. Apart from sport or work a packgirl moved on all fours like a dog so she always looked up to her masters.

Melanie was surrounded by a press of warm bodies, still carrying the scent of soap and shampoo from their after-hunt showers. A few of the more timid said nothing but simply bestowed respectful kisses on Melanie's bottom, in deference to her status as First Girl of the pack. The sensation pleased Melanie more that she let them see.

A barrage of questions assailed her: "I knew you'd run well!" "Was it hard?" "You're almost the last." "Who caught you?"

"Just a minute, you lot!" Melanie said loudly. She'd seen Una hanging back uncertainly from the main group. Melanie shuffled forward until she was face to face with the former First Girl.

"Did you have a good run?" she asked.

"Pretty good, I only just got in."

"Well done," Melanie said.

"You did better."

"Any injuries?"

Una shrugged. "A few scratches and bruises, nothing much. And you?"

Melanie made a face. "Paddle sores. My tits took a bit of a beating and smart like hell."

Una promptly stooped down and gently kissed Melanie's abused breasts, adding a quick flick of the tongue to each nipple. She straightened up and Melanie kissed Una back on her lips, which were as soft as her body was hard. It was partly a show of mutual affection intended to reassure the other girls, but also a natural expression of the bond they shared. Whatever their backgrounds they were united now by the sisterhood of the pack. It was a powerful feeling and Melanie was not yet sure how deep it ran.

She shuffled over and sat carefully down under a tree,

realising how much she ached from her exertions. The rest of the pack crouched down attentively before her. Melanie grinned at them.

"All right. I managed to make it through the farms until I was halfway round the hunting ground opposite the back of the Hall. I was trying to get back close to find a place to hide up. But a middle-aged couple spotted me. I don't know their names. They wore purple sashes."

"The Whitlows," Una volunteered. "They hunt all over the south."

"I thought they were good," Melanie said. "They caught me pretty neatly..."

At that moment Jill crawled through the door, looking pleased with herself but also completely exhausted. She dragged herself over to the group and slumped down at Melanie's feet.

"I am totally shagged out!" she declared wearily.

Gail, her closest friend, laughed and kissed her lovingly, laying herself by Jill's side and rubbing her soft body against her.

"What happened?" somebody asked.

Jill sniggered. "Two teams tried to run me down at the same time. They had me on the ground when they got into a fight. You should have heard the names they were calling each other! The hounds had already been called off and by the time they sorted themselves out I was well away. Took them hours to catch me again."

She rubbed her red and swollen pubic cleft ruefully. "Mind you, they all gave me a good seeing-to when they did. Don't know how I'm going to manage both teams tonight."

The other girls laughed. Melanie said: "So how many are still out?" She counted heads quickly. There were twenty-one, including herself. The pack was twenty-two strong. "Who's still out... Gillian? Where's Gillian?"

"She's never been last caught before," Una murmured.

"Could she have been hurt?" Melanie wondered.

"She wasn't in the sick room when I went past earlier," Una said.

"I just hope she hasn't done anything stupid. Remember, she promised us she wouldn't let the pack down this time."

Genuine concern showed on Una's face. It was quite a change from the contempt with which she had been treating Gillian when Melanie had arrived only a few days before.

"I could go to Alison," Una suggested. "She can ask if there's been any news..."

At that moment Alison herself entered the pound.

"Here she is, girls," she announced brightly, "today's champion vixen!" And she stepped aside so that Gillian, freshly washed and harnessed, could shuffle in on all fours.

"Mr Platt will be along later with the full list of times," Alison continued. "But I can say that he's very pleased with how you all ran. Now you get some rest - you're going to be very busy tonight, remember."

Alison went out and the pack crowded round Gillian. Melanie was concerned. Gillian seemed very stiff and was shivering slightly.

"What happened?" Melanie asked her, looking her over anxiously for some sign of injury.

"I'm just... cold," Gillian said. "I've been hiding in a... pond for hours."

Sympathetically, a couple of girls pressed their warm bodies against Gillian's pale form and she rubbed gratefully against them.

"You look frozen stiff," Melanie exclaimed.

"I didn't want to let the pack down," Gillian said. She looked at Una. "I used your trick. I went past the pond, then... peed up a tree and backtracked, then jumped in so as not to leave tracks. There was an old moorhen's nest in the middle in a pile of sticks and I hid by that. Riders and hounds went past the pond several times following my scent, but they didn't see me. When it was quiet I crawled onto the bank to warm up, but I kept on

57

having to go back in again when I heard hunters coming. I stayed there as long as I could stand it."

Una looked impressed. "That took some guts."

Gillian smiled shyly at the compliment. "Well, it was certainly better than being caught by Arabella."

"Yeah, who's the unlucky one today?" Una asked.

The other girls exchanged glances and shook their heads.

"Arabella didn't catch any of us?" Melanie said. "What team was she in?"

"She was wearing a white sash - hunting on her own," Una explained. "Probably after you, Mel." She suddenly grinned. "She's going to be really pissed at not getting anyone. But at least she can't take it out on us!"

The girls all laughed. Una kissed Gillian. The girl's warming her did the same. Melanie followed them. Gillian's lips were sweet and her eyes were sparkling as she pulled away from her, reminding Melanie that she was the first woman, under the Major's direction, that she had ever made love with.

What followed seemed perfectly natural.

The huddled group moved closer with whispers of flesh brushing against flesh. The kissing spread, becoming more passionate. Gail slithered around on top of Jill until they lay head to crotch and buried her face between her friend's thighs. Swaying breasts were kissed and licked, hardening nipples nipped lovingly between white teeth. Girls were rolling onto their backs and splaying their legs wide in open invitation, while others were mounting their crouching sisters from behind, rubbing their clefts on the springy shafts of implanted pack tails. Emanating from between twenty two pairs of glistening pubic lips, the heady scent of multiple arousal gradually filled the pound.

Amidst the hot press of bodies, Melanie suddenly found herself staring at a wide-open unclaimed cunt, pink and slippery and lovely. Without hesitation she plunged her face into it and began to lick and suck and tongue in wild delight. Hair brushed the insides of her raised haunches and she felt a tongue

58

sliding into the honeypot of her own split peach. A shiver of ecstasy coursed through her. She didn't know who was pleasuring her and, she realised joyfully, that it didn't matter. Reason had surrendered to lust and they were enjoying themselves as only girls who had had all inhibition driven from them could.

Lost in their own pleasure, the pack did not notice Alison and Platt standing side by side in the kennel doorway watching them. Alison, staring the squirming bodies in open fascination, said: "Should we stop them, Mister Platt?"

Platt turned his gaze quickly back to the orgy.

"No, it's good to let a pack have their private pleasures from time to time," he said quickly. "They all ran well today. They'll rest easily after this and be fresh for tonight. Put up the running times list where they can see it, please Alison."

He turned and made his way back to his office, struggling to maintain his dignity. Proud as he was of his beautiful pack, he had not been watching them make love. Like some nervous schoolboy, he had secretly been peering down the open collar of Alison's shirt at the tantalizingly exposed soft upper curves of her breast.

The irony of the situation was not lost on him. He was master of twenty two beautiful slaves whom he could use almost as freely as the Major, if he chose. Yet he lusted after the sturdy form of his sweet-natured kennelmaid; a girl more than twenty years his junior who could never be his.

10: Frustration

The girls had never before seen Arabella so angry.

She returned to the playhouse later that afternoon still clad in her riding gear with a crop in her hand. They didn't need to ask if her hunt had been successful; the expression on her face told its own story.

For fully ten minutes she paced up and down the tiny garden, muttering under her breath and making vicious swipes at the grass with her crop. The other girls could only watch her in silence, knowing nothing they could say would help.

Eventually Arabella seemed to regain a measure of self-control, and asked sharply: "Have you been treating her as I told you?"

"Yes, Arabella, exactly as you said," Belinda said quickly.

"Did she make the proper responses?"

"Yes, every time."

"Has she protested or spoken out of turn?"

"No. She just sits there."

"Bring her here," Arabella snapped.

Such was their haste to obey that they simply tipped the old butt onto its side, dirty water spewing from its mouth, and rolled it out onto the lawn before Arabella. They heard gasps and groans as Sue's body tumbled about the inside, but were too anxious to care for her comfort. They strained to lift the bottom of the butt and Sue's limp form slithered out onto the grass.

She was a pathetic sight. Pale and shivering and grimy from the slime and mildew that had covered the interior of her prison. Her prolonged immersion had bleached and crinkled the flesh of her legs and buttocks, which were ridged with boardmarks from the bottom of the butt.

Arabella gave Sue a shove with the flat of her boot to roll her over onto her back, then lifted the unfortunate girl's chin with her boot toe. Sue's eyes flickered open and she gazed fearfully up at her mistress.

"Well, girl. What has your morning lesson taught you?" Arabella demanded.

"That I'm worth nothing, Mistress... I'm a slave fit only to be pissed on. I live only to serve you... to obey and to suffer for your pleasure."

The tip of Arabella's riding crop traced the cane marks that formed a lattice across Sue's trembling breasts. "We shall see about that, girl." Arabella turned to the others. "Untie her legs," she commanded. "Then clean her up. I'll be back in a minute."

As Arabella went into the playhouse, the others freed Sue's legs. She whimpered as she tried to straighten her numbed limbs and they had to half-carry her over to the old garden pump, where they washed the worst of the dirt from her. Jemima brought a comb from her bag and gently ran it through Sue's tangled and matted hair.

"Are you all right?" Jemima asked Sue fearfully.

"I suffer for my Mistress," Sue replied mechanically.

"Don't waste your time talking to her," Belinda snapped at Jemima. "Let's get her looking clean before Arabella comes back."

"Have you ever seen Arabella looking so angry?" Penny asked in hushed tones.

"No," Belinda admitted. She pinched one of Sue's abused breasts. "Just be grateful she's got this one to take it out on."

They had just finished their task when Arabella emerged from the playhouse. She was carrying a yellowed roll of drawer lining paper, which she unrolled on the grass, forming a rectangle some six feet long.

"See that it stays flat," she said, and went back into the house again.

The girls quickly found pebbles from the flowerbeds to weigh the paper strip down.

"What's she doing?" Ernestine asked nervously.

"How should I know?" Belinda said.

Arabella appeared again, this time carrying an old wooden serving tray and an enamelled bucket. She set the items carefully down at each end of the paper sheet.

The girls examined the curious arrangement. The tray was covered with about fifty drawing pins, each resting with its point uppermost.

Arabella was flicking her riding crop across Sue's back, urging her to shuffle forward on her knees until she was positioned before the tray.

"You will move the drawing pins from the tray to the bucket," Arabella told her briskly. "Your hands will remain bound and you are not permitted to use your mouth. You will continue until all the pins have been transferred. Do you understand?"

"Yes, Mistress."

Jemima was staring at them in confusion. "But how can she do it without using her hands... oh! No, Arabella, that's too cruel!"

But Sue was already obeying her Mistress's command. She spread her knees wide so that her thighs were almost flat and her pubic bush brushed the grass, then dipped her back and thrust out her bottom, opening the cleft of her buttocks and exposing the dark eye of her anus. Bending forward, she deliberately lowered the heavy pale globes of her breasts over the tray. Her nipples were full and erect, as though perversely intent on increasing her suffering to the limit.

Jemima gasped: "No, don't..." and took a step forward.

Belinda caught her arm. "Don't be stupid! This is just another lesson."

The soft balloons of flesh flattened over the tray, impaling themselves onto the points of the drawing pins. Sue's face contorted with pain. They heard her stifled gasp and saw tears welling about her eyes. But gritting her teeth she pressed harder onto the tray, before carefully raising her torso upright.

Her breasts were grotesquely studded with the shiny heads of at least two dozen pins. Some had only lightly pricked her flesh and hung loosely from her, but several had penetrated for half their length and tiny drops of blood were already forming about their shafts.

With great care Sue shuffled sideways until she was opposite the bucket, and lowered her breasts into it. She wriggled her shoulders, setting her breasts swinging and banging into the bucket sides. Dislodged pins rattled metallically. A few of the more deeply embedded pins remained in place, and Sue had to drag her breasts several times across the rim of the bucket to pull them free.

Finally they were gone and Sue straightened up. Her face was set and tear-streaked. Her breasts, naked once more, were pinpointed with spots of blood, showing livid against their paleness. For a moment her gaze flickered to Arabella, as though hoping for some sign. But Arabella's face did not waver from its expression of hawkish intent. The other girls watched in silent disbelieving fascination.

Resolutely, Sue went back to the tray and bent over it again.

By her third trip a dozen pins were left lying on their side on the tray, together with a few that had fallen off onto the paper between tray and bucket. Try as she might, Sue could not gather them.

Sue straightened up and asked meekly: "Please, Mistress?"

"Jemima," Arabella said. "Put the loose pins back on the tray and set them all point up."

Dumbly Jemima obeyed, arranging the pins in the tightest cluster she could on the very centre of the tray. As she looked up her gaze met Sue's, and she saw the slave girl mouth a silent: 'Thank you,' before bending over the tray again.

Two more agonising trips and it was done.

Sue shuffled over and knelt before Arabella, her face pale, her breasts a bloody testimony to what she had just endured. She looked up at her Mistress in shivering expectation, biting her lip, hoping for the words she longed to hear.

Arabella looked down at her uncertainly, her own face clouded, as though searching for something she herself did not understand. A moment passed heavy with possibility. Arabella suddenly shook her head and her expression set again. "That was quite well done," she said coldly. Nothing more.

Sue made a little choking noise.

Arabella ignored her, turning her attention to the girls.

"Tomorrow you will begin searching for the Jones girl. That fool Bailey is never going to find her. But if there's any chance that she's in hiding, or being kept anywhere in the area, I want to know. Perhaps she'll provide more of a challenge."

Sue collapsed onto her side sobbing quietly, not from physical pain but despair. The despair of a slave who can give no more, the despair of knowing that she would never receive the reward for which she had sacrificed so much.

Jemima soaked her own handkerchief under the garden pump and, while the others talked, began gently to wipe from Sue's breasts the blood that had been shed in vain.

11: Entertaining the Whitlows

The lid of the wicker slave basket creaked open.

"Ah, what a pretty picture she makes, Sam," said Mrs Whitlow.

"I can certainly think of worse things to unpack from a trunk," Mr Whitlow agreed with a fruity chuckle.

They were contemplating Melanie, who was curled up on a blanket in the bottom of the basket.

As with all packgirls delivered to the guests' rooms, she was gagged, blindfolded and had her hands bound behind her. Otherwise, apart from her collar, she was in her natural state of nakedness and ready for whatever the Whitlows cared to do with her. She shivered in anticipation. This would be the first time she had served anyone except the Major, and though she dearly wished it was him, she was determined not to disappoint his guests. Her body was ready; her labia slick with natural lubrication, her anus thoroughly cleaned and oiled.

Melanie felt the Whitlows take hold of her and she allowed them to help her stand up and step out of the basket. She felt thick carpet under her feet. The blindfold strap was removed and she saw her surroundings for the first time.

It was a large, comfortable bedroom, lit by pink-shaded electric bracket lamps. Tall pelmeted windows were heavily curtained against the night, while a thick-piled carpet covered most of the floor, leaving only a strip of dark polished boards around the walls. A massive dark oak four poster bed dominated the room, accompanied by a matching wardrobe, chest of drawers and dressing table and a couple of deep armchairs. It might have been a showroom in any stately home or part of a period suite in some plush country hotel - except for the canes with the leather handle bindings lying casually on the bed and the sets of manacles hanging from the carved bedposts.

The Whitlows, dressed in matching wine-red quilted robes and carpet slippers inspected Melanie, running experienced hands over her body as she stood between them. It was an intimate, methodical, yet quite impersonal examination, as though she was a prize animal - which for practical purposes she was of course - rather than a person. The thought gave Melanie the perverse thrill of mingled shame and excitement.

"Ah," exclaimed Mr Whitlow, "I see her nipples are coming to attention nicely."

"Such firm buds as well," Mrs Whitlow commented, testing the resilience of the chocolate dark cones that had hardened to a glossy sheen, "and so well proportioned to her breasts."

They dipped stiff fingers into the well of flesh between her thighs and sniffed the glistening secretions as though judging the bouquet of a fine wine. Her triangle of tight belly curls was fluffed up and they agreed it was the ideal frame for the thick lovelips that nested within them.

"Feel the weight of her buttocks, Sam. Such pliant flesh."

Mr Whitlow slapped and squeezed the full roundness of Melanie's bottom. "But there's muscle there as well, Marjory. That's what gives her body such a fine tone."

His wife had slipped an exploratory finger up Melanie's rear.

"Beautifully hot and tight," she pronounced. "You'll enjoy yourself up there, Sam. How I wish I could share the experience with you."

"You'll have your fair share of fun, my dear, don't you worry. Now, let's warm her up first."

Melanie was turned to face the foot of the bed and her wrists untied. Her arms were extended and fastened to the upper set of bedpost manacles, but not stretched out tight. In the same way her legs were spread just a couple of feet and manacles closed round her ankles. She was secured but allowed some degree of movement.

The Whitlows took off their robes. They were both quite naked underneath. Mr Whitlow's body hair was grey but under it he was wiry, with only a slight paunch. The beginnings of a substantial erection hung between his legs. Mrs Whitlow had slightly over-full hips and her breasts, with cherry-bright nipples, sagged distinctly. But her skin was very clear and hardly wrinkled. The broad blonde bush of hair between her legs was at least an inch deep and seemed never to have been trimmed.

They picked up a leather-bound cane each and slipped the thong handles over their wrists. Mrs Whitlow got onto the bed facing Melanie and knelt right in front of her, so she could feel the warmth of her body. Looking at her intently, Mrs Whitlow undid Melanie's gag, but immediately put a finger over Melanie's lips.

"A little noise is permitted, my dear. But no words, do you understand?"

Melanie nodded.

Mrs Whitlow smiled, bent forward, put her arms about her and kissed Melanie full on the lips. The intensity of the action surprised Melanie for a moment, but then she found herself responding with equal passion. Mrs Whitlow smelled slightly of Lily of the Valley cologne.

Melanie heard Mr Whitlow chuckle. He ran a hand up and down Melanie's smooth back, patted her bottom, then took up his stance and swung his cane.

It was not a hard blow, just enough to send a shiver through the flesh of her buttocks. At Melanie's gasp, Mrs Whitlow disengaged from their embrace, turned slightly to one side and swung her own cane up at Melanie's breasts.

The impact set them bouncing and sent a sharp jolt through her already swollen nipples, but again it was relatively mild; nothing like the punishment Platt had meted out to her on her first day of captivity. Then Melanie understood. This was not intended as a punishment, but as a means of arousal. The Whitlows wanted to see her respond to stimulation. They wanted her body straining against its bonds, showing off the physique that they so clearly appreciated.

She gave them what they wanted.

Under their carefully placed blows she writhed and jerked against her bonds, swivelling her hips and rolling her bottom sensuously. She gasped and moaned and sighed in a show of helpless delight. Her exertions caused sweat to bead on her brown satin skin and the Whitlows licked it off her, interspersed with pats and strokes and kisses.

A sudden surge of joyous pride in her own being infused Melanie. She was healthy and attractive, but above all, she was vitally alive. The Whitlows might be middle-aged, but they had not forgotten how to celebrate life and passion. Their treatment of her was just another way by which she could express her physical prowess, not so different from running in the hunt. In fact it was the natural culmination of the hunt. A sexual perfor-mance taking the place of the killing and feast, with all her strength and agility channelled into giving pleasure.

Mrs Whitlow reached between Melanie's sweaty thighs and felt upward. Melanie rubbed her mound urgently into her hand, groaning imploringly. Mrs Whitlow examined the glistening deposit on her palm with a smile and said: "She's ready, Sam."

They released Melanie from the manacles, turned her about and dragged her up the bed on her back, until they could re-fasten her spread-eagled between the bedposts, her head rest-ing on a plump white pillow. As they looked down at her, Melanie lifted her hips and opened her thighs in a shameless show of need. Her sex gaped wide, the crinkled tongue of her swollen inner lips protruding impudently.

"This little filly is eager for her stallion," said Mrs Whitlow.

"But she must service us both. You mount her first, my dear."

Mrs Whitlow climbed onto the bed, swung round with her back to the headboard, and squatted down over Melanie's face. Her luxuriant bush of pubic hair parted to reveal a deep pink and red cleft extending well up between her thighs. Melanie could smell the heady aroma of the older woman's own arousal as the warm thick lips parted about her face. Melanie's nose slid into the mouth of Mrs Whitlow's vaginal tunnel even as her tongue was flicking out for the love bud rising amid the slippery folds of flesh. Mrs Whitlow ground her hips forward and back, riding Melanie's face with evident delight.

Mr Whitlow climbed onto the bed between Melanie's wide-spread legs and entered her without preliminaries. Melanie gave a muffled gasp as her love tunnel stretched to accommodate the surprising girth of his cock. She felt him kneading her breasts like dough, kissing her throat and then nuzzling into Mrs Whitlow's golden pubic curls. Their tongues met inside the hot slippery folds of his wife's vagina.

Mrs Whitlow turned about so that she faced the headboard and began to ride Melanie's face with increasing vigour. Her husband was raining kisses and tiny nipping bites on her bobbing buttocks even as he rammed himself even harder into Melanie. Almost lost beneath them, Melanie squirmed and bucked and tongued and squeezed with all her might.

They all came within seconds of each other and Melanie was inundated with male and female ejaculate both inside and out. As the spasms subsided they sank into a blissfully exhausted heap.

For half an hour the Whitlows lay sprawled across Melanie, talking softly to each other and exchanging affectionate kisses; occasionally fondling Melanie and telling her she'd been a good girl. It was hardly more attention than a favourite family pet might receive, and yet Melanie felt no resentment. It all seemed so perfectly natural that she was simply content to have served them so pleasurably. The Whitlows drank some red wine and fed a little to Melanie. It must have reinvigorated Mr Whitlow, for soon after he said to his wife:

"Ready for another ride, Old Girl?"

Mrs Whitlow smiled almost coquettishly. "Really, Sam. You are quite insatiable."

"You should know that after all these years. But you've never failed to keep up with me."

"You old tease! Had you something particular in mind?"

"The Mountheath Hotel in 79?"

Mrs Whitlow laughed and reached over to her husband's flaccid penis which lay across Melanie's thigh and stroked and squeezed it encouragingly. "I knew you'd not miss a chance to put this into her tightest hole. Will the poor thing be able to take you?"

"They usually do after a bit of squealing. Are you game for the Old Reliable?"

"I usually rise to the occasion..." She looked down. "As you seem to be doing now."

Melanie was unchained from the bedposts and her hands were strapped behind her once again. Mr Whitlow brought out a leather covered case from the wardrobe and opened it up before her. Inside was a double-ended strap-on dildo of such thickness that Melanie gave a little gasp. This must be the 'Old Reliable'. Would she be able to take it? It didn't matter of course, because she had no choice.

Mrs Whitlow braced her as her husband knelt before Melanie and slid one end of the device into her tremulous cunt. For a moment she thought her tunnel mouth would not stretch wide enough, but then it gave way to the intruder and the thing passed all the way up her, wrenching a little gasp from her on the way.

As the waist strap was secured, Melanie stood with her legs spread wide. She was fearful of bringing them any closer in case the pressure was too much.

She'd never been so completely filled!

The head of the dildo bobbed before her. The fit was so tight that every movement was transmitted back to her inner passage, so it seemed almost an extension of herself. It conveyed a strange sense of potency. Was this what men felt following after their erections?

Mrs Whitlow returned to kneel on the bed. She gathered up a couple of plump pillows and bent over them so that they supported her upper torso. The posture thrust out her pink buttocks towards Melanie. Mrs Whitlow looked at her over her shoulder and gave an encouraging wiggle, at the same time spreading her knees wider.

Mr Whitlow helped Melanie climb onto the bed and shuffle gingerly forward on her knees until she was kneeling behind his wife. Holding the shaft of the dildo he guided it towards the gaping pink lips half buried in the fluffy mass of his wife's pubic bush. Melanie watched in fascination as it slid into the older woman with hardly any resistance, bringing forth only a low sigh from Mrs Whitlow's lips as it sank home to its full length.

Mr Whitlow climbed onto the bed behind Melanie and knelt in turn between her legs. He pulled Melanie's bound arms upwards and ducked inside them, so that she was bent forward to rest on Mrs Whitlow's back. Now Melanie's wrists were crossed behind Mr Whitlow's back and she grunted as her shoulders were stretched backwards to embrace him.

Still bowed over, she felt the head of his cock was nuzzling at the pucker of her oiled anus. She tried to relax her sphincter, knowing what a monster she had to accommodate. She felt herself being forced open wider and wider, and, as Mr Whitlow had predicted, she squealed aloud. Her front passage was already full to bursting. She couldn't take any more! His cock and the end of the dildo were trying to occupy the same space inside her pelvis. Surely she would be torn open!

"You can take it, girl," Mr Whitlow said encouragingly.

Suddenly the head of his cock was inside her and her anal ring was sliding down its shaft with relative ease. She was crammed full and ready to burst. The pressure within her was almost unbearable and the pleasure indescribable. The three had become one, with Melanie the conduit between husband and wife - as though both women were penetrated through by one cock.

Clasping her breasts from behind to control her, Mr Whitlow pulled her back a few inches then thrust hard into Melanie's rear, forcing her to plunge the dildo sprouting from between her legs into his wife. Mrs Whitlow cried out in delight.

"Yes, Sam! All the way. Ream her out. I want to feel you inside her."

Mr Whitlow reached round Melanie, clasped his wife's breasts and thrust again, ramming into Melanie so hard it felt like he was trying to push right through her into his wife's hungry cunt.

The threesome surged to and fro ecstatically. Building up a rhythm, sweat-sheened where their bodies rubbed and pressed together. Melanie added her own efforts to those of Mr Whitlow: thrust hips forward to impale his wife, push hips back to impale herself.

When the tension within her could no longer be denied, a gut-wrenching, mind-searing orgasm of slavish intensity burst within Melanie. Just as befitted the plaything of two loving hedonists.

12: Sally gets an Offer

The brisk ringing of a bicycle bell caused Constable Bailey to open the gates of the police station punishment yard.

"Oh, hallo, Sister," he said, as his visitor drew up.

"I hoped I might catch you, Mr Bailey," said Miss Newcombe. "You're usually here for the end of the morning pillory session."

"Yes, I'd just closed up. What can I do for you?"

"There were a couple of things - if you can spare me a few minutes?"

"Always glad to chat with you, Sister - if you don't mind me getting on with my work while we talk. You'd better come in. Bring your bike."

Miss Newcombe wheeled her bike into the yard and Bailey closed the gates behind her.

The walled yard was where the residents of Shaftwell con-tributed to the process of public shaming and torment that the law decreed appropriate for young women who broke its edicts. By the gate was a box of pillory shot - balls of coloured mud wrapped in greaseproof paper - while in the middle of the yard a girl was strapped to a target board.

The board was tilted backwards at 45 degrees and the girl was fastened to it in a spread-eagled position so that her feet hung clear of the ground. She was naked but, like the board on which she was mounted, covered in muddy multi-coloured splashes and trickles from dozens of pillory shots. From the burst patterns several looked as though they had struck her very hard. Something also extended from between her spread legs to add to her misery.

Miss Newcombe regarded the unfortunate girl with inter-est. "Ah, Sally Potts. She was one of the things I wanted to talk about. But first, I was wondering if you'd had any luck tracing the Jones girl? It seems so extraordinary her disappearing like that."

72

Bailey's large face darkened. "It is that, Sister. I've made enquiries and searched as far as I can, but nobody's seen hide nor hair of her. And there's no reports from other districts."

"Could it have been those men I glimpsed in the woods when she first appeared, the ones she said originally waylaid her?"

"Maybe, Sister. I wouldn't admit it to everybody, but it's got me baffled. A gang bold enough to break a girl out of jail. You hardly ever hear of such a thing, certainly not round these parts. Won't look good on my record, that's for sure. I never lost a prisoner before."

"I'm sure your superiors will understand," Miss Newcombe said sympathetically. "You had her properly secured as far as the means at your disposal allowed. Nobody can blame you."

Bailey brightened slightly. "Well, that's kind of you to say so, Sister. Now, what did you want with Sally Potts?"

"I believe I mentioned, when you had the Jones girl in custody, that I was considering investing in a bondservant. I had thought then about bidding for Jones herself, but now she's gone, perhaps Potts will do."

"But she won't be going to auction, Sister. She's never done anything serious enough to warrant it. Leastwise, we've never caught her."

"I thought I might convince her to enter my service voluntarily. I don't think she's a bad girl at heart. I believe she has possibilities... if she has the proper guidance."

Bailey chuckled. "I think you'll have your work cut out for you there, Sister. A very independently minded little minx, she is. But, if you want to make the offer, I've no objection." He made his way over to a garden hose coiled against the wall.

"I'd better wash her down first," he said, turning on the tap and picking up the end of the hose. "Mind you don't get splashed."

Miss Newcombe watched as Bailey hosed the mud from Sally, revealing a pink body and blonde hair beneath. When he

73

was finished he said: "Let me know when you're done," and went back inside the police station.

Miss Newcombe walked up to the bedraggled girl and looked her over.

Sally was a petite girl of nineteen or twenty, with sharp defiant eyes and pouting, impudent lips. Her hips were slim and her breasts, full for her size, were soft and loose. The object protruding from the reddened lips between her legs was a round flap of rubber, a little like a paddle blade, attached to a spring handle. Around the neck of the paddle was a ring of metal spikes. Any pillory shot striking the blade would set it bouncing freely. From the number of scratches on her thighs it appeared that several had.

"Do you know who I am?" Miss Newcombe asked.

"I've seen you about," said Sally. "You're the nurse at that boy's school. So what?"

"I thought you might need my help."

"I ain't sick."

"But you still need help."

"I don't need nobody's help."

"Really?" Miss Newcombe pointedly looked Sally's helpless body up and down once again, then reached out and wagged the end of the punishment paddle to and fro, making Sally jerk in alarm. "It doesn't look like that from where I'm standing."

"I'm getting out of here today," Sally said. "Then I'll be on my way..."

"To where?" Miss Newcombe interjected. "You have no home, no proper friends. You're a vagabond, a petty thief and a casual prostitute, living by your wits and luck. You don't dare stay anywhere more than a few days for fear of arrest."

"But I'm free!" Sally said defiantly.

"But for how long? What happens when you get arrested for something more serious - as you will inevitably and you know it. You'll get six months or a year of public servitude, perhaps more. You won't be free then."

74

"I'll manage!" Sally blustered, but she sounded less sure of herself. There was powerful conviction behind Miss Newcombe's words.

"Perhaps; until the next time. At the moment the police tolerate you as a minor nuisance, and you make a pretty target in the pillory to fill an empty yard. But once you've had a spell of servitude they won't be so forgiving. You'll just be a little lonely, good for nothing tramp."

Sally tugged futilely at her bonds, discovering that words could hurt more than pillory shot. "It won't be like that!"

"Well, if you're so certain, then I can do nothing for you," said Miss Newcombe with a resigned sigh. "As you say, you'll be released at midday. Of course, I'm sure that Constable Bailey will be wanting to give you something to remember him by before you go - as I'm sure all the policemen who've ever arrested you have done. Do you really want that to be the pattern of the rest of your life? A jail slut to be had chained up against the bars when the local constable's bored - oh yes, I know what they do to you in the cells. You might ask yourself: is that all I want to achieve? Well, goodbye..."

Miss Newcombe turned to leave.

"Wait!" Sally said quickly. Miss Newcombe turned back to her. "What's this 'help' you wanted to give me?"

"I was going to suggest you become my bondslave."

Sally gave a derisive laugh. "How would that help me? Bondslaves are nothing. At least I can hold my head up."

"Sally, most people think you're nothing already, and they don't care if you hold your head up or not. Face the facts. I have a certain position in this community. As my bondservant you would benefit from that by association. It would mean you could walk down the street without people looking out for their washing lines or cakes cooling on windowsills."

"But I'd be a slave no better than what you said I'd end up as anyway. I'd still have to please you like any master."

Miss Newcombe stroked her fingers lightly across Sally's

75

soft stomach, then up to her right breast, which she began to knead gently.

"Of course you'll have to serve me, but it will be nothing you haven't done before and less than Bailey's put you through here. I don't pretend I'm making this offer out of pure altruism. I'd enjoy owning a pretty girl like you - and you could be very pretty with the right grooming. Yes, I'll be strict, but I'll also teach you manners, improve your education and perhaps give you some genuine self respect."

Under her gentle manipulations, Sally's nipple was rising, the areola spreading and darkening. Miss Newcombe smiled at the display.

"You don't seem to find my touch unpleasant," she said. "Think how much easier it will be this way. It will be a private arrangement you'll have entered into voluntarily, say for six months at first. If you don't like it, or if I find you unsatisfactory, then you won't be any worse off than you would have been."

Sally was frowning deeply as her eyes searched Miss Newcombe's face. She said slowly: "If you want me that bad what will you pay for me? Maybe I'll sell myself as a bondslave - the law says people can. Then I'd have something put by at the end of it."

Miss Newcombe laughed. "You're a mercenary little creature. If I had to pay I'd expect a dedicated slave. Would you be worth it?"

Her hand left Sally's breast and slid down her body to the damp tangle of blonde hair between her legs. A finger slipped between soft pubic lips parted by the shaft of the punishment paddle and began to tease the hood of Sally's clitoris. Sally gave a tiny helpless moan and her eyelids flickered closed. She forced the words out: "You'd be taking a chance - just like you want me to with you!"

Miss Newcombe laughed and bent over and kissed Sally lightly on the mouth. She withdrew her finger from Sally's cleft and sniffed the glistening deposit left upon it thoughtfully.

"Maybe you are worth paying for. Shall we allow ourselves a little more time to think it over?"

"All right," Sally agreed cautiously. "But I ain't promising nothing."

"Fair enough. I'll tell Bailey not to move you on for a few days. I live in School House Cottage. I have some errands to run now, but I'll be back there later this afternoon. We can talk further then. Now I'd better let Bailey see to you. I should think he's getting impatient to give you your leaving present."

Just after midday, Sally, still smarting both inside and out from Bailey's farewell, emerged from the Police Station door. She was clothed, for the first time in weeks, in her shapeless old coat and long patched skirt. In her hand was a carpetbag that contained all her worldly possessions. Bailey saw her on her way with a wry grin.

"So you'll be turning over a new leaf, will you Sally Potts?" he said. "Going into bond under Miss Newcombe?"

"Maybe I will and maybe I won't," Sally replied haughtily. "One thing's for sure - you ain't going to have me again!"

"I'll keep a cell warm just in case," Bailey said with a chuckle to her retreating back.

Sally stomped her way through Shaftwell, ignoring the looks of the people she passed instead of staring them out or pulling faces as was her normal response.

As she walked she realised that her clothes itched and smelled, and not just with the stuffiness of storage. At least she'd been kept clean in jail, with all that hosing down. Skin was easy to manage with a bit of soap and water. Pity she couldn't live in skin all year round. It was nice to smell good. She found herself wondering if she could talk herself into being given a hot bath at Miss Newcombe's. Probably, if she sounded pathetic enough.

She cheered herself with thought that she'd have some money soon. She was making for the rendezvous agreed with the Cranborough House boys, where they would pay her ten shillings for not giving them away to Bailey the night they broke Amber out of jail. With that she could... well, she'd think of something.

Walking with a little more spring in her step, she continued on out of Shaftwell along the road leading towards Cranborough House. She'd only gone a little way when she realised she was being followed.

13: Jemima the Detective

Jemima looked up and down the empty road in dismay. Where could Sally Potts have gone? Sally had rounded a bend and Jemima had run to keep up, but when she got there Sally had vanished. How could she go back to Arabella and admit that she couldn't do a simple thing such as following a vagrant like Sally?

When Arabella had set them to finding Amber the previous day, the other girls had been given serious tasks like questioning the station porter or delivery drivers, or making a map of old barns and disused buildings in the area. Jemima, however, had been instructed to follow Sally when she was released in case she knew more than she had told about Amber's disappearance, or even went looking for Amber herself. But Arabella had already interrogated Sally herself, quite cruelly, and had decided she knew nothing useful. Secretly, Jemima suspected she'd been given a pointless job as a punishment for not being strict enough with Sue.

Now it looked as though she was going to fail even in this.

"What you doing following me about, then?" a voice demanded right behind her.

Jemima jumped and spun around. Sally was standing there

with her fists resting aggressively on her hips. Sally hadn't seemed frightening when Jemima seen her naked and chained in the pillory. Now, though she was no bigger than Jemima, she suddenly looked threatening and capable of anything.

"I... I wasn't following you," Jemima stammered.

"Don't piss me about. I saw you jumping behind trees every time you thought I was going to turn round. What are you up to?"

"I... I was worried about you."

"Oh, yeah?"

"When Arabella did those things to your... your..." she nodded desperately at Sally's breasts swaying freely behind her frayed lace-up shirt.

"You mean when she nearly tore my tits off with her chain and clips?"

"Yes. I thought you might have been hurt. I was just following you to say I was sorry and see if you were all right."

A mischievous smile flashed across Sally's face and her manner underwent a sudden change. "Were you really worried about me?" she asked gently.

"Oh yes. Arabella was so nasty. I didn't want to be there, but Arabella insisted. She's like that."

"Well now you can see she what she did. Come on."

Sally led the way off the road into the trees where she had left her bag.

"I beg your pardon?" Jemima said, following uncertainly after her.

Under the shelter of the trees Sally turned round to face Jemima and pulled open the neck of her shirt. Her breasts squeezed through and bobbed free.

"There, see what she did to me?"

Jemima blushed at the sudden exposure. "I can't tell..."

"Come closer. You can't see from over there."

With embarrassed, hesitant steps Jemima walked up to Sally, who lifted her malleable breasts with her palms so that the nipples pointed skyward. "Do you see the bruises on my nips?"

As Jemima bent forward to look closer Sally grabbed her shoulders, spun her round and pushed. Jemima went sprawling backwards onto a grassy bank with Sally falling on top of her. Pinning Jemima's arms to her sides with her knees, Sally grasped Jemima's hair to hold her head steady and wriggled about until her bare left breast was flattened against Jemima's horrified face.

"Now, you're going to kiss 'em better!" Sally rasped.

Jemima's eyes saucered. "No, please!" She struggled, but Sally was stronger than she was and kept her pinioned, enjoying the futile squirming of the girl's body under her own.

"Do it!" Sally commanded.

Jemima's struggles ceased and Sally sensed her surrender. Her face woebegone, Jemima gently kissed the warm globe of flesh.

Sally shifted her position so that her right breast dangled over Jemima's face. "Now this one!"

Again Jemima obeyed. Her lips were very soft.

Emboldened by Jemima's compliance, Sally said. "Now suck my nips until they're hard!"

A momentary flicker of alarm crossed Jemima's face. Her body tensed against Sally's, then relaxed again. She opened her mouth and accepted the nipple Sally thrust into it. Her lips closed about it. Sally felt the curious flicker of Jemima's tongue as it explored the contours of the unfamiliar form. Jemima drew on the teat hesitantly.

"Go on, harder than that!" Sally said.

Jemima's eyes closed and her lips and tongue began working busily, cheeks hollowing as she sucked as she had been instructed. Sally's nipple swelled as blood coursed into it.

"That's better," Sally said.

Jemima's face had relaxed. She looked almost blissful as she sucked away.

She was enjoying it! And so, Sally had to admit to herself,

was she. It wasn't quite what she'd planned.

With an effort she raised her shoulders, pulling her breast free from the warm moist haven of Jemima's mouth and leaving Jemima blinking in confusion. Then awareness returned and Jemima turned her head aside in shame. Sally clasped her chin and twisted it back to face her.

"Just what are you?" Sally demanded. "You couldn't keep your eyes off what Arabella was doing to me and now you nearly come giving me a tit-sucking!"

Jemima's face crumpled in dismay. "I know! I can't help it! I must be very bad. I hated seeing you hurt, but I kept wondering... what it felt like... I'm sorry!" And she broke down into uncontrollable sobbing.

Sally looked down at her in amazement, then shook her head. She was taking her revenge on the wrong person. Though it felt nice, this pretty little mixed-up wimp was too easy a conquest.

She rolled off the distraught girl and wriggled her breasts back inside her shirt. Jemima continued crying. After a minute Sally reached out an awkward hand and patted her shoulder. "All right, you can stop blubbering. I ain't going to do anything else to you."

Jemima sat up slowly, pulled a handkerchief from her sleeve and dabbed her eyes. She glanced guiltily at Sally.

"Please... don't tell anyone about this," she begged.

"I won't if you tell me straight why you were really following me."

Jemima sniffed miserably. "Arabella wants to find Amber Jones and keep her for herself. She wants to train anoth... a slave of her own. She's got us all out looking. I was sent to follow you because... just in case you did know where Amber was. And now I've got to go back to Arabella and tell her how I made a mess of it all..."

She started crying again. Sally sighed in exasperation.

"I told you: stop blubbing! You don't have to tell Arabella

bloody Westlake the truth."

Jemima caught her breath. "I don't?" she sniffed.

Was the girl stupid or just too dumb honest? Sally wondered.

"No," she said firmly. "Well, half the truth, maybe. Did you see the nurse go into the police yard while I was there?"

"Yes."

"Well she wants to save me from going to the bad by taking me under bond. I said I'd think about it. I'm goin' to her house by the school gates to look the place over and maybe talk to her again. So I'll be around here for the next few days at least - and it's been okayed with Bailey, so he won't be moving me on. You tell your precious Arabella all that, but not that I saw you, and she'll think you've been real smart."

Jemima looked a little more cheerful. "I could say that, couldn't I?"

"'Course you could," Sally said encouragingly. "What happened here can be our secret." If Arabella was going to have her followed, Sally thought, she'd rather it was by Jemima. She might even be able to use her to pass something really misleading to Arabella later on.

Jemima was looking pensive again. "Is it strange to feel the way I do... about girls... and being punished?"

Sally wasn't sure quite how to respond. "Depends. The funniest things sometimes makes you hot."

"But did you get excited like that when you were in the pillory... or when Arabella was torturing you?"

"I can get off on a bit of rough treatment," Sally admitted. "But Arabella's a mean bitch, the sort that's never satisfied. She took it too far to be fun."

"She always does," Jemima agreed sadly.

Jemima returned the playhouse for lunch as agreed, so that Arabella could get reports of their progress.

As the weather had clouded over and was threatening rain,

they were all in the old sitting room when she arrived. The other girls were eating their packed lunches while Arabella lounged back in a chair using Sue as a footrest.

Sue was perfectly if uncomfortably positioned to serve such a purpose, confined on all fours by her training harness. Steel rods a foot long with cuff rings mounted on the ends kept her wrists and ankles in close proximity. A three-foot chain connected the two rods, while from the ankle rod another chain ran up under her body and emerged between her breasts to fasten to her collar. These restraints meant that Sue could not straighten her body, and could only move about by shuffling on her hands and knees.

Sue's face was blank of expression, staring sightlessly at the carpet. Her dangling breasts still bore the scratches and prickmarks of yesterday's torture, but there were no fresh punishment marks on her. In a horrible way Jemima understood her evident misery. Arabella could not be bothered to torment her further. She would continue to use Sue as it suited her, but she was no longer truly interested in her.

As she tucked into her own meal, Jemima gave her edited version of her morning's investigations and was secretly pleased to see grudging admiration on the faces of the others for the amount of information she had obtained. By the looks of it they had not found out anything useful. At least what she had discovered was interesting and showed she had tried.

"You have been busy, Jem," Arabella said when she had finished. "It almost makes up for your disappointing behaviour yesterday."

Jemima felt a sudden shiver at the tone of Arabella's words. She saw the others were grinning at her nastily. What had they been talking about before she arrived?

"I don't understand," Jemima said, trying to keep her voice level. "What did I do wrong?"

"You showed too much concern over this," Arabella said, tapping her heel on the piece of human furniture before her.

83

"You started cleaning her up while I was still talking to you."

"But she was bleeding."

"A few scratches," Arabella said dismissively. "There was no need to make such a fuss. You have to learn when to show the proper interest in a slave and when to ignore them. They're here to be used for our convenience, do you understand?"

"Yes, Arabella."

Arabella smiled thinly. "You do still want to learn about training slaves, don't you?"

"Oh, yes."

The other girls sniggered. Jemima gulped.

"Good," said Arabella. "Then since you seem so fascinated by this one, you can try her out and get a proper taste for what owning a bondslave really means. Or perhaps I should say, she'll get a taste for you."

"I don't know what you mean."

Belinda and Penny had risen and stepped quickly over to stand ominously on either side of Jemima's chair. She tried to stand herself but they firmly held her down. Ernestine appeared with a handful of ropes and in seconds they had tied Jemima's arms to the armrests of the chair.

"Arabella - stop them!" Jemima wailed. "This isn't funny!"

"Yes it is," said Belinda.

"It's your own fault for going all goopy over the girl," Ernestine said. "Now you've got to be taught a lesson."

And they began rolling her skirt up to her waist.

Jemima shrieked and kicked, but to no avail.

When her skirt was out of the way they began tugging down her panties. She clenched her thighs together but they slapped and pinched and wrenched them apart until her panties were pulled free of her feet. They then spread her legs and tied them to the feet of the chair so that her private parts were exposed for all to see.

They laughed at her pubic mound and the shy lips below it.

"Now we'll see if you're a girl or a woman," Belinda said.

84

Arabella had turned Sue round and prodded her forward so that she was crouched in front of Jemima. Now Arabella picked up a device that had been lying along the skirting board and which Jemima hadn't noticed before.

It was a broomhandle-sized wooden rod with a trigger grip at one end and a rubber phallus at the other. Running along its length through eyelets was a wire cable, which ended at the base of the phallus in a dangling pair of toothed spring clamps.

Arabella sat in a chair opposite Jemima and extended the rod device. The phallus end slid between Sue's rounded buttocks and butted against her anus. With a sharp shove from Arabella the phallus vanished all the way inside her.

"Put the clips on her," Arabella told Belinda.

Belinda squatted down and fumbled between Sue's legs for a few seconds. Sue gave a little gasp and Belinda straightened up.

Arabella squeezed the trigger and the cable tightened. The pink petals of Sue's inner labia were stretched painfully backwards by the clamps now biting into them, bringing forth another yelp from Sue.

Arabella smiled and looked at Jemima. "That will continue until you come, do you understand?"

Jemima, beyond words, could only nod.

Arabella urged Sue forward with the control rod until her cheeks were brushing Jemima's pale inner thighs and she could feel her warm breath whispering over her pubic hair. Sue flicked a glance up at Jemima and mouthed: 'Sorry'; then nuzzled forward under the urging of her Mistress and kissed Jemima's virgin orifice.

Jemima bit her lip and shut her eyes.

She didn't blame Sue. She was just a tool of Arabella's will.

Both she and Sue were helpless prisoners of their secret desires. Now they were paying the price.

Sue began kissing and licking Jemima's love mouth, gently rousing the petals within into bud and flower. And like a flower a dew was forming as blood pulsed and the delicious knot of pleasure began to tie itself in her loins. Jemima groaned. It was like sitting on the butt again, but this time being able to touch Sue instead of simply looking at her.

Sue's nose was buried in her now slick and glistening cleft. Her tongue was probing into places Jemima herself had hardly explored. Jemima wanted to surrender herself to the pleasure, but she could not. That was the real torture; feeling the unfriendly eyes upon them. She heard them laughing and making rude comments about her and Sue. They didn't want to see or share her pleasure, just her shame.

Sue yelped. Arabella had pulled on the trigger that stretched her labia.

"Faster!" she commanded. "Make her beg you to finish her off!"

Sue had to obey, lapping at her like a frenzied dog, concentrating all her efforts on Jemima's tender swollen young clitoris. And Jemima let the words be dragged from her as she knew they must be if they were both to saved further torment.

"Please... please... make me come... more... I must come now... yes!"

The fireworks of pleasure exploded within her and for a few seconds nothing else in the world mattered.

Then came the terrible fall into utter humiliation.

Released by the contractions of her orgasm, hot urine was spurting from between her engorged lips. And, as with the butt, it was splashing over Sue's face which still rested between her thighs. And Sue, the perfect slave, accepted her wetting meekly while the other girls laughed uproariously at their wretched double humiliation.

Jemima broke down and cried.

An eternity later, as it seemed, Arabella was pinching Jemima's tear-streaked cheeks and forcing her to look her in the eye.

"Learnt your lesson now?"

Jemima nodded.

"Next time don't disappoint me."

Jemima shook her head, trying not to tremble.

For the first time she fully realised how much Arabella frightened her.

14: S.C.R.A.W. is Born.

"I want to see Amber!" Sally said once again. "Is that so hard to understand? I thought you boys were supposed to be smart."

Sally was at the rendezvous near the gates of Cranborough House and had met Jackson, who had handed over the agreed sum of money. Now however he was standing his ground against Sally's unexpected demand.

"You've been paid what you asked, now go away," he told her impatiently. "Amber belongs to us. She's our responsibility, not yours."

"But she's still my friend," Sally persisted. "I want to see she's all right. No harm in that, is there?"

"Everybody knows bondslaves don't get visitors," Jackson said flatly.

"Official, legal bondslaves, maybe not," Sally agreed. "But then she's not that, is she? This is a, what you call it, a private bargain. So now you can privately agree that it's right and proper that I should visit. Unless you want me to think you've hurt her. Then I might go right back to Constable Bailey and..."

"You promised not to tell!" Jackson exclaimed.

"I promised not to tell who really sprung Amber from jail - and I ain't and won't. But I didn't say nothing about what I'd do afterwards if I chanced to come across her, say, in the clutches of some evil gang keeping her prisoner in an empty school-"

"All right!" Jackson stemmed the flow of Sally's fanciful exaggerations. He sighed. "I supposed it won't hurt if you see her. But we'll be watching you, so don't try to help her escape."

"If she's being well treated I won't do anything. She made her deal with you. How she lives with it is her business."

"You'd better follow me. We've got to go round the edge of the grounds in case Sister Newcombe comes along."

Ten minutes later Sally climbed through the trapdoor of the loft and looked around. Amber was roped and chained in her pen. Sally called out cheerfully and ran over and hugged her. Before Jackson's fascinated if embarrassed gaze they kissed deeply mouth to mouth. Then Sally looked Amber's naked and bound form up and down intently.

"Bailey's probably dreaming of having you back in the cells like this."

Amber laughed ruefully and shrugged in her bonds.

"I said I'd probably be trussed up like a turkey the next time we met."

"Have they been treating you right?" Sally asked softly.

"Nothing I couldn't handle," Amber assured her in the same tone. In a normal voice she added: "They're decent lads really, though I could have done with a bit of help handling them..." She grinned. "Well not handling, exactly. They want to try everything three times a day and once at night. But they don't give me a chance to keep up. They're finished before I'm half-way there."

"Young cocks are like that," Sally agreed knowledgeably. "Toss their loads after half a minute of in and outs. Older men last longer. You can really work up a sweat with them..."

She paused and she and Amber both turned their heads to stare at Jackson, who had been listening in silent fascination.

"Do you mind," Sally said haughtily. "This is a private conversation. People who've been brought up proper don't earwig!"

Such was the conviction in her words that Jackson actually looked abashed.

"Er... I'll be off, then. We've got jobs to do, but we'll be free after lunch."

He left, locking the trapdoor behind him.

Sally and Amber looked at each other and giggled girlishly.

Sally settled herself beside Amber and cuddled up as close as her bonds allowed.

"This Sister Newcombe seems to 'ave 'em well under her thumb," she observed.

"I only met her once, but she's tough all right," Amber agreed.

"She came to see me this morning," Sally said slowly. "She made me an offer..."

Sally related what had been said. When she finished she looked at Amber expectantly. "What d'you think? Should I do it?"

"You're asking me? Isn't there somebody who can give you a more informed opinion? I'm only just getting my mind round the idea that people can sell themselves into slavery. I'm a stranger here, remember."

Sally chewed her lip, suddenly looking younger than her brash outspoken manner made her appear. "You see, a bit of what she said was right," she said slowly. "I ain't got anybody else to talk to about it. I know people, but there's none I'd call real friends. You're the nearest thing I got to a proper friend."

The unexpectedly frank admission touched Amber. All they'd shared was a little less than two days in cells or the pillory. There had been some intimate moments, of course, but if that had been enough to make Sally regard her as a friend, the poor girl must be desperate.

Amber bent and kissed Sally. "I'm very honoured that you think of me as your friend." She frowned. "As for your decision, you know best what you'd be giving up. I suppose it would give you security of a sort. The trial period sounds sensible. If it didn't work out you wouldn't have lost much. Why don't you talk to Miss Newcombe some more. Find out exactly what she'd expect of you. If this is all done legally there should be a contract of some sort. Get a copy and read it first."

"I ain't very fast at reading," Sally admitted.

"Then bring it to me and we'll go through it together."

Sally smiled gratefully, looking much happier again. They kissed.

Sally fingers had been idly stroking Amber's stomach as they talked. Now they slipped lower into the valley between Amber's thighs held apart by the spreader bar tied to her ankles.

"Oh... that's nice," said Amber. "Don't stop."

Sally grinned. "Those boys ain't been letting you finish yourself off, have they? Good thing I came along..."

When all the boys returned to the loft after lunch Amber was looking far more relaxed. Not that they noticed. The other four only had eyes for Sally.

"What did you let her up here for?" said Harris angrily.

"You can never trust her kind," added Gosset.

"Why didn't you just send her on her way?" said Bickley.

"Getting in here might be part of a trick to help Amber escape," Parsons warned darkly.

"Look, they're both still here, aren't they?" Jackson protested. "No harm's been done."

"Well let's get her out of here quickly before Sister sees her," said Parsons.

"But will she tell on us?" Gosset said. "She may want more money. Her sort always do."

"Excuse me!" Sally said loudly, scrambling to her feet and pushing her way into the middle of the bickering group of boys. "That's a fine way to talk about your new lodger!"

That statement captured their attention. Before they could recover from the surprise, Sally continued with the air of one letting them into the secrets of her social diary. "I may be wanting to stay around here for a few days. This place of yours doesn't look too bad. O' course I wouldn't stay without payin' rent. That wouldn't be proper. So all you got to do is say how you want to be paid."

The implication of her words slowly sank in. For the first time the boys looked at Sally as something more than a nuisance. She smiled back knowingly.

"We can't do it with her," Gosset said.

"Why not?" Parsons said, looking Sally up and down with growing interest.

"You know what they say... her sort are always a bit dirty."

Sally glared at Gosset indignantly. "I ain't dirty - Bailey gave me a hosing down just this morning. So my clothes may whiff a bit - but clothes can be taken off easy enough if you want..."

Sally stood before them expectantly as the suggestion, with all its exciting implications, hung in the air. The boys licked their lips and exchanged anxious glances.

Looking on as a fascinated bystander, Amber realised how uncertain they were about taking the next step with Sally, despite her virtually offering herself to them on a plate. None of them was willing to make the first move. For all their recent practise with her and what they were learning from the handbook, this was all new to them. Apparently boys could live in a slave owning society and still be nervous and ignorant when it came to dealing with the opposite sex.

Sally made an impatient face. "Course if you ain't up to it, I'll just have to try elsewhere. But you'll be missing one of my specials if you do."

The boys looked lost, slightly awed by Sally's brazen self-confidence. Jackson, clearly unsure of himself, glanced round at Amber as though silently begging for guidance.

"I'm sure it'll be good value," Amber said. "Why not give her a try."

Reassured, Jackson turned back to Sally and took a deep breath. "Grab her," he said quickly.

Harris and Bickley obeyed, each catching hold of one of her arms and pulling it out and a little behind her, so that her body was thrust forward at Jackson. Sally gave an artful little gasp and her eyes widened, as though surprised by the boys' strength and initiative.

"We'll show you whether we're up to it or not," Jackson said.

He untied the lacing of Sally's shirt and jerked the flaps apart. He reached inside, clasped her breasts and as he bent, kissed her in the forceful, open-mouthed manner Amber had taught them. For a moment genuine surprise flickered across Sally's face, then she gave herself up to the intimate contact; responding hungrily with her own lips.

Jackson broke the kiss looking flushed and excited. Amber knew why: Sally put a lot into a kiss.

"What's she like?" Parsons asked eagerly.

"Find out for yourself!"

They took turns kissing Sally fiercely, pinching and pawing while she struggled sufficiently in their grasp to ensure they kept a firm hold of her. Her face showed excitement and confusion, as though she was being overwhelmed by the intensity of the process she herself had initiated. As each boy had kissed her she had felt his growing erection pressing against her and knew there was no turning back now.

When they were done Jackson took hold of Sally's hair and pulled her head back so that she had to look up at him. Her eyes were fearful but defiant, her sulky pouting lips flushed and more provocative that ever. Who could resist dominating such a creature?

"Strip her!" Jackson said.

They tore her loose shirt off over her head and her breasts swung naked and free before them. The boys pressed against her and impatient hands reached out to maul and fondle her mammaries, testing their weight and pinching their rubbery nipples.

Imprisoned by their bodies Sally struggled and pleaded, every word only exciting them further: "No, please, let me go...

Ahh! that hurts. I can't take all of you at once..."

Her long wrap-around skirt with its fraying hem was un-tied and cast aside. Below it were several layers of old salvaged petticoats which they tugged down over her slim hips. She wore no pants and the boys cheered with delight as they exposed the gold of her pubic bush. Struggle as she might, Sally could not prevent curious hands and questing fingers sliding between her thighs and into her cleft from front and rear, testing the way for the forthcoming onslaught.

Sally's legs were parted and her feet were suddenly kicking in the air, still shod in her old-fashioned ankle boots, an incon-gruous contrast to her nakedness. Each taking an arm or leg, the boys lifted her off the ground and carried her over to Amber's makeshift bed. Amber herself, tied to a post at the end of the wooden pen, twisted round to watch the spectacle being played out only feet from her.

As they dropped Sally onto the blankets and wrenched her legs wide, Amber had a momentary glimpse of the gaping, thick-lipped slit between them, the penetration of which was the boys' sole objective. Such a beautiful and vulnerable seem-ing orifice - and Amber knew, quite capable of swallowing all the boys could pump into it without undue exertion.

Sally was giving them what they wanted. They were too inexperienced to appreciate the subtleties of lust yet, so she was letting them master her, control her, use her. It was a rape in all but actuality; a superb performance in all but name.

Four of the boys were lying huddled round Sally, each pin-ning down one limb while running their free hands over her wriggling body. Jackson was standing, pulling down his trou-sers - first again, the prerogative of a leader. His erection sprang free and he almost fell onto Sally, lunging frantically, caught up in the frenzy of primitive lust.

As his cock found its goal, Sally gave a choking gasp and arched her back, clearly stretched to the limit by his entry.

"No...! You're too big... it hurts... let me go!" Sally cried.

But nothing could stop Jackson spending himself inside her now. His smooth strong buttocks rose and fell in rapid rhythm, making Sally's slender frame jerk with each thrust. With a grunt he spent himself and Sally moaned as though acknowledging her defilement.

Craning her neck and twisting about shamelessly, Amber glimpsed the glistening cock shaft reluctantly withdrawing from Sally's interior leaving a gaping fleshy tunnel behind it. Before it had a chance to close, Harris had taken Jackson's place.

Amber watched with complete fascination, jerking at her bonds, desperately wanting to join in. At the back of her mind was the frightening realization that at that very moment she wouldn't have felt any less excited if it had been a real rape with the knowledge that it would be her turn next. Was she becoming a true slave to sex?

As each boy mounted Sally her struggles diminished, as though she was being subdued by each demonstration of their strength and power, becoming a submissive receptacle for their passions. As she weakened, the thrill of conquest and dominance grew within them. The close air in the loft filled with the scent of hot semen, the spicy tang of Sally's lubrication and the acridity of lusty sweat.

Finally Gosset, the last of the five to take his turn with Sally, spent himself and slowly rolled off her. He left Sally lolling splay-legged and limp in their hands, eyes closed, breathing heavily. The flesh of her cunt mouth was red and swollen, her bush matted and smeared with glistening trails, while semen oozed from her cleft. The boys sprawled about her, grinning at her and each other in satisfaction.

"Please, somebody fuck me!" Amber wailed at them in an agony of frustration.

But for the moment even the boys' youthful lust was satiated, and they only looked at her pleading face in amusement. Then Jackson suddenly grinned afresh. He climbed to his feet, stepped over to Amber and undid the rope binding her to the post. Catching her under her bound arms, the spreader bar holding her ankles apart making it impossible for her to walk, he hauled her into a kneeling position and dropped her face downwards between Sally's legs.

"Use your tongue. Lick her clean," he ordered.

And Amber obeyed, burying her face in the hot slippery gash of flesh before her, not caring that she was cleaning up the boys' leavings. Second-hand passion was better than nothing. She could taste a cocktail of their sperm mingling with Sally's juices and lapped it up with such eagerness that Sally gave a gasp and shiver that Amber felt certain was genuine. Her tongue probed the fleshy tunnel the boys had so recently made use of and Sally arched her back and bent her knees a little to open herself wider.

Amber could feel the boys' eyes riveted on her, and she realised she was exposed before them in a different way than before. It was as though she was on a stage performing before an audience, and it felt desperately exciting. Out of the corners of her eyes, she saw the boys' hands busily working the life back into their cocks. Seized by the urge to do the thing properly, she lifted her sticky shiny face from Sally's crotch and gasped: "If you really want to see something... turn me round so Sally can lick me as well."

Willing hands grasped her, lifted and turned her about. Her gaping, hungry cunt descended over Sally's face to be met with a welcome kiss. Amber felt Sally's experienced tongue slide into her and ascended to seventh heaven.

As though from a distance, she heard the boys commenting in awed and slightly strained tones about the spectacle before them. Aroused afresh but unwilling to interfere with their coupling, they were kneeling round them masturbating furiously as they talked.

"Look... what she's doing now!"

"The other one likes it... see her face."

"There was a chapter in the book... about the things you

can get two girls to do to each other..."

"But how long... will this one stay?"

Amber felt the first hot jet of sperm splash across her back and redoubled her efforts. The two girls came noisily to the accompaniment of splatters of applause in praise of their performance. Then the twice-drained boys slumped across them, the weight of their bodies pressing them even more tightly together, and for a time there was no sound in the loft except for ragged breathing.

Finally voices penetrated the blissful haze fogging Amber's mind.

"That was... great!" Gosset panted.

"See, there wasn't any harm in letting her come here," Jackson said, sounding vindicated.

"We've got to keep her," Parsons said firmly.

Speaking from between Amber's thighs, Sally said: "You've changed your tune. Want me to stay now, do you?"

"Yes... please," Parsons replied almost humbly.

The huddle of bodies broke up, the boys recovering their trousers while Amber was sat back against the plank wall. Sally used a rag soaked with water from Amber's washing bucket to clean both of them up. The boys watched benevolently.

Recognizing they were in a malleable mood, Amber took the opportunity to say: "You see what fun you can have with two girls. Think how much more you could do with three. Now, what about going after the outsider that Arabella's secretly holding?"

"What's this about Arabella?" Sally asked as she wiped semen from Amber's hair.

"Remember when she questioned me while were in the police yard pillories? She asked if there might be a fourth outsider girl around somewhere. But there's only two of us here as far as we know - myself and the black girl Major Havercotte-Gore's got - so it looks like Arabella's holding one secretly. I suggested to the boys that they might like to pinch her from

Arabella as a way of getting their own back for all the grief she's given them. They'd get another slave and Arabella couldn't complain about it to anyone, which we reckon would seriously annoy her."

"Count me in," Sally said. "I'd love to see somebody wipe the smirk off that mean bitch's face." She glanced at the boys. "Got any ideas how you're going to do it?"

The boys looked doubtful. "Well," Jackson said. "We'd have to find out where she's keeping this other girl first."

"She must be hidden somewhere on the Hall estate," Parsons said thoughtfully.

"We guessed that, you dope!" Gosset said scathingly. "But there's woods and fields and dozens of outbuildings and barns and such. Even if we could get in after dark, it could take days, weeks even, to search it all."

"We can't afford to wait that long," Amber said impatiently. "You might get caught, or Arabella might get rid of the girl before you found her. When we make the snatch we must know exactly where we're going. What we need is some inside information." Her brow furrowed. "Who knows Arabella well enough to spy on her?"

The boys looked at each other and shrugged. "She's got a lot of county-set friends," Harris said. "But I don't see how we could find out anything from them."

"What about people locally?" Amber asked.

"There's only really the Snooties," Jackson said.

"The only one I met was called Belinda," Amber said. "And she seemed a hard little piece and pretty loyal to Arabella. I don't see that we could find out much from her. Are they all like that?"

"Pretty much - except for Jemima Moncrief, of course," Gosset said. "She's pretty soft really. I think she got close to them because she thought it was safer than being outside where they might pick on her."

"There's always one like that in any gang," Amber said.

"Now, how can we find this Jemima?"

"Oh, I can get you Jemima whenever you want," Sally said lightly.

They all turned to stare at her. "Do you know her?" Amber asked.

"'Course I do. She was with Arabella when she came to ask me about you escaping. She's soft all right. Didn't like what Arabella did to try to make me talk."

"Did she hurt you?" Amber asked in dismay. "Sally, I'm so sorry."

Sally shrugged. "I've had worse. Anyway, now Arabella's told Jemima to follow me about in case I lead her to you. But I caught her at it and, er, we talked a bit. She seemed pretty sorry for herself. I gave her a story to tell Arabella that would make her look good and she agreed. I think she's frightened of Arabella."

The boys were nodding in sympathetic understanding.

"And you think she'll keep tailing you?" Amber asked.

"It keeps Arabella happy and she knows I don't care. If I hang around the school gates she should turn up soon enough."

"Do you think she'd tell on Arabella?" Jackson asked eagerly.

Sally frowned thoughtfully then nodded. "Yeah, if she's handled properly."

Amber looked at the boys. "Well, do you want to try it?"

They nodded. "That's what we were trying to do when we first caught you in the woods," Jackson said.

"Right. Down with Arabella and the Snooties!" Harris said excitedly.

Amber laughed. "If we're going up against her whole gang we should have a name too. Something that says what we're about."

"Form Six against Arabella," Bickley suggested.

"We're not in Form Six, but we want our share of any revenge too," Amber reminded him.

"That's right," said Sally. "I want to see her get a taste of her own medicine."

"What about: 'The Party for Revenge on Arabella'," Parsons offered.

"We're more a secret society than a party," Amber said. "There should be an acronym in it somewhere. The Society Against Arabella Westlake... no. What about: Society for Co-ordinated Revenge on Arabella Westlake. SCRAW for short. That has a sort of tough ring to it."

The boys nodded in approval. Jackson rapped the wooden floor. "I call the first meeting of SCRAW to order," he announced. "First item on the agenda: Jemima Moncrief."

"I think I know how we can get her on our side," said Sally, "but she's got to be handled just right..."

15: The Conversion of Jemima.

"You look like a sorry piece of work."

The unexpected words startled Jemima out of her despondent reverie. Jerking her head up she saw Sally regarding her with a not unkind smile.

Jemima scrambled up from the bank on which she'd been sitting. "I didn't hear you coming."

"You wouldn't have heard a circus marching past." Sally noted the red rims around Jemima's eyes and the slight puffiness of her cheeks. "Arabella been giving you a hard time?"

"No... I mean... yes."

"Want to talk about it?"

"I... can't. She's just been... firm with me."

Sally shook her head. "Beats me why you put up with her."

Jemima bit her lip. "I sometimes wonder myself."

Sally looked about her thoughtfully. A horse and cart clopped along the lane and passed them by, the driver giving the two girls barely a glance. "Are you still supposed to be following me?"

"Yes, though I don't think Arabella really expects me to find anything useful. But it keeps me out of her way."

"You never know," Sally said. "Let's go this way."

They started off along the lane. After a minute Sally asked: "So how did you get mixed up with Arabella's lot?"

Jemima sighed. "I never meant to. They're not really my sort. But Arabella likes having girls round her she can show off to, the way she can't with her older friends. I think she sometimes likes making fools of us, but she's so forceful it's impossible ever to say no to her. And she's from such a good family, my parents think it's wonderful that we're friends. If only they knew what she can be like..."

"Scares you, does she?"

Jemima nodded miserably. "Arabella always takes things too far. She's never satisfied. One day she'll... well, I'm frightened that somebody may get badly hurt."

They walked along the road past the gates of Cranborough House. Opposite the arm of woodland that enclosed the school grounds, Sally turned off the road and headed through the trees. Jemima followed her without comment, head down and lost in thought.

A hundred yards in they came to a fallen tree. Sally patted the gnarled trunk. "Let's sit here," she said, and Jemima obeyed meekly.

Sally looked Jemima squarely in the face. "How would you like to get your own back on Arabella?" she asked bluntly. "Maybe fix things so she never bothers you again?"

Jemima looked startled. "I wouldn't know how."

"But you'd like to?"

Jemima looked about fearfully, as though frightened they might be overheard. "Oh, yes, I'd like to," she admitted in a hushed voice.

"Thought so. See, there's some people, a secret society sort of thing, who'd really like Arabella to take a fall. And they think you might be able to help them."

Jemima's eyes widened. "Help... b...but how? What can I do?"

"Maybe a fair bit. The first thing they want to know is where Arabella's keeping the other outsider girl."

Jemima clapped a hand to her mouth in horror. "How did you know - I mean, I don't know what you're talking about." She tried to stand up, but Sally caught her by the wrist.

"So she has got another outsider. Don't mess me about, I can see it in your face. Well?"

Jemima collapsed, clutching her head in her hands. "Yes," she groaned. "Arabella made us promise not to tell anyone. I knew it was wrong. Now we're going to get into terrible trouble "

"No you're not!" Sally said firmly. "I'm not going to tell on you. Nobody has to know anything... not if somebody was to steal the girl away from Arabella first. All we need to know is where she's being held."

Jemima looked at her with hope and fear mingled on her face. After a moment's agonising indecision she shook her head. "No. I...I can't tell! I want to... but I'm not brave enough. If Arabella ever found out..."

"But suppose you couldn't help yourself. Then not even Arabella could blame you. Not that she'd ever need to know. It would be your secret."

Jemima hesitated. "What do you mean?"

Sally scowled. "There's a word. It means talking about things just to try them out: a for-instance. High-po-something."

"Hypothetical?"

"Yeah, that's it. Let's talk hypothetical. Let's say... you was kidnapped!"

Jemima gave a sudden shiver. Sally saw her irises swell hugely. "Yes?" she said in a tiny voice.

"You're in some quiet spot somewhere just like this and two or three strong men jump out of the bushes and take hold of you. Now there ain't nothing you could do about that, is there?"

"I'd... scream out."

"You'd be gagged."

"I'd struggle."

"You'd be tied up real tight."

"What... what would they do to me?"

"Only what was needed. Take you somewhere secret and make you tell them where the outsider girl is. Nothing cruel... well, just a little bit, maybe. Probably try shaming you first. Treat you like a girl in the public pillory."

Jemima gulped, but her eyes never left Sally's face. "Would they... take my clothes off?"

"Yep. So's to make you feel more helpless and so they could get at you better. They'd touch all your secret places and you couldn't stop them. They'd spank you and keep on and on until you couldn't take any more and told them what they wanted. You'd have to tell them in the end but nobody could blame you."

"And... afterwards. Would they just... let me go?"

"Of course. Because they'd know you'd be too ashamed of what happened to tell anyone. And they could always pick you up again and give you more of the same if they wanted to find out anything else about Arabella's plans. And you couldn't do anything to stop them."

"No," Jemima agreed faintly. "I couldn't do anything... could I?"

If she saw Sally give a quick signal with her hand, Jemima didn't show it. If she heard Jackson, Harris and Bickley creeping up behind her she made no sign. Only when the sack was thrown over her head did she begin to struggle. But by then it was far too late.

"Jemima Moncrief. You are a prisoner of SCRAW: the Society for Coordinated Revenge on Arabella Westlake."

102

Jemima sat in an old chair in the middle of the loft. The sack had been removed but a blindfold covered her eyes. Her hands were tied behind her back and her ankles were bound. Four of the boys stood silently at the ready around her, while Jackson and Sally stood in front of her. Amber knelt on all fours by their side a rope leash about her neck.

Jackson, who had the deepest voice amongst the boys, was carrying out the interrogation, prompted by whispers from Sally. He had managed to add a gravelly menacing undertone which was obviously having the desired effect on Jemima.

"You will tell us all about the outsider girl Arabella is illegally keeping," he continued.

"I can't tell you anything!" Jemima said tremulously, her head twisting blindly as she tried to focus on his voice.

"Then we shall have to make you tell us," Jackson warned her.

"I know," Jemima said, then added in a curious tone: "I have no choice."

Sally whispered in Jackson's ear. "First we're going to take your clothes off," he said. "You'll be naked. We'll be able to see every bit of you. Do you want that?"

"You've... got to do what you have to," Jemima said with a shiver.

"Strip her!" Jackson ordered.

The other boys lifted Jemima to her feet, undid her bonds and began pulling at her clothes. She fluttered in their grasp like a trapped butterfly, twisting and pulling but never coming close to breaking free. The buttons of her pinafore dress were undone and it dropped about her ankles, exposing white, lace-trimmed panties. She kicked feebly as her shoes were pulled off, leaving behind her white ankle socks.

She began to protest, her voice rising to a shrill: "No! Don't! Let me go... I can't tell you anything... Please ughhh!"

A hard rubber ball was forced into her mouth, stretching her lips and exposing her white teeth as they bit into it. Her words were reduced to indistinct moaning, mewing sounds as she tossed her head from side to side, as though trying to shake the ball loose.

Her blouse was pulled off, revealing a popper-fronted bodice. The boys ripped it open, bringing forth a muffled gasp from Jemima as her breasts spilled free. Another tug disposed of her panties and Jemima was stripped naked but for her socks.

The boys reached up to ropes dangling from a beam over Jemima's head and encircled her wrists in broad leather cuffs. Pulling on the free ends of the ropes which were doubled round the beam, they drew her slender arms up until she was standing on the balls of her feet. Her clenched thighs were parted and her ankles were fastened to the spreader bar they had used earlier on Amber. Jemima twisted in her ropes, whining and gurgling. She was stretched painfully taut, almost all her weight hanging by her wrists, with her squirming toes barely touching the ground.

Only when she was securely displayed before them did they step back to admire their newest captive.

Jemima's elfin face with its slightly uptilted nose was half-hidden beneath her blindfold and distorted by her ball gag. Her shoulder length light brown hair was in fetching disarray after its sacking. The elongation of her slim body pulled the skin taut over her chest so that her ribs showed white. The same force lifted her small breasts so that they stood out as perfect, slightly rounded cones, shivering with every movement like pink jellies. Each was capped by a neatly rounded pale brown nipple, the crowns of which had little puckers in, like tiny mouths. The flesh of her flat stomach swelled with her rapid breathing, the pit of her belly button was deep and sharply defined. Her buttocks were pale and apple-firm. Her hips still had something of the narrowness of adolescence, tapering to slimly rounded legs and knees that turned inward in a futile attempt to bring them decently together.

Below her tremulous navel was a surprisingly thick and

wide fluffy delta of pubic hair that divided about the cleft of her vulva, which seemed almost overlarge in comparison to her slender frame. The crinkled and slightly flushed brown tongue of her inner lips pouted enticingly.

The boys ran their hands over Jemima's warm, helpless body, squeezing, caressing and gently pinching. Her nipples were rolled, her pubic hair tweaked, fingers tickled her slit. She bucked and twisted at their touch for a few seconds, then gradually went limp, moaning slightly as though surrendering to the inevitable. The boys grinned at each other. One layer of her natural privacy had been breached on the path to her complete subjugation.

Sally whispered in Jackson's ear.

"You're a very pretty girl, Jemima," he said aloud. "We'll enjoy torturing you. We'll make you dance in your ropes. A little bit of pain and a little bit of pleasure until you can't tell which is which and then you'll tell us everything. Want to say anything now?"

Jemima slowly shook her head.

They smacked her with homemade paddles of leather flaps nailed to lengths of bamboo, making her firm jelly-moulded breasts shiver and her tight bottom clench. Her nipples flushed into hard little cherries that sprang up masochistically for more every time the paddles cut them down. Red stripes radiated out from them across her breasts, matching those across her stomach, thighs and bottom. As Jackson had promised, Jemima danced in her rope bonds like a tormented puppet, wailing and shrieking behind her gag. Then with a shudder she went limp, hanging from her arms with her head lolling, as though lost in an ecstasy of pain.

Jackson flicked Amber's leash, and she obediently shuffled forward until she was kneeling between Jemima's widespread legs. Lifting her head she nuzzled into Jemima's furry nest and planted a kiss on her pouting cunt lips. Jemima jerked in surprise at her touch and tried to twist aside. The boys took hold of her buttocks and thighs and held her still. Amber began to probe deeper into Jemima's virgin orifice.

"You see," said Jackson. "We can make this nice or nasty for you."

Jemima's stomach was palpitating as her breathing grew more rapid, much to the fascination of the boys who watched its rise and fall from inches away. She stopped pulling back from Amber's tongue and began to work her hips to and fro.

Jackson jerked on Amber's leash, pulling her head out from between Jemima's thighs. There was a glistening film around Amber's nose and mouth and she was licking her lips. A groan of what might have been frustration came from behind Jemima's gag.

"That's enough pleasure," said Jackson. "Now we want to use some clothes pegs on you..."

They clipped four of them to Jemima's body: one to each nipple and one to each outer lip of her vagina. Jemima squealed as she felt them bite into her tender flesh, then squealed again when she discovered strings were tied to each peg. The boys arranged themselves round her and began pulling on the ends of the strings.

At first they pulled at random, determining the limits to the elasticity of Jemima's flesh and seeing how far they could stretch her before the pegs slipped off. Then they amused themselves by stretching her breasts into almost perfect cones, or pulling to each side of her so that her breasts were stretched towards her armpits.

Similar tricks could be played with her nether lips. With two of them pulling the fleshy petals apart at the same time as Jemima let out muffled shrieks of pain, it looked as though her cunt was mouthing her words, which set the boys chuckling.

They added more pegs to her lips and tied the strings around her thighs so that she was stretched out like a flower, revealing the secret glistening pink inner folds of her sex and the tiny dark virgin mouth that led to her interior. Amber was pushed forward again to lap and tease her. Jemima shivered and jerked in her bonds, gurgling incoherently.

"You don't like Arabella, so why are you helping her?" Jackson demanded.

Jemima shook her head wildly, her body bucking, grinding herself into Amber's face. Recognising the signs, Sally jerked on Amber's leash, pulling her away before Jemima came. Jemima hung in her bonds panting miserably - tormented and unfulfilled.

"You asked for it," Jackson told Jemima ominously.

They tied a rope about the middle of the spreader bar, threw the end over a beam, and hauled on it until Jemima's ankles had been pulled up level with her wrists. She hung in the air on her back, her cunt mouth stretched by the clothes pegs gaping even wider; open for all to see.

The loft windows were covered with sacking, turning the interior into a gloomy cavern. The boys put brown paper bags with cut-out eye and mouth holes over their heads. They'd have been comic in daylight, but they were menacing in the near darkness. Two of them picked up electric torches and held them ready. Jackson picked up a large glass jar and held it before Jemima's face. This was the ultimate torment and something Jemima had to see for maximum effect.

They removed her ball gag and pulled off her blindfold.

Jemima blinked, disorientated by her position and the darkness and the pleasures and torments she had already been put through. Macabre faces seemed to float about her. Something hung above her face brilliantly illuminated by torch beams. Her eyes focused.

The jar held a dozen fat glistening earthworms.

She recoiled, trying to turn her head away, but unseen hands forced her to keep looking at the creatures.

"This is your last chance, Jemima," Jackson warned her.

"No... I can't..." she gasped through dry stretched lips.

He upended the jar and rammed it quickly down over her

107

right breast, which slid easily into its mouth. Jemima shrieked in disgust as she felt the worms wriggling about on her still smarting skin.

"Tell us everything!"

"No..."

Jackson twisted and pulled the jar off, her breast coming free with a slight pop, and scooped the worms back inside.

"Well, if you won't cooperate, there's only one other place for these to go..." He turned to look between her legs.

Jemima's eyes widened in utter horror. "Oh... no! Please don't. Ahhhh"

Jackson rammed the jar between her thighs. The rim squashed against the peeled-back flesh of her cunt and the worms tumbled onto the folds and clefts of Jemima's private grotto and began to investigate its strange contours. The boys' torches illuminated every detail.

Jemima jerked and bucked wildly and the other boys had to fight to hold her still.

"I'll bet they tickle," said Jackson.

Jemima screamed in horror. The worms were spreading out, insinuating themselves into the deeper crevices, coiling about the erect nub of Jemima's clitoris, hardened by the thrill of her distress.

"How long before one of them finds that little hole and wriggles inside you?" Jackson wondered aloud.

"No!" Jemima gasped. "I'll tell you everything! Only take them away... please!"

"Promise?"

"Yes, yes anything!" Jemima sobbed. "The girl's called Sue... Sue Drake! She's in the old playhouse... Ahhh"

Jackson pulled the jar aside and scooped away the worms. Sally's practised fingers took their place, bringing her in seconds to the brink of pleasure.

Jemima's breath rose in a series of short gasps, then she shrieked in relief as her orgasm broke. Her stomach pinched in and her buttocks clenched. From out of her gaping cleft her pee pulsed and spurted in a long arc, glittering brilliantly in the torchlight.

The boys laughed and cheered at this ultimate show of surrender.

The fountain diminished to a few drips. Jemima's gasps of pleasure subsided into wretched sobs of despair. She turned her head aside and screwed up her eyes. "No... not again!" she groaned.

"For God's sake comfort her," Amber hissed urgently to the boys.

Sally was already stroking the young girl. "It's all right, really. Don't worry."

The boys clustered round Jemima, uncertainly patting and caressing the flesh they had so recently abused.

"Girls sometimes wet themselves when they start experimenting with sex," Amber said with every ounce of reassurance she could muster. "There's nothing wrong with you."

"It was... pretty," Jackson added.

"Yeah, we enjoy watching girls pee," said Gosset.

"And it was great fun torturing you," said Harris. "I thought you were really brave to last as long as you did."

"You looked really nice hanging by your arms all naked," Bickley said.

"We'd really like to do it all to you again," Parsons concluded.

Jemima's tear-streaked eyes fluttered open and she blinked up at the strange masked faces arrayed about her. "Is... is it really all right?"

"You did fine," Sally told her. "You heard what this lot said. You want more of the same, stick with us."

Jemima's eyes widened at the thought.

"But you must swear the oath first," Jackson said.

They untied Jemima and made her kneel before them. She shivered slightly, excited and frightened, eyeing Amber's naked and leashed form with fascination.

"Jemima Moncrief," said Jackson solemnly. "Do you wish to serve the Society for Coordinated Revenge on Arabella Westlake."

Jemima took a deep breath. "Yes... please."

"Do you promise never to reveal the meeting place or identity of any member of SCRAW to anybody outside the society?"

"I promise."

"Do you swear to obey all orders given to you by your masters in SCRAW, and to accept all punishments they may give you?"

Jemima gave a little shudder. "I do."

"Are you ready to serve your masters?"

"I... am."

Jackson pointed at Amber, who turned about to present her rear to Jemima. "This girl is our bondslave. Kiss her bottom and stay on your hands and knees while you do it!"

And Jemima obeyed, carefully kissing each cheek of Amber's upturned bottom.

Jackson pointed at Sally, who hiked up her skirt to expose her pubes.

"Kiss her cunny mouth," Jackson ordered.

Again Jemima obeyed, exchanging a quick, blushing grin with Sally as she did so.

Fly buttons were popped open and five rods of flesh sprang out like flagpoles.

"Kiss each of our cocks," Jackson ordered. "And say 'Master' each time you do..."

Jemima started at the sight of her first erections. Then her fear turned to curious wonder... and she obeyed.

And when she was finished and knelt demurely before them once more, her pretty face flushed with the thought of what she had done, they took off their masks.

Jemima gave a little gasp when she saw their faces. "Oh,

it's you... masters."

The boys smiled down at their new compliant slave, thinking of the delights to come.

Then Jemima told them everything about Arabella and Sue.

16: Preparations

"Will the boys... our masters, I mean, want to put their thingies, you know, inside me sometime?" Jemima asked hesitantly.

Amber smiled, amused by the girl's naivety of speech.

"They're called 'penises', properly speaking, though the boys call them 'cocks' or 'pricks'. Yes, I think they'd love to put them inside you. They wanted to earlier, but Sally thought you needed to be broken in gently. You're a virgin. The first time should be a bit special. Don't worry, it'll happen soon enough. Right now we've got to concentrate on getting these things finished."

It was a couple of hours since Jemima's initiation into the service of SCRAW. She and Amber were working busily in the loft. They were both naked and chained to posts by their ankles, with enough slack to allow them to fetch tools and other items from the selection the boys had brought up.

They had all been shocked by Jemima's graphic description of the torments Arabella was putting Sue Drake through. Jemima had ended with a plea to rescue Sue as soon as possible, before Arabella inflicted some serious injury on her.

The idea of rescuing a genuine damsel in distress appealed to the quirky side of Amber's nature, and she'd have done it even if it hadn't also been a means of getting back at Arabella. None of the others had needed further encouragement to agree they should make the attempt, and they decided to do it that very night. Jemima had insisted, with surprising stubbornness, that she would go with them. She knew the Hall grounds and the best route to the playhouse, and she said that when they found Sue, she could reassure her that they meant her no harm.

If Jemima was to participate in the rescue and consequently

be out all night, she had to have an alibi. Sally took up Miss Newcombe's offer and went to School Cottage to look over her possible new home. While she kept her occupied, the boys took Jemima into the school office to use its phone. She made two calls; one to her home to tell them Arabella had invited her to stay overnight at the Hall, the other to the Hall itself to leave a message for Arabella saying she was feeling unwell and had gone home. Jemima admitted that Arabella might think she was simply making an excuse to keep away after the humiliating treatment she had received earlier, but doubted Arabella would care. None of the other snooties were likely to check up on her. As to her parents, they would be flattered to think she had been invited to stay over at the Hall.

When the calls had been made, the boys brought Jemima back to the loft and secured her with Amber. They then went off to continue their assigned jobs about the school and to prepare for tea, leaving Amber, advised by Jemima, to plan their entry to the Hall grounds and make whatever special equipment they needed. The boys also left their copy of THE CARE AND TRAINING OF BONDSLAVES with them. There were diagrams of certain devices within it that they wanted Amber and Jemima to make using the tools and materials they had accumulated in making the Training Horse the previous day.

It was as they were working on this task, shaping rope, wire and leather, that Jemima asked about the boy's intentions. Free to reveal her secret feelings at last, questions were pouring out of her. After pondering Amber's answer for a moment, she asked: "Will it hurt?"

"Only briefly. Nothing like the paddling you've already had. And you'll probably bleed a little, but that's quite normal first time." She looked at the younger girl closely. "Are you sure this is what you want?"

Jemima smiled, her eyes sparkling. "Oh yes. I know it now. Anyway, I can't help myself. It's what I am." She blushed. "I've had dreams about this sort of thing happening to me, though I

112

didn't know enough to make them very accurate."

"And how does reality measure up to your dreams?"

Jemima looked about her at the loft, the Training Horse standing in the corner and the ropes and chains hanging from the walls of Amber's pen. "Oh, this is much better! It feels like the right sort of place for what's happening to me... to us. I like it here working like this, now I know what I am and what's expected of me. I don't have to play Arabella's games or be made to hurt anybody." She frowned. "But it was exciting to watch it happen. Even when I hated what Arabella was doing to Sue, I couldn't take my eyes off her. And I like to be tied up and punished myself. Sally said she could enjoy that sort of thing as well. Do you?"

"I'm getting to like it more than I did," Amber admitted dryly. "It's fun if it's done properly with sex mixed in with it. The boys are learning."

"Knowing you're helpless is exciting, isn't it?" Jemima said brightly. "Thinking of all the things they might do to you - like in the book."

The slave training book had fascinated Jemima even more than Amber. She had leafed through it as soon as the boys had left; shocked, amazed and utterly absorbed. As soon as they had finished what they were making she wanted to look further.

Jemima was frowning again. "But why is it different when Arabella does it? I came when she made Sue lick my cunny - I couldn't help myself - but I didn't enjoy the rest of it much." She blushed. "But it felt so different when you were licking me in between the smacking and the clothes pegs. Why?"

Amber considered. "Maybe because there's a point to it with the boys. They like playing with you and seeing you suffer. You feel that. It helps you find the pleasure in it all for yourself. I think Arabella's mean at heart. You know you can never satisfy her. All you're left with is the pain."

Jemima's face darkened. "Sue said we can't choose who

masters us. I think she loves Arabella in a way. She'd do anything for her if she got a little love back."

"Poor kid," said Amber.

A little later the trapdoor opened and Sally climbed up into the loft. She brought cheese, apples, bread and a sweet cake for each of them from the village. They tucked in hungrily.

"How did your meeting with Miss Newcombe go?" Amber asked Sally between bites.

Sally looked thoughtful. "She showed me about her cottage. It's quite a nice place. There's a little bedroom sort of tucked in under the roof that she said I could have. I never had my own room before. Then we talked about what my duties would be. Doesn't sound so bad. I think she'd be strict, mind."

Amber looked at Sally with interest. There was a wistful tone in her voice that she hadn't heard before. "Yes," she agreed. "She struck me as being pretty tough when I met her. But do you think you can keep her occupied tonight? This job's going to take some time. We have to be sure she won't make her rounds and find the boys missing."

"No trouble," Sally said confidently. "She wants me, I could smell it. I'll make her show just how much. That'll keep her out of your way."

17: Night Moves

Miss Newcombe opened the school's timeworn front door of black oak to find Sally standing in the pool of radiance cast by the porch light.

"Oh, Sally. This is very late for you to call."

"Well, see, I thought about what you said earlier, and there's something really important I have to find out."

"Can't it wait until morning? I was just about to go to bed."

"No. This is something we have to get straight right now. Well, you going to keep me standing out here all night? Maybe you think I'm going to nick the silver?"

"Of course not..."

"Not worth it, eh? Just plated?"

Miss Newcombe was forced to smile. "I simply mean that I'm not sure that it's proper for me to receive private visitors at this hour. There are five boys on the premises that I am responsible for. They should be asleep by now and I do not wish them disturbed."

"Well I don't plan on waking them. It's you I come to see."

"Then I suppose you'd better come in."

Sally looked about her at the entrance hall. The school coat of arms was hung on one wall over a half-filled trophy cabinet. Everything else was sombre dark-polished wood.

"Cheerful place," she observed. "Ain't you got a room of your own here?"

"Well, yes, but..."

"Come on, then. Up here, is it? She started up the main stairs with Miss Newcombe trailing at her heels.

In their dormitory, the boys listened while the two sets of footsteps passed along the corridor. Only when they heard the distant click of Miss Newcombe's door closing did they throw back their bedclothes. In a moment they had slid one of the dark wooden wall panels that lined their room aside. From the cavity between it and the old rough stone wall they extracted a homemade rope ladder and a bamboo pole with a hook on one end. They had made the devices months earlier to allow them to get onto the roof and so gain access to the skylight over Miss Newcombe's bedroom, which had afforded them many interesting sights. Tonight the ladder and pole would help them enter the grounds of Markham Hall.

Two minutes later they were dressed in the old dark trousers and jumpers they had been wearing for work and were letting themselves out onto the fire escape. From the foot of this it was only a twenty yard dash to the old stable block which had served Cranborough House when it was still a private residence. Using the keys they had been given while clearing the building, they let themselves inside and swarmed up the ladder to the loft.

As they entered they found their slaves putting the finishing touches to their body camouflage. Amber had thinned down some shoe polish the boys had provided, and using scraps of rag, she and Jemima were artistically smearing themselves with brown and black stripes and spots. As a result their skins now looked as though they belonged to some species of exotic big cat. The effect was so striking that the boys paused to admire them, fingering and stroking them curiously. Jemima looked shyly proud as the boys turned her round to examine her efforts, clearly excited by being handled so intimately.

When they were satisfied, Harris handed over Jemima's shoes and Amber's trainers, which was all they were allowed to wear on the night's adventure.

"Have you brought my set of lockpicks?" Amber asked, as she pulled her trainers on. "We won't get very far if you've forgotten them."

Jackson pulled a flat leather case from his pocket. "I've got them. I'll give them to you when they're needed, not before. Just in case you think of using them to try to get away yourself."

"As though I would," Amber grinned.

Jackson caught her by the hair and hauled and twisted until she stood on tiptoe. He slid his free hand up between her legs, took hold of her delicate inner labia between thumb and forefinger and pinched.

"Sorry, Master!" Amber gasped in pain. "Your slave shouldn't have spoken out of turn. Please forgive her."

"Don't pretend you wouldn't take any chance to escape," Jackson said, pinching a little harder and enjoying the contortion of her features. "We're not stupid. That's why we had you make the harnesses."

116

"We have," Amber winced again. "Look, they're over there. We did the best we could with what we had. They're almost exactly like the diagram in the book."

While Jackson kept hold of Amber, the other boys examined the two creations of old leather, cord, rings and buckles.

"They look all right," Bickley reported after a minute of tugging and twisting joints and knots. "Bit rough in places, but they won't get out of these in a hurry."

Jackson let go of Amber. His gaze passed over her to Jemima, who was looking on with wide-eyed fascination. "Don't forget you belong to us," he told them sharply. "We all want to get this Sue Drake away from Arabella, but that's so we can have her. She'll belong to us, not you. You're our tools, that's all. We're using you to guide us and open locks. You do exactly as we tell you from now on, understand? Now, beg to have the harnesses put on you."

Amber quickly knelt down and extended her arms towards him with her wrists crossed; a classic gesture of submission.

"Please Master, I beg you to bind me so I can be made to serve as your tool," Amber said. And by her side Jemima echoed her words, copying her gesture exactly.

Jackson nodded, and the boys began fitting them into the harnesses. Amber saw Jemima's chest rising and falling rapidly with excitement, her nipples hard and pointed. How she's loving this, Amber thought. So do I, if I'm honest, she amended mentally as leather rasped against her flesh. The familiar fluttering, stomach churning thrill was rising inside her again. Why had she made that silly remark in such a mocking tone? To bring just that sort of response?

In a minute it was done and they stood side by side, harnessed and helpless; ready to go where their masters led them.

Broad padlocked collars and belts encircled their necks and waists. Leather gag straps closed their mouths. Cuffs on their wrists were linked by a rope threaded through a ring on the back of their belts. When this was slack it allowed their arms some freedom of movement to perform simple tasks. When it was pulled in and the middle of the loop hung over a hook fixed to the back of their collars, their arms were automatically pulled behind them into a restrained position. Any resistance only tightened their collars.

From a belt that ran about their chests just below the undercurve of their breasts, two straps ran vertically up over their nipples. These straps were split down the middle for part of their length, allowing their nipples to poke through, held in place by the tendency of the slit in the thick leather to close. The upper ends of these straps were tied to cords that ran through a ring on the front of their collars where they were joined to leather leashes. When the straps were allowed to follow the natural curves of their breasts the slits gaped slightly and the pinching of their nipples was bearable, but any tightening of the leash straightened the straps and brought the edges of the slits painfully close together.

The boys spent a couple of minutes experimentally tugging on Amber and Jemima's leashes and listening to their muffled squeaks of pain and seeing their faces screw up behind their gags. When they were assured their slaves would follow where they led, they gathered up their equipment and, by the light of hooded torches, stole silently out into the night.

Miss Newcombe's bedroom was situated close by the school sickroom, and was where she stayed overnight when required. It was a small neat room with a single skylight set in the sloping ceiling, it was simply furnished with an iron frame bed, side cabinet, single armchair and dressing table. On the dressing table was a three panelled mirror, a hairbrush and a few pots and jars of cosmetics. Before it was a small ladder-backed chair. A circular rug was laid beside the bed. A robe and sensible modest nightgown hung on the back of the door.

Sally took all this in as she dropped her carpetbag in the corner. "This'll do, I suppose, though your cottage would be more cosy."

"Sally, you can't be thinking of staying here for the night. I thought you had some lodgings arranged."

"I do, but there's something I gotta know first, or else I can't decide about your offer. You still want me as a bondslave, don't you?"

"Yes, but this is not the time or place to..."

Sally stepped forward quickly and before Miss Newcombe could protest, kissed her forcefully full on the lips. After a moment's instinctive resistance, Miss Newcombe melted into Sally's embrace, put her own arms about the smaller girl and returned the kiss with passion.

When they finally pulled apart slightly for air, they were both flushed. Sally grinned approvingly.

"That was good. I thought you really liked women better than men."

"Oh, I like men well enough," Miss Newcombe said easily. "But there are more... possibilities with women and sex."

"And if I was your slave you'd want to try them all out on me."

"Of course," Miss Newcombe admitted candidly. "Owning a pretty thing like you, who wouldn't? But I do want a presentable servant as well. I think you could be one with the right encouragement and training. And... I do genuinely want to save you from the path you are taking. It would be such a waste."

Sally considered for a moment. "How much do you want to save me?"

Miss Newcombe frowned. "What do you mean?"

"If you get me as your bondslave you get everything. I want to find out if you can take what you plan to deal out. I've got to know you understand what I'd be going through if I served you. You say you want to save me - show how much you really mean it! Prove it wasn't just fancy words so you could get a bondslave on the cheap."

"I still don't quite know what you mean."

Sally opened her carpetbag and showed Miss Newcombe what was inside. Miss Newcombe's eyes widened. "Oh... I see."

"Well? Are you up to it?"

Miss Newcombe's bosom rose a little faster under the blouse of her uniform. "I admit the idea is... intriguing. But really, this isn't the right place or time."

"Why not? Who's going to know?"

"Technically I'm on duty."

"Nobody's sick, are they? You'll be here if you're needed.

"But the boys. If they should hear anything..."

"Trust me. They won't hear a thing."

The rescue party made their way around the outskirts of the sleeping village of Shaftwell. They flitted through woods and dashed noiselessly across narrow lanes, keeping well clear of the few distant yellow rectangles of windows and pinpoints of street lamps.

Overhead the stars shone through gaps in the broken clouds. The air was dew-dampened but mild.

To Amber it was even more unreal than when the boys had led her from the police station to the school only a few nights before. Now she had a companion in bondage. She glimpsed Jemima's shadowy form as she scampered willingly after her masters and felt the warmth of her body as they crouched down together while the boys scouted ahead.

Nighttime clandestine activity was nothing new to Amber, but never had she done anything like this. It was crazy nonsense, absurd - and desperately exciting. Her senses seemed to be razor-sharp. Never had she been so aware of her body. Her naked exposure and utter helplessness combined with the fear of discovery was uniquely arousing. She could feel herself getting wet. She hoped the boys would be able to spare some time for her tonight.

After almost three quarters of an hour they came upon the indistinct mass of a high wall running through a belt of sparse tree. This was the boundary of the Markham Hall estate.

Now the boys let Jemima guide them to the spot they were after. With her leash trailing over her shoulder she led them along the wall, moving with the confidence of one who had played in those woods since childhood. The narrow beams of their torches occasionally played across her rounded bobbing buttocks. She's like some eager bitch dog following the scent for her master, thought Amber.

They came to a cluster of trees and Jemima stopped and gave an excited whine. This was where they would scale the wall.

Miss Newcombe knelt on the rug beside her bed. Her hands were clasped behind her head and her knees were spread. She was stark naked.

Sally walked around her carrying a short length of bamboo in her hand, the tip of which she was running over Miss Newcombe's body. Though she was a good ten years older than Sally it didn't show. Her skin was clear and pale, but tinted with the lightest of golden tans. Her breasts, a shade lighter than the surrounding flesh, hung proudly, capped with firm pink nipples. Her waist was trim and her hips were full. The thick curls between her thighs had been trimmed back to a neat oval over bare pubic lips.

"Are you ready to begin?" Sally asked, the tip of her bamboo tickling a trembling nipple.

"Yes, Sally," Miss Newcombe said.

"No: 'YesÇMistress.' Tonight you're my slave... what's your first name?"

"'Jane'... Mistress."

"Well, Jane, now you're going to find out what it's like to be me," Sally told her ominously, continuing to circle round so that Jane's eyes flickered left to right, trying to keep her in sight as long as possible while at the same time holding her head still as she had been ordered. "The first thing you got to learn is

121

that waiting's different if you're a slave. See, I can keep you like this for hours if I want, and you've got no say in it. Soon you start to ache, but you can't move. You want to pee, but by now you're too knotted up to let it go, and if you wet the floor you might get a special hard thrashing for making a mess. It ain't fair, but who cares? Inside you're going crazy, not knowing what they're going to do with you, wanting to get it over with at the same time as you hope it'll never begin, even as you feel your insides turning to water. It can get so bad that you beg them to do something." She lifted Jane's chin with her bamboo. "You ready to start begging yet?"

"I beg... to serve my Mistress as she wishes."

Sally grinned and flicked the bamboo across Jane Newcombe's back, bringing forth a gasp of pain.

"Right: get onto that bed, Jane - move!"

Perched atop the wall looking into the grounds through the overhanging branches, Amber saw a grey stretch of fields, beyond which was the bulk of the Hall, picked out by a light burning over the portico and a few glowing upper windows. She just hoped the Major was sleeping soundly tonight.

The ladder was repositioned and the boys descended into the grounds. Amber and Jemima followed carefully after them. Immediately they were down the cords linking their wrists were pulled tight, dragging their hands behind their back once more, and hooked to their collars. A pinch on their nipples told them their leashes were still held in firm hands.

Jemima waited in an alert crouch while the boys rolled up the ladder. Then Jackson patted her encouragingly on the rump and she set off again, leading them towards the dark smudge of a hedgerow.

Sally finished tying the last knot about Jane's ankle and stood back to admire the effect.

Her slave for the night was stretched out on the bed, her

arms pulled upwards and her wrists bound with many loops and turns of rope to the iron-frame bed head. Her legs were parted invitingly and her ankles were equally heavily bound to the uprights at the foot of the bed. It was a lovely sight to see a nicely spoken, educated, correct lady spread and vulnerable like that. Suddenly Sally felt a thrill of unfamiliar power course through her. Well why shouldn't she be in charge for once?

She picked up her bamboo and slashed it sharply across her slave's tender exposed stomach. Jane gave a choking gasp. She tried to curl up around the burning stripe of pain, but the ropes held her back. The first flicker of true apprehension crossed her face.

"Hurts, does it?" Sally asked her. "Well there'll be a lot more of that before the night's out. Now pull on the ropes."

Jane tugged lightly at her bonds. The cane swished again. There was a sweet crack of bamboo on flesh and a second more vivid scarlet line appeared across her flat stomach.

"Harder!" Sally ordered. "You can do better than that!" She slashed the bamboo across Jane's body so that it cut into the undersides of her the soft mounts of her breasts, sending them bouncing and shivering. "Come on, try to get free. Find a bit of slack. Maybe you can slip a hand loose." She cracked the bamboo down low across Jane's stomach so that it brushed her pubic hair. "Don't you want this to end?"

Jane was now bucking and twisting, straining frantically at her bonds in a hopeless effort to escape the steady rain of blows that were scouring her body.

Sally didn't relent until Jane was panting heavily from her exertions and sweat was beginning to bead in the hollow of her throat and between her breasts. Her belly and breasts were no longer an unblemished golden-pale, but mottled with criss-cross lines of burning crimson. Her wrists and ankles were as firmly fastened as before, but the skin around them was chafed and raw.

"Well?" Sally demanded, lifting Jane's chin with the tip of

the bamboo.

"I... I can't get free, Mistress," Jane choked. "I'm sorry... I tried."

"Are you secure, then?"

"Yes, Mistress."

"How long will you stay that way?"

"Un... until you free me, Mistress."

"What are you?"

"Your slave, Mistress."

Sally smiled. "Now you're beginning to learn what it's like to be really helpless. I can do anything I want. To you I'm the most important person in the whole world. You don't have to like me, but you'd better learn to please me, and bloody fast!"

Jane's eyes were locked onto her now; the fearful despairing look of a slave to her absolute mistress.

Slowly, Sally began to take off her clothes.

The front door of the playhouse opened after a few seconds of Amber's skilfully application of her lockpicks. The boys' torches flashed about the cramped interior as Jemima led them through the tiny hall to the stairs. Amber glimpsed a bike with loaded panniers leaning against the wall of the lounge. From its design it obviously did not belong in this version of England.

Jemima gave a pleading whine and Jackson undid her gag.

"Sue - it's Jemima," she called ahead of her as they started up the stairs. "It's all right. We've come to rescue you!"

Her naive words brimmed with concern and conviction.

They squeezed into the small, bedroom, torch beams swinging about wildly. Amber glimpsed the whites of a pair of fearful, confused eyes staring back at them over the top of a leather gag strap. Then the torches steadied and focused, illuminating a pale figure lying on a wooden frame bed.

Sue Drake had been secured for the night in a posture of cruel torment.

She lay on her back, arms and legs spread and chained to the four corners of the bed. Coarse string had been looped several times about the base of each of her full breasts, causing them to stand up like swollen mushrooms. So tight was the binding that the pale balloon-like globes had taken on the purple tinge of congested blood. The free ends of the string had been drawn up and over a pulley hanging from a hook screwed into a beam of the low ceiling. The string then ran downwards again where it was tied halfway along the shaft of a broom handle which projected out over the foot of the bed at an angle of some thirty degrees. Dangling on a loop of string from the handle's end was a cast iron weight of the sort used on old-fashioned pan balances.

The other end of the broom handle was thrust between Sue's thighs and into the tunnel of her vagina. It was prevented from sliding too far into Sue by a cluster of nails which had been driven through the broom handle at various angles some inches below its tip. The spiked ball thus formed pressed against the soft folds of Sue's cleft, parting and stretched the tender lips, exposing its glistening coral pink interior.

For a moment they stared in amazement at the cruel but ingenious arrangement, realising how the iron weight added a terrible tension to the arrangement, simultaneously stretching Sue's tortured breasts while driving the end of the broomhandle deeper into Sue's gaping cunt mouth. Any movement of her body would only increase the pain to one part of her anatomy or the other.

Then Jemima broke the spell by darting forward and kneeling by the bed.

"It's all right," she told Sue. "I know we look strange. But we've come to get you away from Arabella. You'll be happier where we're going."

Amber knelt down and began working on one of the padlocks that held the chains in place about Sue's ankle. She winced as she saw how red-raw and bruised the skin was under them.

The boys were removing the string bindings and broom handle as quickly and gently as they could. Jackson pulled the gag from Sue's mouth, and Jemima showered her with passionate kisses, murmuring: "Don't worry, it'll be all right..."

Sue seemed, dazed, unable to comprehend what was happening to her. Her head jerked about woodenly as she took in the strange group of people clustered about her. She blinked at Amber and the deft clicking of her lockpicks and suddenly her eyes seemed to come into focus.

"No... you mustn't," she said. "I belong to Arabella."

Even as they gaped at her in astonishment, her voice rose to a frightened scream: "Don't take me away from her!"

18: The Bonds of Submission.

Sally sat astride Jane's hips as though straddling a horse. Their open thighs faced each other so that their pubic hair, dark blonde and black, brushed and merged. Sally leaned forward, kneading Jane's warm soft breasts gently, rolling the nipples between thumb and forefinger to keep their hardness. Every so often she would dip her head and kiss her slave deeply. Jane responded with passion. Their tongues twined and fondled.

"Feel better now?" Sally asked, looking down at Jane's flushed face.

"Yes, Mistress. Thank you for the lesson, Mistress."

"Oh, that's just the beginning. What you just had was the sort of thrashing a bondslave might get for breaking a plate. That's nothing." She looked at her slave thoughtfully. "You said this morning that you knew the sort of things coppers did to pillory girls. Ever heard of 'sucking wood'?"

"No, Mistress," Jane said warily.

"Sometimes, on wet days when there's nothing better to do, and a policeman wants a bit of fun with you but can't be bothered to get it up, he makes you do it with his truncheon instead.

126

Sally felt a shudder of apprehension pass through Jane's body and smiled. "Don't worry, they didn't have any truncheons down the village." She reached over and pulled something else from her bag. "But this ought to do as well." It was a cucumber.

Jackson had his hands over Sue's mouth, stifling her screams for help. He looked about at the others, clearly dazed by her unexpected reaction. Why was the girl they'd come to rescue screaming for her brutal mistress to save her from them? Even Jemima seemed unable to calm Sue and tears were filling the younger girl's eyes.

"What's the matter with her?" Harris said.

"She can't really want to stay here," said Gosset.

Amber made several urgent squeaks to gain their attention and finally had her gag removed. "She can't help herself - she's been conditioned to obey Arabella!" she gasped, realising even as she spoke that the boys were unlikely to understand the term. She continued: "If someone's held captive long enough they can start identifying with their captors, even loving them in a strange way, despite how they've been treated." She looked at the marks all over Sue's abused body and thought of what Jemima had told her of Sue's submissive nature. Yes, a girl like this could very well fall under Arabella's influence.

"But what do we do about it?" Jackson snapped desperately. "We can't take her with us like this. Even if we tie her up and carry her, how do we get her over the wall? We'll have to leave her."

"No!" Jemima wailed.

"No, what you must do is teach her that you're her new masters. I think she wants to be dominated, but also cared for. Show her you'll be better at that than Arabella."

"Here and now?" Jackson looked baffled. "How?"

Amber smiled. "Masters, you know how..."

Now Sally rode Jane like a horse, making her buck and toss

in a desperate attempt to accommodate the cucumber that was stretching her front passage and jutting out bizarrely from between her vaginal lips. Again Sally reached behind her and grasped the vegetable, twisting and working it round in a stirring motion, then ramming it a little further up into her sweating, trembling slave.

"That's better, you can do it!" Sally told her. "Suck it hard! It'll get softer the more you try. What're you griping about? This is easier than a truncheon."

Jane came with a series of ever shorter rising gasps and a final groan of pleasure and release that sounded as though it had been wrenched from her soul. Sally felt the cucumber jerk in her hands as it was gripped by spasming vaginal muscles. Then Jane's eyes closed and she went limp, lost in a post-orgasmic swoon.

Sally smiled down at her, fingering her own sticky slit. This was exciting.

She gave Jane a couple of minutes to recover, then slapped her cheeks to regain her attention. Jane's eyes flickered open. She looked dazed by what had happened.

"That was good," Sally told her. "Now you're going to tongue me out."

She turned herself about until she was facing the foot of the bed and settled down onto Jane again, squatting down, pushing back her bottom and spreading her knees so that her gaping pink love mouth ground into Jane's face. Sally felt Jane's tongue dutifully slip into her cleft and begin to work away at her hardened clitoris. Meanwhile she enjoyed the sight just inches before her eyes of the cucumber rising grotesquely out of Jane's cleft. Her labia were shiny wet and rimmed with green flecks of vegetable skin. Sally pumped the cucumber up and down a few times, then began to lick the vegetable flavoured with the juices of a school matron.

Sue writhed and jerked at her chains as the boys raped her,

biting on the gag strap they had put back in her mouth to mute her cries. And as they mounted her they whispered in her ear:

"Who's inside you now? Not Arabella."

"She doesn't really love you."

"You're too pretty to be wasted on an ungrateful piece like her. Come with us."

"We'll treat you properly."

"Look, we've got two girls already. They like what we do. Ask them."

And once each boy had spent himself inside Sue, he held her tossing head steady and kissed first her gag-split lips then each of her tortured breasts, telling her truthfully how much he had enjoyed her.

Amber and Jemima huddled in a corner side by side, their arms restrained and their leashes thrown over their shoulders and tied about their ankles to ensure they did not wander. Once again Amber felt her sense of reality askew. They were watching a gang-bang hoping it would bring a girl to her senses enough to realise her salvation lay with a bunch of lads who would keep her as a sex slave.

Yet it was really happening and she was hoping it would work. From what Jemima had told them, simple straightforward sex was the last thing Sue had been having. The kisses might help as well. Amber felt proud about having taught the boys about them. Sue must be hungry for such simple pleasures. Judging by the state of her, the sooner they got her out of Arabella's clutches the better. She really would be better off belonging to the boys. Not that Amber could blame Arabella for wanting to keep Sue. She had that special vulnerable beauty that just begged to be mastered...

Amber shook her head, but she couldn't deny the excitement the idea had roused within her. She wanted Sue as well... as her own slave.

She glanced at Jemima.

The girl was watching the hard cocks ramming into her

friend with unblinking, hungry, fascination. Amber realised that the thing Jemima most wanted at that moment was to be in Sue's place receiving the same treatment. She'd offer up her virginity on a plate to the boys without a second thought.

What a crazy place this was.

Gradually the fight was driven out of Sue and she lay unresisting in her chains as the boys pounded away between her legs. Perhaps it was simple exhaustion. Hopefully it was the automatic response of her nature to the boys' attentions. Their honest lust for her must be more appealing than Arabella's cold and frightening dominance.

The last boy withdrew, leaving Sue dazed, slick with sweat and breathing heavily. Her pubic hair was matted with sperm and her already abused cunt lips were red and swollen. Jackson dragged Jemima forward once more.

"Get her to see sense!" he hissed, glancing at his watch and calculating the time it would take them to get back to school. "We can't wait any longer."

Jemima kissed Sue's flushed cheek. "Please come with us, Sue. If you don't Arabella might really hurt you. You know she doesn't love you... but I do. We can be together. They'll make us do all sorts of lovely, naughty things. Please?"

Sue slowly turned her beautiful face to Jemima, searching her eyes in hope and wonder - and then burst into tears.

It was the release of some inner emotional dam. The boys, still adjusting their trousers, actually looked embarrassed. She had been absolutely naked to them physically, but this was something deeper.

Slowly the tears subsided. Sue turned to the boys, biting her lip in trepidation. "Please take me away from here," she begged. "I'll be very good, I'll do anything you want."

The boys grinned.

"Masters," Amber said quickly. "It might confuse Arabella further if we take all of Sue's things with us, including her bike downstairs. It's what Sue would do if she got herself free and ran off. Arabella won't know what's happened to her then."

"Right, we'll do it," Jackson agreed. "Now get those chains off her."

As Amber set to work again she decided there was no need to mention that, if she guessed right, there was another of the puzzle box phalluses amongst Sue's possessions.

Jane was so stiff and numb when Sally finally removed the cucumber and released her from her spread-eagled position, that it was easy, if painful for her, to be arranged in a new and quite different posture.

Jane groaned as she was re-bound, and asked plaintively: "Mistress, what are you doing now?"

"Teaching you not to ask so many questions!" Sally said sharply. "Slaves don't ask, they just obey. You talk too much. I'd better do something about that." She finished tying her. "The sickroom's next door, ain't it?"

"Yes, Mistress. But please don't..."

But Sally had already gone out of the door.

The rescue party climbed wearily back up into the loft. Harris and Bickley, who'd been carrying Sue's bike and loaded panniers, dumped them gratefully in a corner.

Sue, a rope collar and leash round her neck and her hands bound behind her back, blinked uncertainly at her new home. She looked desperately tired, Amber thought. Of course, she'd had no proper exercise or sleep for days, either being worked to exhaustion or confined and bound for long hours. Her latest emotional wrench combined with the strain of the 'rape therapy' she had undergone and the walk back from the Hall had been almost too much for her.

Jackson looked at his watch. "We'll have to get back to the dorm and get some sleep. Sister's going to have more jobs for us tomorrow."

"Leave Sue to us, Masters," Amber said. "When you come

131

back in the morning she'll be ready and eager to serve you again."

The boys removed the girls' harnesses and chained them by the ankles once again. They untied Sue's ropes then kissed her in a suitably masterful fashion, holding her by the hair with one hand while clasping a handful of plump buttock with the other. They looked at each other, grinned, and took it in turns to kiss their other two slaves in the same fashion. Jemima blushed with delight, clearly considering kisses of that intimacy to be a major step forward on her road to adulthood.

Then the boys climbed back down the ladder. The last sight they had was Sue's curious expression as they closed and locked the trapdoor behind them.

Weary but very content, the boys crossed the stretch of gravel to the fire escape and climbed back up to their dormitory. Once inside they stowed the rope ladder and pole behind the wall panel and changed by torchlight back into their pyjamas, conversing only in whispers. They were sure Sally was distracting Sister Newcombe as planned, but they didn't want to risk making unnecessary noise.

It was just as they were settling under the covers that, without any warning, the door of the dormitory swung open and the overhead light was switched on.

They jerked upright with hearts leaping, only to see Sally, naked as the day she was born and brimming with brazen self-confidence, stride impatiently into the dormitory.

"I thought you'd never get back," she said. "How'd it go?"

They goggled, momentarily lost for words, nonplussed by the sight of her. Inside the school, their own dormitory even, a naked girl seemed shocking. An acute sense of guilt and impropriety overcame them.

"You can't come in here!" Gosset said, unconsciously pulling his bedclothes modestly up about him.

"Be quiet!" Jackson hissed. "Sister will hear you!"

"Oh, she won't hear anything," Sally assured them. "Now

how'd it go?"

"Fine," Jackson said hastily. "She's in the loft with the other two and nobody saw us. Now please go away!"

Parsons was frowning. "Why won't Sister hear us?" he asked. "What have you done with her?"

Sally grinned mischievously. "Just teaching her a lesson about slavery. Want to see?"

The boys exchanged uncertain glances.

"Come on!" Sally said. "It's perfectly safe. She won't know you're there. Just don't say anything."

Curiosity made such an invitation impossible to refuse. They climbed out of their beds and followed after Sally's pale, impudently rolling buttocks as they led them along the dimly lit corridor, through the door to the infirmary and up the short flight of stairs to Sister Newcombe's bedroom. Outside the bedroom door she put her finger to her lips, then ushered them silently inside.

Jane Newcombe was standing on the floor facing the foot of her bed. Her legs were spread very wide and tied by the ankles to the feet of the iron bedframe. More ropes round her thighs secured them to the top rail, holding them absolutely rigid. Her upper body was bent sharply forward at the hips, held outstretched by ropes about her wrists which were tied to the top rail of the bed's headframe. Her reddened breasts dangled freely, nipples swollen and pointed. But the strangest sight was Miss Newcombe's head, which was swathed in crepe bandage, wrapped firmly about her eyes and mouth and crossing several times over her ears, so that only her nose and locks of tousled hair were visible.

The boys gaped at the sight in jaw-dropping disbelief. The woman they had fantasised over and secretly spied upon for months was displayed before them in the most provocative manner they could imagine.

Sally waved them forward and gestured that they should bend down to look between Jane's parted legs and admire the fleshy, split-peach of her sex that pouted from underneath the swell of her cane-striped buttocks. They saw her lovelips were stained green and sticky with drying juices, odorous with the animal scent of female discharge.

Testicles that had emptied themselves into Sue little more than an hour before were tightening under swelling erections that were straining to be released or thrusting proudly through pyjama trouser vents. The boys' faces showed sudden desperate need for release.

Sally smiled and patted Jane on the bottom, causing her to flinch as well as her bonds allowed. Muffled by her bandages she evidently did not realise Sally had returned to the room. Sally bent over Jane's bandage-swathed head and said loudly:

"Now you've had a rest, it's time you found out the most important lesson about being a bondslave: anybody can have you. We're going to pretend that those boys you're in charge of aren't sleeping quietly in their dorm, but have come in here and found you like this..." The boys gave a shocked start of surprise at her words. "They wouldn't see a school matron, just a slave nicely set up for use. And that's just what they'd do."

The expression on the boys' faces was almost comic as realization dawned. Sally picked up what had been a firm cucumber but was now rubbed yellow and softened for half its length.

"Now you've worn it down a bit, this old cucumber is going to stand in for their hard young cocks, understand?"

Jane was slow in responding so Sally picked up the bamboo and slashed it across her buttocks. The pale globes clenched inward at the burning blow and Jane nodded her cocooned head vigorously.

"That's better," said Sally. "I expect you to work at milking it just like it was a real cock. I'll feel if you're not trying. And you got to do it five times, understand?"

Jane nodded.

Sally pointed at Gosset, indicating he should take off his

pyjamas.

Gosset gulped, then with trembling fingers obeyed. Sally pulled his hands behind his back. "She mustn't feel anything but your cock touching her," she whispered in his ear.

Sally rubbed the end of the cucumber up and down Miss Newcombe's cleft, teasing the soft folds into readiness.

"Here comes the first one," she said loudly.

Before he realised what she was doing, Sally had taken hold of Gosset's erect member with a practised hand and fed it into the waiting slit.

A look of wonder and delight passed over Gosset's face as his cock penetrated the hot succulent tunnel of flesh. He began to work his hips back and forth, straining to fill Miss Newcombe to the hilt, watching in fascination as tiny shivers crossed the flesh of her buttocks with every thrust he made. His dreams had come true. He was savouring the ultimate forbidden fruit, he was fucking his school matron - and she would never know!

Standing at Gosset's side, Sally reached round and flicked the bamboo across Jane's dangling breasts, setting them bouncing and swaying. Gosset gave a stifled gasp as he felt Miss Newcombe's ribbed passage contract about him. The extra tightness accelerated the inevitable. Gosset's face contorted, his buttocks clenched as he spasmed, discharging his load into the receptacle intended for it by nature.

Gosset sagged and reluctantly withdrew his cock from its exquisite lodging place, a few drops of semen from his penis head falling to the floor.

Sally beckoned to Harris...

When the boys had all made use of the innocent object of their lust and had returned to their dormitory completely satiated, and no trace of their presence remained in the room, Sally released Jane Newcombe. The older woman slumped exhausted onto the bed, her hand sliding between her thighs to probe, very carefully, the swollen lips of her vulva.

"I never knew a cucumber could feel like that, Mistress."

"You can call me Sally again. The lesson's over."

Miss Newcombe, her face flushed from her exertions, looked at her intently. "Well, have I passed your challenge? Do you believe my offer is genuine?"

"Yeah, I think so."

"And? Will you be my bondslave?"

"Give me a couple of days to think about it."

19: A Slave's Slave.

"I've been giving them lessons," Amber said modestly, by way of explanation for the kisses Sue had received, as they watched the boys close the loft trapdoor and heard the padlock click on the other side.

Jemima threw her arms about Sue and hugged her. "You see, they're really nice. You can be their slave and they won't be beastly to you like Arabella."

Sue was bewildered, blinking at their naked, camouflaged bodies. "I... don't understand. What are you doing here like this, Miss Jemima?"

Jemima beamed a happy smile, still hugging Sue. "Just call me 'Jemima' - or 'Jem' if you like." She giggled. "We're both slaves now."

"We haven't been properly introduced," Amber said. "My name's Amber Jones." Automatically she held out her hand and automatically Sue took it. The image of how odd they must appear; two naked women with chains around their ankles shaking hands so formally, struck them at the same moment. They grinned foolishly into each other's faces, then broke into helpless laughter.

"I'm... I'm Sue Drake!" Sue choked out.

"Pleased... to meet you!" Amber replied, struggling to control herself.

"Sorry... but I haven't laughed... for days!" Sue gasped. Then her face crumpled and the tears began to flow again.

"Get a blanket over her to warm her up and give her some food!" Amber told Jemima urgently.

Five minutes later Sue was huddled in blankets and seated between them on Amber's makeshift bed, chewing on bread and cheese. Sue wiped her eyes with an unsteady hand.

"I'm... sorry about that. But after what's happened... after what Miss Arabella did to me. At first I thought was going mad. Then I realised what I am..."

"It's all right," Amber reassured her. "This is all strange to me as well. I think we come from the same place. If I guess right, you came across a black lacquer box somewhere called Hoakam Woods?"

Sue's eyes widened. "That's right! You know about that?"

Amber smiled wryly. "It kind of belonged to me. Nevermind, it's a long story. I just wondered if you still had the, uh, phallus that brought you here?"

"Oh... that. It was with my things in the playhouse, I remember... but I haven't seen it since then."

Jemima had been following their conversation with a curious frown. Now she spoke up: "Do you mean that rude sort of statue thing that was sticking inside you when we found you?"

"Yes!" Amber interjected. "Do you know what happened to it?"

"Arabella took it with her after she looked through Sue's things," Jemima said. "I suppose it must be in her room in the Hall now."

Amber gave a disappointed sigh.

"Is it important?" Jemima asked.

"It might be. Don't worry." Amber smiled reassuringly at Jemima. "It's not your problem. Now we'd better get ourselves cleaned up and get some sleep. You've got to go back home looking bright and fresh tomorrow morning, remember?" She saw Sue's puzzled look. "Jem's a sort of part-time slave," she

137

added helpfully.

Sue shook her head tiredly. "I really don't understand any of this."

"Well, it's like this..." Amber began.

With interjections from Jemima, Amber explained their relationship with the boys and their mutual desire for revenge on Arabella, while they soaped and scrubbed the camouflage off their skins. Sue listened intently. When they were done, Sue turned wondering eyes on Jemima.

"You really did all this, let yourself be tortured and made a slave, to get me away from Arabella?"

Jemima blushed. "I was frightened Arabella would really hurt you, but I just wasn't brave enough to stand up to her... well, you know what I am. When I found out what our masters - the Cranborough House boys, I mean - wanted, I realised I could let them make me tell them about you. It wasn't hard..." She stared at the floor in embarrassment for a moment. "You can see that I like being treated this way, even if it is wicked and wrong. But that's why I couldn't keep my eyes off you while Arabella was doing all those terrible things. Then when you were in the water butt and I..."

Sue leaned over and kissed Jemima. "Thank you," she said simply. "I knew what Arabella was, but I could never have left her, even if I'd been free to." Sue turned to Amber. "And thank you for opening all those locks."

"It's a hobby of mine," Amber said with a smile. "Hey, don't I get a kiss too?"

Sue obliged and Amber revelled in the soft warmth of Sue's body and the electric tingle as Sue's heavy breasts brushed across her own nipples. After long seconds they drew apart and Sue looked at her uncertainly.

"You're not like us, are you?" she said.

"What do you mean?"

"I've discovered my true nature over the last few days. I'm naturally servile, a submissive, a masochist, call it whatever you like. It would be stupid to pretend otherwise after what I let Arabella do to me, and loved it... most of the time, anyway. From what Jemima says I think she's the same. But I don't feel you're the type to let people just walk over you."

"In case you hadn't noticed, I'm the boys' slave, and they've done a pretty good job of keeping me in my place."

"But some of the time she tells the boys what to do," Jemima volunteered.

"And get punished if I say too much," Amber pointed out. "But you're right, I'm not a total submissive - though I've found out it can be fun for a while as a sort of game. But I'm not planning to make a career out of it."

"I think," Sue said slowly, "that there's comfort in surrender to somebody with a stronger will, just accepting what happens. You don't have to work to please your master; you leave all the complicated decisions to them and simply obey. It's a way of being important to somebody without threatening their position. As long as you find the right person."

"That's the danger, isn't it?" Amber said.

"Perhaps the danger's part of it. Maybe that's what I'm looking for."

Amber nodded. "Sounds like you've given it all some thought."

Sue smiled ruefully. "I've had a lot of time to think lately. Arabella didn't make it easy to sleep at night."

"So I saw," Amber said grimly. "I don't know how you stood it."

"Oh, some of the time I was in ecstasy. I think the pain was giving me a high. I loved the feeling of being treated like dirt, being so absolutely degraded. But I found there has to be a point to suffering. You must know that your pain is being balanced by somebody else's pleasure, or else it's just meaningless. Then it really hurts." A hunted look came into her eyes. "If she'd just said... she loved me..."

Sue looked close to tears again. Jemima hugged her tighter

and Amber embraced them both.

"Well the nights are usually more comfortable here," Amber assured Sue cheerfully. "Forget about Arabella, it's the boys you must think about serving now, and they'll want you fresh in the morning. Look forward to plenty of sex, bondage and light torture. After the sample they've already had you'll go down a bomb, I promise you. No problem about being appreciated there."

Sue smiled. "That sounds... wonderful."

"Let's get some sleep then. I hope you don't both mind sharing. There aren't the blankets to make up more than one bed."

"It'll be warmer," Jemima said quickly, her face shining at the thought of sleeping beside Sue.

"Yes, it will, won't it," said Amber.

They arranged the bedding, then Amber stretched to turn off the light switch, which her ankle chain just allowed her to reach, then burrowed back underneath the covers by touch. Sue lay in between Jemima and herself. Amber slid an arm across Sue as casually as she could manage and rested her head very nearly on her shoulder. Sue made no protest. They formed a huddle of warm female flesh, the scents of their bodies mingling. Amber felt content. Nobody should sleep alone. She shifted her arm slightly so that it rested against Sue's breasts.

"I know this is stupid... but I can't sleep like this," Sue said suddenly.

Amber sighed, pulling away. "I'm sorry..." she began.

"I don't think I can take this much freedom anymore," Sue continued in a small voice. "I'd like to feel under control... restrained. Please?"

Amber got up and switched on the light again. She looked down at Sue's anxious face. Jemima was frowning at her uncertainly. Yes, Amber thought, Arabella really had broken Sue in completely.

"Of course," Amber said gently. "Fortunately you've come

to the right place."

Using spare rope she bound Sue's arms to her sides, crossing ropes over her chest and stomach so she could feel their constraint, and making figure-of-eight loops to fasten her wrists to the tops of her thighs. Then she spread Sue's legs and tied her ankles with lines running out from the sides of the pen, taking care not to abrade her skin any further, then put enough tension on the ropes to hold Sue in place without being painfully stretched.

And there Sue was, little more than two hours after being rescued, back in bondage. She looked helpless, very beautiful and quite content. Amber felt an ache in her loins and a hot slickness between her love lips, reminding her that it had been several hours since she'd had sex. And there Sue was...

She realised that Jemima was looking at Sue with much the same expression as her own. The younger girl definitely had the hots for Sue, though in this world they'd probably still call it a 'crush' or 'pash'. It would be cruel to cut her out.

On the other hand they were both self-confessed natural slaves...

Amber picked up another length of rope. "Come here, Jemima. Turn round... that's it."

Jemima offered no resistance as Amber tied her hands behind her back.

"Now get on top of Sue and have sex with her," Amber told her. "I know you want to."

Her face radiating daring and delight, Jemima obeyed, kneeling and slipping between Sue's parted legs and wriggling up her body. Her small conical breasts squashed against Sue's soft full mammaries. Face to face they kissed. Instinctively Jemima began to work her hips up and down, rubbing her cleft into Sue's. Their pubic hair whispered as their bushes intertwined.

"That's it, harder..." Amber took a firm hold of Jemima's smooth buttocks and helped her grind more forcefully against her lover. The girls began to make tiny throaty noises of delight. Amber slid a hand between their thighs and into the pulsating, squirming fleshy tunnels of their kissing lovemouths and felt the hard nubs of their clitorises in perfect contact. She reluctantly withdrew her hand from this delightful haven and found it wet with their passion. Both girls had such full deep clefts despite their difference in build. Was it a sign of their intense sexual natures?

"All change!" Amber said suddenly.

With a heave she half lifted Jemima off Sue and turned her about. Before Jemima could protest, Amber had her kneeling astride Sue with her head pushed down between Sue's thighs. Immediately Jemima nuzzled her face into the hot cleft and continued eagerly with her tongue the work she had started.

"Can you still taste the boys' come in there?" Amber asked as she straddled Sue so that she faced Jemima's upturned bottom. "You'd better get used to that."

Amber squatted down and ground her already dripping peach into Sue's face, settling herself into place so that Sue's tongue could find her clitoris. Jemima's mound, blossoming from between the taut smooth columns of her thighs, bobbed before her; its swollen sticky lips pouting from their hairy nest. Amber clasped Jemima's hips, bent forward and buried her face in its scented depths.

As she kissed and sucked and lapped, Amber revelled in the feel of the two bodies she had arranged for her pleasure. It gave her such a delicious sense of power.

She lifted her head for a moment to draw breath. "Now you're both the slaves of a slave," she murmured.

Three girls locked in a perfect loving triangle of flesh. What would the morning bring them?

20: A Little Sport.

It was before nine the next morning when George Platt, cap clasped respectfully in his hand, entered Major Havercotte-Gore's study.

"You wished to see me, Major?"

"Take a look at this, Platt," the Major said, sliding a paper across the desk to his head keeper.

It was a notification of a public bondslave auction. Prominently displayed was a photograph of two identical naked blonde girls standing in chains. Under the picture was a list of their particulars. Platt studied these for a minute, then perused the picture more closely with a critical eye.

"We don't see many twins put up for sale, do we, sir?" he observed. "They certainly look pretty enough. Fine for show and bedding no doubt, but they seem a might slim for the hunt. I don't reckon they'd have the stamina."

"That's what I was thinking," the Major agreed. "But it says they're proven runners. If they were up to it they'd make splendid additions to the pack and bring it up to full strength."

"Well, I'd like to see them for myself first, sir." He looked at the paper again. "Specially with that high a reserve price."

"That's the trouble, Platt. Look at the date of the sale - today at three o'clock in Exeter. This confounded notice has been lost in the post for a week!"

"Doesn't give much time to check them over, even if you can get there before the start, sir."

"Which is why I want you to come with me. If we leave within the hour we can just make the connection to the West Coast Express. Have the trap made ready for the station and tell Alison she'll be in charge of the kennels for the day."

"Right you are, sir."

"Now; where's Arabella? She'll have to see to our guests. Bad show to leave your house while you've got people staying, and with the Ball tomorrow!"

"I'm sure they'll understand, sir," Platt said. "Most of them being keen hunters themselves, they know you can't pass up the chance of adding fresh blood to a pack."

The first suspicion Arabella had that something was wrong was as she put the key into the front door of the playhouse. The door was shut but not locked. Surely she had locked it behind her when she had left last night. She was scrupulous about security where slaves were concerned.

She stepped into the house, automatically looking about her. Sue's bike was no longer resting against the wall of the sitting room. A sudden dread filled her and she raced up the narrow stairs three at a time and burst into the bedroom where she had left Sue. The shackles hung loose, the padlocks were open and the bed was cold and bare.

Arabella tore through the tiny house, searching for Sue in every cupboard and corner, but in her heart she already knew the truth. The playhouse was empty. Her slave was gone.

"Pity you have to dash off like this just now, sir," said Thomas to the Major.

"Though we quite understand how it is," Gerard added quickly. "Can't miss the opportunity to acquire prime girlflesh."

"I hope you find something as rare as that brown vixen of yours," said Thomas. "Shame we missed her run in the hunt. Hope we'll see something of her this time."

Thomas and Gerard's steamer taxi had just deposited them at the front door of the Hall, where they had met the Major on his way out.

"I'm grateful for your understanding, gentlemen," the Major replied. "I should be back before dinner. Until then Arabella will look after you... if she condescends to put in an appearance. Ah, there she is at last... Arabella! Come here, please!"

Arabella had appeared, walking with heavy steps along the drive, swishing her riding crop angrily at the gravel. She barely acknowledged her uncle's call, but turned listlessly towards him.

"Arabella," the Major said as she slouched up to them, "I've been trying to find you for almost an hour..." He caught sight of her face. "What is the matter with you, child?"

"You look as though you've found sixpence and lost half a crown," Gerard said.

Arabella's lips pinched as though she was controlling herself only with a tremendous effort and her eyes shied away from theirs. "It's... nothing," she said, aiming another cut of her crop at the innocent gravel. "It doesn't matter."

"Well, do try to look a little more cheerful," the Major begged. "Remember we have got guests in the house. Now I'll be away for most of the day. I've made my excuses but please see that everybody is properly entertained."

"Yes, uncle," she mumbled, still scowling.

At that moment the trap, with Platt already inside, rattled across the gravel and drew up before them. The Major climbed aboard, gave a quick wave and they were off again along the drive.

Thomas and Gerard watched until it was out of sight, then turned to Arabella.

"Well, how have things been, Old Thing?" Gerard asked her. "Have to say you don't look much brighter than when we left."

"Yes, how did the hunt go?" Thomas said.

Arabella's face darkened further. "Don't talk to me about the hunt!" she snapped.

Thomas and Gerard, old acquaintances of Arabella, knew her moods well enough not to pry further.

"As you like," Gerard said easily. "Only we were saying to you uncle that we hoped to see more of the new brown girl - Melanie, isn't it? - while we were here. Did she run as well as you hoped?"

Arabella's riding crop slashed the gravel again, then paused as a gleam came into her eyes. "Is Platt going with my Uncle as

145

well?" she asked lightly.

"Why yes," said Thomas. "He wants him along for his opinion. Sound thinking. Got a good eye for sporting flesh has Platt."

"And they'll be away most of the day?"

"That's right - just as your Uncle said."

A broad smile appeared on Arabella's face. "So, you'd like to see how well Melanie can run, would you?"

Alison Chalmers looked critically about the keeper's office to check everything was in its place. It was the first time she had been left in charge of the kennels for so long, and she wanted to show she was up to the job.

At the moment the girls were all out working so there was little to do. But later there would be the lunches to oversee and the work reports to make out, and there always had to be somebody on call in case one of the girls had an accident. They were valuable property and Alison took her responsibility towards their care very seriously.

She walked though the connecting door to the Examination and Sick Room. All was as it should be. The barred cell at the end of the room which enclosed a pair of iron-frame beds had fortunately seen little use for months.

She passed through into the Harness Room, redolent as always with its heavy smell of leather and polish - and paused as a memory surfaced.

In here only a few days before she had secretly watched Platt giving Gillian special training. Gillian had been in trouble for refusing a guest the use of her rear passage. Platt had given her a proper thrashing as a punishment, of course, but later he had bound her over a trestle in the Harness room away from the other girls and had taught her how to open her bottom hole to penetration. First he had used an anal plug, then his finger... and finally his penis.

It was the first time Alison had seen a mature male member standing erect, and she'd felt embarrassed and guilty... but also fascinated. She had continued to watch as Platt had given Gillian a lesson in sodomy, tactfully encouraging her to perform to order. Alison wondered if she would ever be that skilled at handling pack girls, and wished she could learn Platt's special blend of firmness combined with a deep understanding of the bondslave mind.

Her reverie was interrupted by somebody calling her name.

Alison went out into the yard and found Arabella, clad in riding dress, slapping her riding crop impatiently into her gloved palm.

"There you are, Chalmers. Bring Melanie here at once."

"Melanie's working in the gardens, Miss Arabella."

"Then send somebody for her or fetch her here yourself!"

Alison hesitated. She knew well enough Arabella's reputation for occasionally mistreating the girls. If it had been up to her, Alison would not have let her near any of them in her current mood, far less a prize specimen such as Melanie. But Alison had been given no specific instructions to refuse such a request, and with both the Major and Platt away, Arabella was mistress of the Hall and so entitled to use the girls as she wished.

"I'll fetch her myself, Miss," Alison said, and hurried off.

When Alison returned ten minutes later with Melanie on a leash and her hands bound behind her back, Arabella was holding a bundle of items she had evidently taken from the Harness Room. Arabella's eyes gleamed as Melanie appeared, and Alison felt a slight tug on the leash as the slave girl instinctively held back. But Alison handed over the loop end of the leash nevertheless and watched as Arabella led Melanie out through the yard gates.

As they disappeared, Alison felt a sudden shiver. She hoped she had done nothing wrong.

Melanie's stomach was churning at the thought of being in Arabella's power as she was led through the passage to the

147

stable court. From their very first meeting it had been obvious Arabella had designs on her, and after hearing stories of her behaviour from the other pack girls, she had no desire to find out what they were. Fortunately the Major had kept Melanie for his own use, and of course Arabella had failed to win her in the hunt.

But what now?

Thomas and Gerard were waiting in the courtyard already mounted on their horses. Even though they were both carrying long handled paddles like those she had seen in the hunt, the sight of them was reassuring. She knew they were both gentlemen and sportsmen. Surely they wouldn't allow Arabella to treat her too badly.

Arabella's own mount had one of the wheeled frames that were used to transport exhausted packgirls back from the hunt hitched to the back of its saddle. Why did she need that, Melanie wondered?

"There's our pretty brown vixen all ready for a bit of sport," Gerard said, running his eyes appreciatively over Melanie's naked body.

"She's even better than I remember," Thomas agreed. "You've been training her hard, Arabella."

"We train all our girls hard," Arabella said, slinging the bag of equipment she had taken from the harness room onto the frame and then mounting her own animal. Trailing Melanie behind them on her leash, Arabella and her companions rode out of the courtyard and across the gravel drive.

Beyond the garden gate they set out across the fields at a gentle trot. Melanie had to run briskly to keep up, and with her hands tied behind her this accentuated the bounce of her breasts and the roll of her hips. Arabella watched her intently. If Arabella just wants to show me off to Thomas and Gerard that's fine, Melanie thought.

They reached the woods where Arabella halted the little group. She unhitched the frame from her horse and left it leaning against a tree, then looked at Melanie.

"Now, you are going to give Mister Thomas and Mister Gerard some sport," she told her. "They never had their reward for capturing you the day you arrived, remember?"

"Yes, Miss Arabella," Melanie answered brightly, her heart leaping with relief and her nipples hardening and standing up even as she spoke. "I shall be honoured to serve them."

"Good. But first we need to warm you up..."

Arabella rode up and down the field leading Melanie along behind her while Thomas and Gerard took turns to ride past and smack Melanie with their paddles. The enticing targets of her unprotected breasts and buttocks naturally received most of the blows. Melanie gasped at each stinging impact and her eyes misted with tears, but she tried to show her mettle by maintaining her stride and accepting the punishment bravely, as she would in a real hunt. It was just the prelude for what was to come, the thought of which was already lubricating her lovelips.

The 'warming' session ceased when Melanie's chest was heaving and she was sheened with sweat. With her tender flesh flushed and tingling, Arabella led her into the shelter of the woods.

Thomas and Gerard dismounted.

"Free her hands, Arabella," Thomas said. "It's only sporting."

For a moment Arabella seemed ready to argue, but with a shrug she complied, releasing Melanie's hands.

Briefly freed of her bonds, Melanie stood between the two men, ready to enact the culmination of the hunt - the capture and subjugation of the prey.

The men circled her, grinning in anticipation. Melanie smiled back, feinted to one side, then lunged in the opposite direction, trying to get between them.

She managed to run five yards before Gerard, with a diving tackle he must have learned on the rugby field, brought her down. His hands caught her ankles and held her fast, despite her desperate kicks and twists. Thomas's heavy body fell across her back and bore her down. Then she was wrestling with them, three figures rolling on the ground, the men grunting and cursing in frustration and delight as they clasped Melanie's sweaty, dirt-streaked naked body and strained to control her.

"By God, but she's strong!" Gerard exclaimed.

"Secure her, Arabella, quickly!" Thomas pleaded.

With a heave the men rolled Melanie over and forced her arms behind her back. There was a slight jangle of chain and she felt handcuffs click about her wrists. Her flailing legs were stretched wide apart. Arabella pushed a spreader bar between them and snapped the spring lock cuffs mounted on its ends about her ankles.

With a whimper of defeat, Melanie ceased to struggle and lay still; a pinioned animal panting for breath, her chest heaving. Her body ached and her skin smarted, but inside she felt a glow of satisfaction. She knew she had given good sport.

The hunters sat back on their heels for a moment to catch their breath and to examine their prize, turning her round between them. Their touch was firm, but not ungentle, and they praised her even as they handled her intimately.

"Well run, girl," exclaimed Thomas as he squeezed her warm full breasts experimentally; pinching and lifting a dark, plump nipple and letting it snap back, watching her flesh tremble and still.

"Thank you, Master," Melanie panted.

"Yes, a fine show," agreed Gerard, running his hand over the smooth swell of her belly, teasing the deep pit of her navel, then sliding his fingers into the tight, dark curls and moist recesses of her cleft. Hands ran down the curve of Melanie's slender waist and out across the fullness of her hips.

"Fine strong haunches," said Thomas.

"Lovely full rump," Gerard commented, his fingers digging into her flesh and parting her buttock cheeks firmly. Melanie felt the surprising coolness of the air touch the tender pucker of her anus. "A dark, tight little hole here, that might repay investigation in due course," he concluded.

Melanie heard Arabella laugh at his remark. Twisting her head around she saw Arabella seat herself in the hollow of two great splayed roots of an oak tree. She was going to watch as the men used her.

Gerard grasped her hips and pulled Melanie backwards and up onto her widespread knees. Thomas knelt before her, unbuttoning his bulging riding breeches, releasing a thick, purple-headed penis, which seemed to spring to attention before Melanie's eyes. Gerard gave her a little push and she toppled helplessly forward. Melanie could smell saddle leather and the heavy male scent of his arousal as he lowered her head onto his erect member. She closed her eyes and opened her mouth. Hot, hard, silky flesh pushed past her lips. She sucked and licked dutifully. Thomas pressed her head down further and she swallowed the head of his rampant tool, feeling her throat bulge. A tug on her hair and she was allowed to pull back enough to draw breath. She began to work her tongue and lips harder round his organ, rolling down his tight foreskin to expose the smooth plum at its head.

Behind her, Gerard opened his fly buttons, and she felt the head of his erection brush across her bottom. Then he grasped her hips firmly and drove into her moist slit, stretching the fleshy sheath to accommodate him. She gasped as he penetrated her, and almost choked on Thomas's cock.

Arabella sat on the oak root with her legs splayed and her hand working busily under her skirts. Her eyes were wide and intent on the scene before her.

Thomas and Gerard worked Melanie's bound and helpless body to and fro between them, falling into a steadily increasing tempo. Back and forth, back and forth, the pistons of flesh plunging remorselessly inside her. Just time to take a breath as Thomas's thick rod cleared her throat, even as she was impaled by Gerard's longer shaft reaming into her cunt again.

151

The raw lust grew within Melanie and a warm knot began to tighten in her stomach. How perfectly natural it all was after the pain and exertions of the hunt and capture. She was their prize, properly won and now to be enjoyed... and to enjoy.

Thomas came first: hot sperm spurting down her throat. She ground her face into his stomach as he spent so that her nose was buried in the tufts of pubic hair peeping through the vent of his soft linen underwear. Melanie felt Gerard's urgent ejaculation blossom forth inside her and knew her own need had to be satisfied. Desperately riding his last thrusts into her slit, she came herself; bucking and jerking wildly, pulling at her bonds, and finally collapsing onto the grass.

Exhausted and happily satiated she lay there: a packgirl at peace. The living trophy of the hunt and her captors united briefly by their spent passion.

"Now it's my turn," Melanie heard Arabella say brusquely, "How's her tongue, Thomas? I hope you have warmed her for me. Over here, girl. Crawl!"

Still in a post-orgasmic daze, Melanie obeyed automatically; awkwardly bracing herself by pressing her face and chest into the grass until she could lever herself upright enough to shuffle forward on her widespread knees, moving in undulating jerks rather like a caterpillar, squashing and scraping her tingling breasts across the grass. She was aware of Gerard and Thomas watching her progress from behind, and realized what a sight her raised and naked bottom and widespread thighs must present to them. Even as she edged towards Arabella, she felt Gerard's sperm start to ooze from her lovemouth and trickle down the insides of her thighs.

Arabella watched her uncomfortable and humiliating approach with a strange mixture of impatience and delight. When she was close enough she thrust out her boots.

"Kiss them!" she commanded.

Painfully, Melanie levered herself upright enough to lift her head from the grass, acutely aware that she was thrusting out her hips and bottom even more than before to keep her balance. She felt the mens' eyes upon her helplessly exposed cleft as she bent forward and kissed the shiny black leather toes of Arabella's boots. Arabella smiled, then suddenly parted her legs wide and drew her skirt up to the tops of her thighs, so that Melanie found herself staring up between the two shapely columns of pale flesh to the nest of golden curls at their apex and the swollen vaginal lips that they framed. So Arabella wanted her to lick her out. Well that wasn't so bad.

But Arabella was edging her bottom forward even as she leaned back. The dark pucker of Arabella's anus appeared from beneath her mound of Venus.

"I want your nose in my cunny slot and tongue in my bottom hole," Arabella said.

Melanie faltered, instinctive revulsion at odds with her training to obey.

"Well?" Arabella demanded, in a more menacing tone.

"Please... Miss Arabella... I've never done that to anyone. Let me please you in some other way..."

Even as she spoke she was bracing herself for the expected slash of Arabella's crop. But it didn't come. She looked fearfully up into Arabella's face only to see a cold smile of triumph.

"Obviously you need further training," Arabella said, seeming to relish every word. "I'll show Uncle how girls should be broken in. Something severe is called for. I think the thistles in the fallow field are tall enough to serve."

"I say, that's a bit steep, Arabella," Gerard exclaimed. He and Thomas were standing now, brushing off their clothes. "Give the girl a thrashing if you must, but don't start that again. You know the trouble you got into last time."

Sickening realization dawned on Melanie. Arabella had planned this all along. She'd just been searching for the excuse to do something terrible to her to prove her methods of training, which she'd been pestering the Major about since Melanie's capture. Fear broke down Melanie's inhibitions. Stupid for her to have hesitated. She was a slave girl. She was meant to obey.

"Please, Miss Arabella," she said cravenly. "Forgive me. I'll do it now." Melanie tried to push her head between Arabella's thighs, but Arabella caught her collar and held her back.

"Too late, girl. It's the thistles for you. Thomas, Gerard: give me a hand with her."

But now both the men were looking at Arabella in stern disapproval.

"Sorry, Arabella," Thomas said firmly. "We won't have any part of this."

"Look, you've already given her a fright, now let the girl please you," Gerard advised.

"No, she must be punished properly!" Arabella insisted.

"Well you can't take her through the thistles without us - and we're not helping you."

And the two men mounted their horses and rode away through the trees.

Arabella looked at them go with a face contorted by both rage and disbelief. In that moment Melanie saw the naked soul of the spoilt child that lay beneath the adult exterior. Then Arabella turned back to her.

"Don't think you've got away with this," she warned Melanie ominously. "You're going to go for a ride you'll never forget!"

21: The Thistle Ride.

Jemima cautiously opened the front gate of the playhouse garden.

She was holding a handkerchief over her nose ready to give a convincing demonstration of sniffles, adding credence to the message that she had sent to Arabella yesterday reporting her indisposition. Actually Jemima did not want to be here. She wanted to be in the school stable loft, sharing in everything that she knew even now the boys were doing to Sue. But she had promised to find out what Arabella's reaction to Sue's disappearance was and what she might do in response. So Jemima had gone home as soon as she had been released, told her mother what a nice night she had spent at the Hall, and then hurried back here. She was looking forward to making her report to the boys. Amber had advised her to be a little reluctant to speak, and Jemima secretly thrilled at the thought of what they would do to her to persuade her.

There was nobody in the playhouse, but she heard voices from the back garden and went through. Belinda, Penny and Ernestine were sitting out on the lawn.

"There you are," said Belinda impatiently as Jemima appeared. "Where did you go to yesterday afternoon?"

"I didn't feel well," Jemima said quickly, displaying her handkerchief for all to see. "I left a message for Arabella telling her I was going home. Er... where is she?"

"We don't know," Ernestine said. "Everything was open when we arrived, but there was no sign of Arabella."

"And she's taken the girl with her," Penny added with a scowl, "so we haven't anything to do."

"Oh," said Jemima, finding herself a seat. She thought for a minute, then said hesitantly: "of course, we did used to play at lots of other things before we found Sue. Why can't we try them again?"

"Huh!" said Belinda contemptuously. "Those were children's games. We're too old for that now - except you! You'll always be a silly girl, Jem."

Just then the backdoor of the playhouse opened with a bang and Arabella strode out into the garden. Her face was set, her eyes were gleaming. Before they could say a word her gaze fastened on Belinda.

"Come with me!" she snapped in such commanding tones that Belinda jerked to her feet without question.

"What's happening?" Ernestine asked.

"And what have you done with our slave?" Penny added.

Jemima's heart thudded, fearful that Arabella would somehow know she had been responsible. But Arabella didn't spare her a second glance.

"She's gone," Arabella said simply. "We'll talk about it later. This is more important. Come on, Belinda."

And the two of them walked briskly away, leaving the other girls to exchange puzzled glances.

Melanie tried to move to ease the pain, but her bonds were too tight. She moaned but could not cry out: a gag strap stretched her lips back with cruel tension. Her bared teeth chewed on leather.

She was tied with her back to a tree, her arms wrenched out behind her and pulled upwards so high that she thought her shoulders would dislocate. There was a rope around her middle, cutting into her stomach and pinching it in painfully tight. Her legs were pulled wide apart and back around the tree, with her knees bent so she could not support her weight. Only her bonds held her upright. Her bonds... and the stick.

Arabella had rammed one end into the grass between the tree roots so that the stick leaned inwards at an angle. The top end was cleft in a 'Y' fork, like an extended thumb and forefinger. The 'finger' was lodged in her vaginal passage which was distending under the weight of her body, pressing up against her bladder. The 'thumb' was gouging into the upper fold of her vulva, pushing the cleft mound of soft brown flesh upward beyond its natural limits, stretching it agonisingly into a vertical grin. Her perversely aroused clitoris ground against hard wood. Arabella had smiled when she inserted the stick. It was a symbol of her power over Melanie; a reminder of her subjugation.

Now disgust mingled with Melanie's fear and pain. How could she have been so stupid as to refuse her? The only consolation was that something like this would have happened sooner or later. Arabella would have made more and more taxing demands of her until she rebelled. She had obviously been looking for an excuse to punish her - 'training' her as she thought of it. At least Thomas and Gerard had refused to help. But they had still left Melanie to her fate. Perhaps it wasn't done to interfere with the punishment of another person's slave. Not polite. Not good manners.

Melanie found herself crying. The warm companionship of the pack, her delight at serving the Major, the challenge and joy of the hunt; all were melting away before the stark realization of her utter helplessness in the face of Arabella's malevolence. How had she let this happen to her? She had to get away... but to get away was wrong. She was a slave.

She heard the beat of hooves. Two horses! She twisted her head around in the wild hope that it was Thomas and Gerard returning. But it was Arabella, together with a dark-haired girl perhaps a couple of years younger than she was.

They dismounted and walked up to Melanie. The new girl looked her over in wonder, but also with a touch of the coldness Arabella showed.

"Oh, she is beautiful," she said, turning Melanie's head from side to side and squeezing her breasts. "I can see why you wanted her for yourself. Does she really run as well as they say?"

"Yes, but she needs more obedience training."

"The sort of thing you did to the Drake girl?"

Arabella smiled cruelly, looking Melanie straight in the eye. "Better than that. Help me get her onto the frame."

They pulled the cleft stick out of Melanie and released her bonds, leaving the rope ends bound about her wrists and ankles. Melanie fell forward onto her face, her arms and legs numb and useless. They dragged her over to the packgirl frame which was lying flat on the grass. Resting her on the netting they tied her face down, her hands fastened over her head to the bar at the apex of the 'A' frame which hitched over the back of a saddle and her feet on the rests over the axle.

"Now unhook the net," Arabella said.

Belinda obeyed, leaving Melanie hanging in a bow from her wrists and ankles, her stomach and breasts brushing the grass. Mutely she watched as they fitted rods from the pack Arabella had brought with her to either side of the frame top, forming extended 'handles' about five feet long. Loops of leather trailed from the handle ends.

They brought their horses up and positioned them close together and lifted the frame by the handles and rolled it forward so that they could hook the leather loops over their western-style saddle pommels. Now Melanie hung suspended from the frame between the two horses, hanging at an angle of some forty-five degrees. The girls mounted up and Arabella looked across at Belinda.

"You've always boasted you were a good rider," she said. "Can you follow my lead and hold the frame steady between us?"

"Of course," Belinda replied confidently. "Where are we going?"

"Just across to the next field. You'll see. Ready?"

They set off. The frame rattled along between the two horses. Melanie swung limply from her ropes, her breasts bobbing and swaying with a heavy fluid motion. Arabella watched her with triumphant eyes. They passed out of the woods and along the top of a field and through a gate. The field beyond had been left fallow. Most of its lower slopes were covered in clusters of bright green spear thistles, some already standing four or five feet high, though not yet in flower.

Belinda laughed at the sight. Melanie whimpered and began pulling futilely at her bonds, shaking her head desperately.

The riders urged their mounts into a trot and then a canter, sweeping down across the field and into the thistle patch with their helpless victim suspended between them. The hoofbeats of the two horses became a pounding roar in Melanie's ears. She shrieked behind her gag, then turned her head aside and

158

screwed up her eyes as she ploughed into the first clump of thistles.

The plants broke against her naked, unprotected body with a swish and slap, their hollow stems popping as they fell, raking along the length of her before being scythed by the frame's axle. Vicious inch-long thorns stabbed and tore at her out-thrust breasts and stomach like spiked flails, leaving beaded trails of scarlet streaked down her body. Shorter, finer thorns broke off in her brown flesh, each forming a burning point of pain. Her body contorted in reflex, muscles over her shoulders and back lifting and hardening. Her buttocks became glossy, perfectly rounded hills, clenching inward as though to close the deep cleft between them. Thighs swelled, calves bunched, tendons stood out in sharp definition as she strained magnificently at the ropes that bound her to the frame, hopelessly trying to shrink away from the agonising onslaught. Under the pressure Melanie's bladder cut loose, spraying a convulsive stream wildly across the grass.

From the safety of her saddle, Belinda laughed at this loss of control and dignity. Arabella watched each twist and jerk the tortured woman made, her eyes straining as though trying to take in every thistle point as it struck home.

Then they were through the thistles and the two horses were slowing to a trot, then a halt. Melanie's head dropped limply onto her chest as though in a faint. Incoherent gurgling noises came from behind her gag. Arabella dismounted and ran eagerly round her horse to inspect the effects of her punishment at close quarters.

Melanie was hanging trembling in her bonds, her head hanging loose, her fingers and toes clawing feebly at the air. The front of her body was a mass of longitudinal grazes and fine streaks of blood, mingling with splashes of sap from the thistle stalks. The insides of her thighs glistened with urine. The upper slopes of her breasts, driving into the thistles almost full-on in her suspended position, had suffered the worst. They bristled

159

with broken spines like pincushions. One large spine was actually embedded in Melanie's left nipple. A bright red globule of blood was rising about its point of penetration.

Arabella grasped Melanie's hair and tugged her head upright. Melanie's face was frozen in a mask of pain, her eyes half-closed. Arabella pulled the gag strap from Melanie's mouth. Her jaws remained parted, teeth still bared, a drool of saliva dribbled from her lips. On the strap were the marks of her teeth where she had half-bitten through the leather.

Arabella took in every detail of her abused body and smiled, savouring her slave's distress, feeling elated at the change she had wrought in her.

"Oh, you are so beautiful," she said softly.

Then she slapped Melanie's cheeks repeatedly and hard, until Melanie's eyes flickered open and focused fearfully upon her.

"Well, girl? How do you feel about licking my arse now?"

The question slowly penetrated the shocked layers of Melanie's mind, still spinning in the waves of fire rising up from her tormented flesh. All her dignity and self-respect had been obliterated by the ordeal of her ride. Those few seconds had broken her spirit more easily than she could have imagined. It was more than the pain she had suffered, it was the fact that it could be inflicted upon her so casually. It was proof of her absolute subjugation to Arabella's will. Arabella was her Mistress, she was her slave. She could escape the pain and the fear of more pain by agreeing to serve her. How simple it was.

Melanie fought to keep her voice steady. "I... I would be honoured... to lick your arse, Mistress."

"And Miss Belinda's?"

"Any... anybody you wish, Mistress."

"You wish to serve me?"

"Yes, Mistress."

"Will you do anything for me?"

"Anything... everything... please let me show you, Mistress!"

160

Arabella considered for a minute, then said to Belinda: "Help me untie her."

Melanie found herself blubbing with shameless relief. She kept saying: "Thank you, thank you..." to Arabella as she freed her, actually feeling gratitude to the person responsible for her suffering. A tiny part of her raged impotently against her cowardice, but the need to be free was overwhelming. If she was free she could pull out the agonising thorns and put dock leaves on her burning flesh. And she would serve her Mistress and be so good she would never, ever, need to punish her like that again...

It was several seconds before she realised that she was being re-tied to the frame in a new position.

"Mistress...?" she croaked.

Arabella smiled. "You said you would do anything for me..."

As Thomas and Gerard rode across the sweep of gravel before the Hall, they saw the Major descending from the trap that had taken him to the station hardly two hours earlier. By the time they trotted up the trap had set off again carrying Platt in the direction of the stables.

"Didn't expect to see you back so soon, sir," Thomas to the Major, who was standing on the steps of the front door.

Major Havercotte-Gore scowled. "The Express never arrived. Engine trouble, apparently. Waited around hoping for another train, but there's nothing that could get us to Exeter in time."

"Bad luck, sir," Gerard said.

"Well, it can't be helped. We'll have to manage with two girls short for a little longer. Hope there'll be enough of them for the Ball. I wanted the decorations to look particularly fine this year."

"I'm sure everything will go swimmingly, sir," said Thomas.

They chatted for another minute, then the Major turned to

enter the house. But he was stayed by the sight of Platt dashing through the archway of the stable court towards him, with an anxious looking Alison at his heels.

"Good Lord, man," the Major exclaimed as he reached them. "What's the matter?"

"I'm afraid Miss Arabella has taken Melanie out to the woods... in the company of Mr Thomas and Mr Gerard."

The Major fixed the two young men with an enquiring gaze. "Well, gentlemen?"

Thomas answered. "That's quite right, sir. Arabella invited us and we had a little sport with Melanie - and very fine she was too."

"And where is she now?" the Major asked impatiently.

The two men exchanged awkward glances. "Afterwards, Arabella wanted to punish the girl for not pleasing her," Gerard said. "She, er, talked of thistles."

"No!" exclaimed the Major.

"But we wouldn't have any part in it," Thomas assured him quickly. "And it needs two for that sort of game."

"But that's the trouble, sir," Platt interjected. "Alison says Miss Arabella took out a horse for Belinda Jenkyns to ride half an hour ago."

The Major's face flushed with rage and dismay. "Gentlemen, we need your horses this instant!"

Melanie hung on the frame, her feet above her head and her back nearest the ground, her spread ankles tied to the supporting rods. Her wrists were bound to the footrests while her head hung downward, trailing her hair in the grass. Melanie's bottom now twisted and swayed where her breasts had been on the previous run. Her thighs spread in grotesque welcome, her lovemouth gaping, exposing its coral-pink interior as though perversely eager to receive its chastisement.

The frame bounced between the two horses as they galloped across the field and into the thistle patch. Melanie's scream

162

rose above the pounding of hooves as the taller thistle heads lashed across her inner thighs, funnelled inward to the plump purse of flesh at their apex. Taller plants bowed over and slapped down on her mound, raking through her pubic hair and leaving spines and fragments of leaf entangled in the tight black curls. Dozens of spines every second were pricking and tearing at her most sensitive flesh, delicate inner labia twisted and tugged as though by many tiny pins. Thicker stems rasped deeper through her cleft, clawing at her clitoris, then ran on downward to cut a searing line between her buttocks. Fine streaks of blood appeared about her inner thighs, around the curve of her bottom cheeks and down the smooth skin of her back.

With a tremendous pain-driven effort, Melanie arched her body to lift her groin above the thistles. Arabella's long switch cracked out, cutting across the taut muscles of her stomach and beating her down again. There was to be no escaping her punishment.

In all the ride lasted little more than ten seconds, but they were the worst seconds of Melanie's life. Her screams continued far longer.

Then they ran clear of the thistles and the riders slowed to a halt. The two girls looked at the twitching, sobbing, bedraggled figure slung between their mounts. They felt the thrill of power course through them at the thought of what they had done to such a beautiful creature.

"Now she really knows what it is to be punished," Arabella said, her eyes sparkling.

"She'll never dare disobey you after this," Belinda added.

"She might, but no matter. I want more of a challenge than Sue provided. But for the next few days, I certainly don't think she'll give any trouble. Now, we had better..."

"Arabella!"

The ferocious cry rang out over the hedgerows. Arabella and Belinda twisted round in their saddles to see the Major and Platt gallop through the upper field gate and race towards them.

163

"Damn!" said Arabella quietly.

The riders came to a halt only yards from them, their mounts snorting and kicking up a spray of earth.

The Major was purple with rage, while Platt almost fell off his horse in his haste to get to Melanie. He crouched down by her side and lifted her head with remarkable tenderness, muttering: "Dear Lord, what have they done to you, girl?"

They all heard the faint rasp of Melanie's reply: "I... submitted... first time round... Mister Platt... but they did it again... please don't let them do it again... please!"

Platt took in her scratched and torn body, then cast such a venomous glance at Arabella and Belinda that they shrank back in alarm. Pulling out his clasp knife he began cutting Melanie free.

The Major spoke, clearly fighting to keep his voice under control.

"Arabella, you will go to your room and stay there until I say otherwise. This may have to be referred to the police."

"But we were only breaking her in, training her..."

"You call this barbarism training! Now do as you are told."

"But the Ball tomorrow...!"

"There will be no Ball for you. Now go, or must I have the servants take you there by force?"

Platt had Melanie free and she rested unsteadily on her hands and widespread knees; too weak to stand, unable to lie or sit because of the thistle spines that bristled over most of her body. Platt was trying to support her as best he could, but there was hardly any place he could hold her comfortably. His eyes once again found Arabella's face and she read the utter contempt in their depths.

Arabella mutely unhitched the carry frame from her saddle and rode off.

The Major turned to Belinda, who had been looking on trembling and white-faced.

"Miss Jenkyns," he said in brittle tones. "I have no doubt

my niece led you on in this, nevertheless you should have known better. You will return your horse to the stables and then leave my land. You are no longer welcome here. Do you understand?"

Belinda gulped, nodded and rode off after Arabella.

Only when they had gone did the Major dismount and kneel down by Melanie's trembling figure.

"My poor brown vixen," he said, gently stroking her hair.

And there were tears in his eyes.

22: Punishment and Reward

"And then Belinda went home," Jemima said breathlessly. "She looked really frightened. So we went home too - except I came back here."

It was lunchtime. Jemima was in the loft, standing naked with her arms stretched over her head by cuffs and ropes. A red blush on her pretty bottom and about her shapely little breasts showed where the boys had been 'encouraging' her to give a report on her morning's spying. It was the mixture of pain and pleasure she had been promised the previous day. A second rope was slung from the beam over her head. Tied at both ends, its middle passed tautly between her legs, vanishing between the lips of her sex. Jemima was rubbing herself on it as she talked so that a dark stain was spreading along the rope. Her nipples were so hard and swollen they looked as though they might burst.

The loft was silent for a moment after Jemima had finished, except for the sound of chewing. Miss Newcombe had allowed the boys to make themselves a sandwich lunch today as she had errands to run. Sally had brought some food from the village for Sue and Amber. The entire membership of SCRAW was therefore congregated to hear Jemima's story.

"She deserves worse than being sent to her room after what she did to the brown girl," Jackson said angrily.

"Maybe the Major'll give her some proper punishment after the County Ball's over," Harris suggested.

"Hope so," said Gosset.

Amber agreed with their sentiments. She would not wish what Arabella had done on her worst enemy, even a policewoman who'd once tried to arrest her. She began to feel very sorry for Melanie Kingston. Then she noticed self-conscious and slightly guilty looks from the boys as they glanced about them at their growing harem in the loft. Jemima, working herself gently to an orgasm on the rope; Sally, sitting on the floor eating an apple, her legs provocatively crossed so that her skirt had ridden up to reveal an absence of underwear; Amber herself sitting in a corner of her pen, her arms and legs spread wide and tied to the walls; finally Sue, strapped to the training horse with their sperm still oozing out of her, their gaze lingering on the marks her body still bore. Understanding their train of thought, Amber said quickly:

"Don't worry, Masters. What you're doing to us is quite different. We know you'd never be as irresponsible as Arabella."

The boys looked relieved but still uncertain. Jackson said: "But what do we do? Now this has happened we'll never know how much we hurt Arabella by stealing Sue from her. She's got other worries."

Amber had been thinking furiously as he spoke. She had to keep them interested. She said carefully: "But you still want to personally take revenge on Arabella, like you were planning when you caught me in the woods? Not just for this, I mean, but for getting you into trouble last term."

"Of course, but how?" Jackson said. "We can't get at her while she's in the Hall."

"But perhaps you can get her to come to you," Amber said, "and get yourself another girl into the bargain."

"Have you got a plan?" Gosset asked, with a barely suppressed eagerness that gladdened Amber's heart.

"At the moment it's half a plan. For the rest, Jemima will

have to do some reconnaissance..."

Melanie lay on her back on the Examination Room table, her eyes closed and head turned to one side as though asleep. Her arms were loosely cuffed to the top of the table, her legs bent at the knees and spread wide, her feet strapped into the stirrups. Alison and Platt worked over her removing thorns with pins and tweezers, washing and disinfecting her scratches, putting plasters over the larger cuts and tears. Fortunately none was so deep as to need stitches, but there were still many nasty gashes.

Alison was tending to Melanie's breasts, her pretty, open face contorted in dismay at the flawless ripe globes which had been so terribly marred. A simple lashing would have left clean, purposeful weals that would heal in a few days. This was careless and wanton.

"How could Miss Arabella have done such a thing?" Alison said dismally, for the fifth time.

"That's her way," Platt replied simply. "There's a cruel, wild streak in her, though her family are of the best. You'd hardly think she and the Major were related."

Platt was working between Melanie's widespread legs. With a torch and a large magnifying glass mounted on a stand, he was painstakingly examining every square inch of her abused lovemouth, its lips held apart by spring clamps, carefully removing broken thistle spines. Some were even embedded in the mouth of her vaginal passage. Instead of a delicate pink, the inner flesh was red raw. He applied a soothing cream as he worked to take out the heat. He could also see spines sticking in the crinkled ring of her anus, but at least the Major's favourite orifice did not seem otherwise seriously damaged.

"It's all right, girl," he said reassuringly to Melanie when she flinched as another thorn was pulled from the folds of her most delicate skin, "soon be over."

Guilt was obviously weighing heavily on Alison, for she

suddenly blurted out: "It's all my fault! I should never have let Miss Arabella take her. But how I could have refused? She's so... commanding!"

Platt saw the genuine distress in her face and his heart softened. "It wasn't your fault, Alison. She did have the right to take her. You couldn't have known it would come to this."

"But I had a feeling. There was a nasty look in her eyes. You'd never have let her take Melanie out like that, would you Mister Platt?"

"No, but then I've had more experience with the world than you, Alison. You'll learn how to stand your ground. I promise, next time you're left in charge, you'll have the Major's authority not to let anything be done with the girls that you're not happy with."

"If the Major will ever trust me with them again," Alison said miserably.

The visitor was shown into the Major's study.

Major Havercotte-Gore had enough to occupy his thoughts at that moment without entertaining unexpected callers, but good manners required that he be polite, especially if the visitor was female. He rose to greet her with hand outstretched.

"Good afternoon, Miss Moncrief. Jemima, isn't it? Please take a seat."

Jemima sat shyly on the edge of the chair as though anxious not to disturb anything about her. She looked very fresh and bright in her light plain frock, white socks and polished patent shoes. In her hand was a small posy of flowers.

"I'm so sorry to call on you like this, Major Havercotte-Gore," she said hesitantly. "But I felt I had to come... to apologise."

The Major looked surprised. "Apologise, Miss Moncrief? What have you to apologise for?"

Jemima lowered her eyes as though ashamed. "For what Arabella did to your bondslave Melanie."

168

"But that was none of your fault. It was all the doing of my unhappy niece and Belinda Jenkyns."

"But you see, Arabella has talked to us about Melanie for days. She kept on about the... the things she would like to do to her. I feel I should have known something like this would happen when she got the chance. I should have... warned you."

"My dear Miss Moncrief, you could have done nothing to prevent this. If anybody else is to blame it is myself. If I hadn't been in such a hurry to leave this morning, I would have thought to give instructions about how the girls could be used in my absence."

"Oh, please don't blame yourself either, Major," Jemima said. "Everybody knows how much you care for the girls you own. It must be terrible to see one hurt like that."

The Major felt touched by her understanding. "It has certainly been a great shock. Melanie's going to be unable to serve for several days, I fear. It's going to leave me with even fewer packgirls for the Ball. But that's my problem, Miss Moncrief."

"Do please call me Jemima, Major."

The Major felt himself smiling rather foolishly. "Certainly, if you wish... Jemima."

Jemima held up her posy. "I hope it's all right. I brought them for Melanie. I thought they might cheer her up a little."

"That's most kind of you."

The Major felt himself unexpectedly warming to Jemima. He realised she had grown since he'd last seen her. Where there had been a girl there was now a young woman. Quite an attractive one as well, in a slightly impish way. And there was something engaging about her manner (such a contrast to Arabella). Deferential, almost meek, but at the same time, somehow... provocative? Yet she also seemed to brim with innocence.

Jemima had been glancing round the study. Now she pointed at some photographs on the wall. "Oh, you have pictures of your slaves. May I have a closer look? Thank you... oh, aren't they beautiful? This must have been taken at last year's Ball.

Look at them all laid out like that, and so cleverly decorated. It must be so hard for you to arrange. And then catering for all those guests..."

And the Major found himself explaining what was required, all the weeks of planning, the conferences with his staff, hiring extra servants for the day, decisions about the menu... As he escorted her to the kennels, it was only natural for him to show Jemima the Ballroom and describe how the girls would be placed.

By the time they reached the kennels Melanie was asleep on the Sick Room bed. Alison found a jar for Jemima's flowers and with some wire they were hung on the bars where Melanie would see them later. Platt was flattered by Jemima's interest in the workings of the kennels, and soon found himself showing her around his little kingdom.

When Jemima at last left the Hall a couple of hours later the Major stood on the front steps to wave her goodbye. He felt immeasurably cheered by her visit. In fact, he couldn't remember when a young person had last been such delightful company. How had such a sweet girl ever been drawn into Arabella's circle? he wondered.

His brow furrowed. Arabella. Yes, he felt ready to face her now.

Arabella paced up and down her room like a caged animal. Every few minutes she glanced angrily out of the windows. The bright fresh day beyond mocked her. She should be outside riding, not confined and shamed like some stupid child.

Even the servants hadn't had the nerve to meet her eyes when they had brought her lunch in on a tray. They must know what had happened. Were they secretly laughing at her? What would Thomas and Gerard think of her now? And Belinda would not have kept her mouth shut, so the girls must know. How long before the whole county knew?

And all over a few scratches on a bondslave.

If only her Uncle hadn't come back early she could have had Melanie cleaned up and presented as a properly broken-in packgirl, justifying everything she'd done. The trouble was her Uncle was too soft on them. Even Platt had looked ridiculously concerned. How could they care so much about a creature that was simply meant to give pleasure? Begin caring for others that much and you might get hurt yourself. It was a stupid weakness.

Without a warning knock the door opened and the Major strode in.

Arabella turned to him with eyes flashing. "Uncle, you cannot keep me..."

"Shut up, Arabella!" the Major snapped. "You will not say another word unless I give you leave!"

Arabella's mouth shut. There was an edge to his voice that penetrated even her cocoon of self-interest and allowed for no dissent.

"I'm now going to do something I should have done before this as your guardian," the Major continued. "Something my brother-in-law, God Rest Him, should have done years ago as your father..."

Only then did Arabella realise he was carrying a short plaited leather thong whip.

She shook her head in disbelief, but she could already feel fear supplanting her anger. He couldn't really mean it...

The Major pointed to the foot of her bed. "Kneel down there and raise your skirt!"

She took a step back from him, biting her lip.

The Major slashed the whip through the air so that it struck the bed with a startling crack.

"Either you do as I tell you this instant, or I will call in the servants to do it for you!"

He meant it!

The colour draining from her face, Arabella obeyed; kneeling down over the edge of her bed. With trembling hands she

171

reached behind her and drew her skirt up over her hips. Elastic gartered stockings encircled her thighs, lace-trimmed purple silk knickers stretched over the swell of her buttocks.

"Take down your drawers," the Major said.

With a shudder, Arabella hooked her thumbs around their waistband and pulled them down around her knees.

For a moment the Major surveyed her exposed bottom with the dispassionate gaze of a connoisseur of female flesh.

Her buttocks were creamy smooth and quite flawless. They did not have quite the firm muscular swell that rigorous training developed in a packgirl, but they were adequately strong. Peeking from their cleft undercurve was the golden-fuzzed mound of her pudenda.

"It shall be seven strokes," he told her. "The pattern you used when you still had some sense - not like the travesty you inflicted on poor Melanie. Perhaps it will serve as a reminder..."

The whip hissed through the air and corded leather bit into her soft skin with a pliant crack! Her bottom lifted and her flesh shivered. Arabella buried her face in the bedcover to stifle her shriek of pain.

"She had broken, submitted, yet you continued," the Major said.

Crack! went the switch again. Now Arabella was clenching fistfuls of cloth in her hands.

"That was simple cruelty. When the lesson has been learnt you stop, do you understand?"

Arabella was nodding desperately even as the third blow landed.

Crack!

She bit a fold of the bedcover to stop herself screaming aloud.

The Major changed his stance and struck her again.

Crack!

"Packgirls can be taught to behave properly..."

Crack!

"Perhaps that's why I like their company."

Crack!

"I would never use this on a packgirl," he told her, "but then a decent packgirl would never have warranted it!"

Crack!

The last blow fell and the Major stepped back to inspect his handiwork.

Arabella's bottom was no longer the flawless thing it had been only minutes before. Two raw 'X's marked the centres of the fleshy curves of her buttocks, framed by two parallel horizontal cuts scored on the rounded slopes above and below them. Running through the middle of both 'X's and bridging her cleft was a final slash of scarlet and purple. Where the marks crossed, beads of extravasated blood were appearing on the welted skin.

"You will stay in your room until you are fit for decent company," he told her. "In the meantime you will receive no callers, nor have the use of any bondslaves. The servants will be instructed not to speak with you more than is absolutely necessary."

The door closed behind him and a key turned in the lock. As Arabella sobbed into her sheets, a drop of blood fell from the undercurve of her buttocks onto the carpet.

"...and Alison has to stay in the kennels tomorrow night and sit with Melanie while she's in the Sick Room, so she'll miss seeing the Ball. Melanie was going to be the main tablepiece, but now they're going to have to choose one of the other girls... I think that's all... Oww!"

Jemima was relating what she had discovered that afternoon. It was after teatime in the loft. The boys had an hour to themselves before they had to go to their dorm and get ready for bed, so while ostensibly 'taking a walk' they had come to hear the latest news. Jemima had struggled delightfully as they stripped her, then tied her hands behind her back and feet to the spreader bar. The bar was then hoisted on a length of rope up

173

over a beam so that Jemima hung upside down with her legs apart and her inverted breasts jutting out enticingly. Paddle smacks on her conveniently exposed inner thighs and bottom sent her twirling merrily, while pinches and tugs on her nipples set her swinging to and fro.

With her crotch almost at eye level, the boys were curiously probing the hidden depths of its thick-lipped upturned mouth. Jemima's subsequent bucks and jerks added greatly to her gyrations.

Amber watched them play with their willing victim with half a mind as she digested the information Jemima had brought with her. The scheme which had floated nebulously in her thoughts for days was now taking on a definite form. If the Ball went according to the schedule Jemima had laid out, it was possible. But they'd need to get to the Hall early in the evening, so Miss Newcombe would already have to be taken care of.

"Can you keep Miss Newcombe occupied again tomorrow night?" she asked Sally. "She's got to be out of the way so we can get to the Hall in time to take care of Arabella."

"Suppose so," Sally said. "Though I'd like to see Arabella get what's coming to her with me own eyes."

Sue, who was secured next to Amber, said hesitantly: "I'd rather like to see that myself, if it's possible."

"Yeah," Sally said. "We want to know she suffered good and proper!"

Amber frowned. "Maybe we can work something out. Let me think a minute..."

"Masters!" Jemima begged loudly. "Please take me! I don't want to be a virgin any longer!"

The boys laughed at her frustrated need as they clustered round Jemima's suspended form; finding unexpected pleasure in denying her the release she craved. Sally grinned mischievously. She got up and went over them and said something to the boys, then bent down and spoke softly to Jemima. Amber saw her eyes widen and her already flushed face grew even redder.

The boys looked at each other uncertainly, then Gosset unbuttoned his flies and released his straining erection. Standing before Jemima's inverted body he caught her by the hips to stop her swaying, dipped his hips and pushed forward. Jemima's mouth opened obediently and his shaft slid between her lips and down her throat. Clasping her buttocks and pulling her to him, Gosset hesitantly bent his head over Jemima's glistening grotto.

"That end don't bite - stick your tongue in her!" Sally urged. "She's a nice clean girl - enjoy her."

Gosset buried his face in the pretty pussy before him and began to kiss and lap at the treasures within, even as Jemima sucked and lapped at his cock. Amber smiled benevolently at the sight of the two teenage lovers joined in their suspended sixty-nine, knowing that this would only serve as an appetiser for the boys when her own turn came later. And as she watched the last pieces slotted themselves into place.

If Jemima could draw a plan of the kennels, and the boys believed Melanie was still in danger from Arabella... If they accepted Arabella might have something of value to trade for Sue, but as long as they didn't appreciate the importance of the phallus to Amber's own plans...

Yes, it was blatant and daring, but it would work!

Jemima didn't have to work hard at pleasuring Gosset. In a minute his hips jerked and he spent himself in her mouth. And like a good girl she gulped it all down with a blissful expression on her face. Gosset pulled out of Jemima to make way for Harris to have his turn.

"Have her quickly, Masters," Amber said aloud. "We've got to clean Jemima up and send her home early. She's got an important letter to post and then she'll need her sleep. We all will. Here's the plan..."

23: The Day of the Ball

The next morning at breakfast, which the boys had to prepare themselves and which was consumed in the school's echoing dining hall, Miss Newcombe entered with a frown on her face. Guilt immediately re-surfaced in their minds about the outrageous liberties they had taken with her the night before last, and they exchanged anxious glances. Miss Newcombe had been perfectly normal the previous morning and had shown no sign of the sexual torture she had endured or that she suspected their involvement, but the fear that somehow she would find out the truth lingered.

Miss Newcombe took her seat at the head of the table where they had laid her place and sipped at her tea, looking preoccupied.

Jackson asked hesitantly: "Is their anything wrong, Miss Newcombe?"

She blinked and looked up at them.

"It's rather unfortunate. I had a telephone call from Dr Gideon while you were washing. A patient of his, a Mrs Sayward at Hitchen's Farm, over Boxley way, needs continuous nursing. The regular nurse has been taken ill and he was hoping I could fill in for her tonight. I said as it was urgent I would help if I could find a suitable person to take my place here, but so far I've been unsuccessful..."

They did not hear the rest of the sentence as their minds were overwhelmed by the disastrous implications of what she had said. If somebody else was employed to watch over them tonight there was no chance they could be distracted as planned. Anybody Miss Newcombe trusted to deputise for her was certain to be a zealous type. The boys would have no option but to be in bed at the proper time and stay there. There would be no way they could carry out their raid on the Hall.

It was the thought of what they might be losing that galvanised Jackson to speak up. "You don't need to find anybody to babysit us, Miss Newcombe. We can look after ourselves, you know."

Miss Newcombe smiled. "I appreciate you are only trying to help, Anthony, but the school regulations require a member of staff, or some responsible adult, to be on the premises at all times pupils are in residence."

Parsons said quickly: "But you've been leaving us here on our own sometimes while we've been working."

"Strictly speaking I should not have left you for any time at all," Miss Newcombe admitted. "However there is a great difference between and hour or two during the day and the entire night."

"But if somebody badly needs looking after you must go to them," Gosset said. "That must be more important than school regulations."

"Please trust us, Miss Newcombe," Jackson said solemnly, "You gave us the bondslave handbook because you thought we were old enough to know about that sort of thing. Well, aren't we also old enough to take care of ourselves for just one night? We're not children anymore. We can be responsible - if we're given a chance."

Miss Newcombe's brow furrowed and she regarded them intently with her cool sharp eyes. The boys held their breath, desperately hoping that their faces showed only earnest intent and an honest desire to please.

"If I was to agree to this," Miss Newcombe said slowly, "you realise nobody must ever know you were here unattended. Should anything untoward occur in my absence..."

"Then it would be our fault," said Jackson firmly. "We'd own up to everything. We'd say... we'd say we tricked you into thinking that somebody was coming here to keep an eye on us."

"We wouldn't ever do anything to get you into trouble," added Harris, and the others nodded. That was one thing they could be absolutely truthful about.

177

Miss Newcombe took a deep breath, then smiled. "Very well. I shall tell Dr Gideon that I will be able help him. Now eat up your food. You have floors to clean today..."

"You've got some visitors, Melanie," Alison called out gently.

Melanie rolled stiffly over to face the bars of her sickroom cell and saw Una and Gillian kneeling at Alison's feet. Alison clipped their leashes to the bars, said they could have five minutes with Melanie, and walked away. They pressed their faces to the bars and peered through at her.

"How are you?" Gillian asked anxiously.

"The rest of the girls want to know when you'll be back in the yard with them," Una said.

"It's not the same without you," Gillian added.

Melanie smiled tiredly. "Thanks. Tell them I miss them and love them too."

"Was it... bad?" Una asked.

Melanie threw back her blanket so they could see her body adorned by dabs of cream and sticking plasters. The multiple tracks of her numerous scratches showed clearly even on her brown skin. Gillian caught her breath and Una uttered several choice expletives to describe Arabella.

"Luckily none of the cuts are very deep," Melanie assured them. "But there were so many thistles hitting me so hard it felt like I was being flayed. Even worse, I didn't know if Arabella would ever stop..." Melanie lowered her eyes, shamed by what had happened but wanting them to understand. "I'd submitted to her, I would have done anything she wanted - and she still kept on! I found out what it meant to be really helpless in somebody else's power. Not helpless and excited, like we were waiting for the hunt to start. Just plain shit-scared." She gave a shudder, then realized her visitors were looking at her in dismay. She forced a smile. "Don't worry. I'll get over it. Sorry I'm going to miss the Ball, though. The Major doesn't want everybody seeing me like this."

"We know," Una said. "Platt said I'll be taking your place on the table. Last three to be caught in the hunt, see?"

Gillian gave a slightly forced smile. "Which means I'll be the centrepiece. I just hope none of the guests know me."

"Don't start that again," Una warned her. "Just be pleased somebody thinks you're worth putting on show."

"I'll try," Gillian promised.

"Time's up, girls," said Alison, coming back into the room with the Major at her side. "The Major wants a word with Melanie."

Una and Gillian were led away. The Major unlocked the cell door and sat on the end of Melanie's bed. Melanie tried to adopt a servile posture as she had been taught, but he motioned for her to stay as she was. She lay back with her legs respectfully parted. He gently stroked the inside of her thighs while examining her with troubled eyes.

"My dear girl," he said at last, "I'm so sorry for all this."

"It's not your fault, Master."

"But as your owner, your well-being is my responsibility. Bondslaves can only be subjected to lawful and reasonable punishment. What Arabella inflicted upon you was unacceptable... unlawful." He looked at her deeply for a moment. "You may, if you so choose, bring an action against her for assault."

Melanie saw the pain in his eyes. "But you'd like me not to?"

"For the sake of the family name, I'd rather this incident remained as private as possible. But I will do nothing to prevent you. If it helps, I should say I have already punished Arabella severely. She will not sit down in comfort for a week. In addition she is denied all social contact until I deem otherwise - that is a severe blow to Arabella's self-esteem, I assure you."

He saw Melanie's expression of confusion and shook his head. "There, there my pet. Don't trouble yourself..."

His hand slid up her thigh and his fingertips traced the plump lines of her lovemouth and circled the crinkled pit of her anus. For a moment Melanie's eyes closed in instinctive pleasure at his touch, then she flinched as he stretched open a half-healed cut. Automatically she shied away and tried to close her legs.

The Major removed his hand with a look of angry despair.

"I will never forgive Arabella for this! She has destroyed that wonderful trust between us. You were so proud to serve me!"

"I'm... still proud to serve you, Master!"

"Are you? Doubt makes you hesitate. Curse Arabella!" He puffed out his breath. "Well, we must hope for the best. Let's get you fit again first. Meanwhile, I shall inform Arabella that you are considering making a charge against her. No reason why she should not suffer doubt as well. Then we shall see..."

Bickley brought the news of Miss Newcombe's unexpected call of duty to the three girls when he opened up the loft after breakfast.

"It'll make things simpler," Amber agreed, after thinking it over for a moment while rubbing the sleep from her eyes. "We can all set off in good time and Sally won't have to keep Miss Newcombe busy." She frowned. "As long as we're sure she'll be away all night."

Bickley gave a smug grin. "Don't worry, we already thought of that and got Sister to tell us exactly how long she'd be. That's easy because she's very careful about her work and always lets us know what she's doing. She says she'll ring up the doctor late this afternoon to check she's still wanted. If she is she'll be cycling over to Boxley, so she'll leave at seven and won't be back till gone nine tomorrow morning."

"Okay, then it looks like it's all on," Amber said.

"So I can see Arabella get stuffed good and proper!" Sally said delightedly.

"Yes... if you still want to do it that way," Amber said.

Sally shrugged. "At least people won't be chucking things

at me. I might even make a few bob out of it for a change."

Amber smiled at her friend's mercenary enthusiasm, then turned to Sue. "Still want to go through with it? You won't mind people seeing you like that?"

"After what Arabella did to me I don't think I have any modesty left," Sue said simply. "It'll be worth it to see her face when the time comes. Anyway, from the way Jemima describes it we'll just be part of the background. A Ball sounds quite exciting, actually. I'd like to see more people." She smiled ruefully. "I've hardly got about much since I came here."

"It's settled, then," said Amber. "When Jemima gets here we'll tell her there'll be a slight change of plan. I hope she remembers to bring those old clothes of her sister's she promised. Then we'll get started on the costumes for the boys - I mean, our Masters," she corrected herself quickly, looking up at Bickley. "You've got to look right for this. Now we hope Arabella plays her part..."

Arabella sprawled miserably facedown across her bed. Even the softest chair was too much for her burning bottom.

She had tried to read a book, but gave up when she realised she had read the same paragraph three times and still could not remember what it said. She had too much on her mind: shame, frustration and the gnawing uncertainty over whether or not Melanie would press charges.

She could not believe it would come to that. Her fate decided by a bondslave! Despite everything, her Uncle would never allow it... would he?

Eventually she turned to opening her mail in the hope it would take her mind off her own troubles. Her Uncle had permitted her to receive letters, but any replies could only be the briefest acknowledgments for the sake of politeness.

Unfortunately, all that her correspondents seemed to want to talk about were plans for holidays, shopping expeditions to the city and who was dating whom. All part of the life from which she had been so unfairly excluded! She screwed them up and threw them aside in disgust.

Then the last letter in the pile caught her eye.

It was addressed in anonymous capital letters on a cheap envelope and bore a local postmark. The single sheet of paper within was neither headed nor signed, and read simply:

BRING THE PHALLUS STATUE THAT YOU TOOK FROM SUSAN DRAKE TO THE PLAYHOUSE TONIGHT AT EXACTLY EIGHT THIRTY AND YOU MAY HAVE THE GIRL BACK UNHARMED.

Taped to the bottom of the sheet was a golden lock of Sue's pubic hair.

Arabella gaped at the letter in astonishment.

That it could only have been sent by whoever had taken Sue was obvious, but what did they want with the phallus? Was that what they had been after all along? Could it be more valuable than she had thought?

Stiffly she got up from the bed and went over to a drawer, took out the phallus and examined it closely. If it was real ivory then it was worth a few pounds, but no more. As a sexual toy she knew it was useless because she had tried it. So why did they want it badly enough to exchange for a potential slave girl?

Anger boiled up within Arabella once again. It was all a reminder of another unfairness perpetrated upon her. Had the letter been sent simply to taunt her? In any case, how could she do anything about it in her present circumstances?

Wait!

Of course, if she wanted she could sneak out tonight because all of her Uncle's and the servants' attention would be on the Ball. And it might be worth the risk because it could prove a chance to redeem herself. The Markham girlpack was short of suitable slaves. Sue was an unclaimed outsider and a wonderful natural submissive already broken in. Arabella was sure she could be trained to run. What a gift she would make to her Uncle! Surely he would think better of her then.

She would go to the rendezvous. She had nothing to lose - but she would take precautions.

It was late morning when Major Havercotte-Gore was informed that Miss Moncrief had called again. Despite his pre-occupation with last minute preparations, he happily made a few minutes free to talk to her. However his face fell when Jemima entered his study and he saw she was accompanied by two young women.

One was a stranger; a buxom blonde with pretty open features wearing a faded dress. She was looking about her with slightly nervous curiosity. The other girl was also blonde, but with a face he knew all too well.

"I'm sorry to trouble you when you're so busy, Major," Jemima said quickly, "but we thought we might be able to help you out tonight." She clapped a hand to her mouth. "Oh, my manners! These are my friends Sue and Sally."

"Miss Potts and I," the Major said with brittle formality, "have already met. She has come up before me in court on several occasions, when it has been my sad duty to sentence her to the public pillory."

Sally grinned. "That's all right, Major. I don't hold it against you."

"How considerate of you, Miss Potts," replied the Major dryly.

"I know Sally has been in trouble before, but she's really trying to be better now," Jemima said earnestly. "And we really think we can help you."

"I appreciate your offer, Jemima," the Major told her gently, "but we have all the serving staff we require."

"Oh, we didn't want to do serving," Jemima said brightly, "we want to be decorations in the Ballroom - like your packgirls."

The Major had rarely been taken so completely by surprise. For several seconds he could only gape in mute astonishment at the three young women lined up in front of his desk. Finally he recovered his voice.

"Jemima, do you... do you realise what you're saying?"

"Of course, Major," Jemima said cheerfully. She pointed at the wall. "I've seen your pictures remember, and everybody knows girls are put on display on special occasions. And you did tell me that you were short of girls, especially with Melanie hurt."

"Yes, but... Nevermind. It's out of the question!"

"But don't some women volunteer to become bondslaves?" Jemima persisted. "If I committed a bad crime I'm old enough to be sentenced to bondservice, aren't I? You might even buy me yourself... if you thought I was pretty enough."

The Major found himself put absurdly on the defensive. "Be that as it may, young ladies from good families do not make such offers!"

"I ain't from a good family," Sally interjected with a grin.

"I've got no family," Sue added.

The Major was determined not to be deflected. "But what would your family think, Jemima?"

"Oh, I already told them I was helping you out and they were very pleased," she said lightly. "And they'd never need to know what I'd really be doing because nobody will see much of our faces, will they? It'll be our secret. Mr Platt and Miss Chalmers would have to know about us, of course, but your guests would just think we were more of your bondslaves."

"Nevertheless..." the Major began, but Jemima continued blithely:

"It would only be for the evening and nobody would be able to do anything to us except look." She giggled coquettishly, glancing sidelong at the others. "And we don't mind that. Really, we'd be honoured to do it."

184

"They'd be honoured, I'd like ten bob," Sally said in a businesslike fashion.

A disquieting thought appeared to strike Jemima. "Unless... you don't think we're pretty enough, Major? Do you want to see us undressed?"

"Jemima, really, this has gone far enough!"

He was too late. Buttons were popping, dresses were being pulled over heads and cast aside, slips fell with a whisper. In seconds there were three naked young women lined up before his desk waiting for his approval.

It was impossible, and absurd, not to look at them.

They were three very attractive young women, he had to admit. Sally stood with her hands provocatively on her hips, a slight knowing smile playing about her impudent lips. All in all a challenging little minx. Sue had, he now realised, an exceptionally beautiful, almost angelic face, tinged with an appealing anxiety; please like me, it seemed to say. Jemima was flushed and bright-eyed with girlish excitement, returning his look with a devastatingly direct gaze. Bared breasts trembled as three pairs of nipples stood up at attention. Navels swelled with the girls' rapid breathing. Smooth flanks framed fluffy pubic deltas, through which peeped thick, soft vaginal lips. He saw the sparkle of moisture and realised he could smell their excitement at being exposed. Despite his years of assessing and handling female flesh he found the novelty of the situation had also had a stimulating effect on him, and thought it best to remain seated behind his desk.

He realised the girls were waiting for some response.

"Clasp your hands behind your heads," he said slowly.

And they obeyed.

He watched their breasts lift through the smooth interplay of muscle and flesh and felt the unique thrill that came with controlling things of beauty.

"Turn round."

They did so obediently, and he was presented with a row of

delightful posteriors. Oh, the pleasure he could have between those cheeks! He checked himself. This was not the time or place for such things. Regrettably these pretty creatures were for show only.

"All right, turn back," he said. When they faced him once more he smiled and shrugged in gallant surrender to the inevitable.

"As you wish, Jemima. You, and your friends, shall be put up in the Ballroom. You had better come back here at five o'clock to be prepared. Meanwhile I shall inform Platt that there will be three temporary extra decorations." He saw Sally's expectant expression and nodded. "Ten shillings it shall be, Miss Potts - for which I expect impeccable behaviour."

"I always give value for money, Major," she said.

The girls laughed. Sue and Sally reached for their clothes. Jemima said joyfully: "Oh, thank you, Major. We'll be ever so good, just you see!" A look of decision crossed her face. She turned and whispered a few words to the others. They grinned and hurried out of the study still adjusting their clothes. Jemima pointedly shut the door behind them and turned the key in the lock, leaving herself inside and still naked. She faced the Major with the full force of her innocent but knowing gaze, even as she trembled with excitement and trepidation.

"Jemima... what is it?"

She took a deep breath and knelt down gracefully before him, extending her arms with her wrists crossed. "Please," she said meekly, her eyes sparkling. "I don't want to be the only virgin on display tonight. Do please oblige me, sir. Take me as you would one of your packgirls..."

He opened his mouth to protest, only to realise that, once again, her words were absolutely genuine. She wanted him to be the first to breach her. Well, who could refuse such a touching request?

"I shall be honoured to oblige you, Jemima," he said.

He took her hand and guided her round to the back of the

desk until her thighs were pressed against the drawers, then bent her face down. The Major pressed carefully on the decorative wooden inlay surrounding the green leather desktop. There was a click and two sections lifted half an inch above the rest. He pulled on them and curved steel bands shaped like opposing halves of an arch rose up on either side of Jemima's head and locked over the back of her neck. The Major drew her arms out to her sides and secured her wrists with similar smaller bands released from the desktop. He spread her legs and locked her ankles on either side of the kneehole with more of the concealed clamps.

Now Jemima was perfectly positioned for ravishment; secured and immobile, with her rear pushed out towards him.

The Major squeezed and fondled her buttocks, delighting in their warm elasticity and silky texture. He fingered the dimple of her anus with a smile. Some other day, perhaps. His hands slid downward, cupping the plump warm purse of flesh between her thighs. Ahh, such a full deep cleft for one still young. He felt between the lips, finding aromatic slippery wetness bedewing his fingers.

She was ready and eager for him. Still, that didn't mean he shouldn't do things properly. He picked up a ruler.

"Do you know that packgirls often have their bottoms warmed up before sex?" he said.

"Yes, sir... please."

The rapid light, crisp smacks put a rosy glow on Jemima's bottom cheeks, causing her to make instinctive but futile jerks against her restraints while giving voice to a series of delightful yelps and whimpers. It focused all her attention on the most sensitive part of her body as a reminder of her exposure, of the use to which she was going to be put and her utter helplessness to do anything but serve her master.

When he judged her buttocks were blushing to perfection, the Major cast aside the ruler and released his straining manhood. Taking a firm hold of Jemima's slender hips, he pushed

187

his shaft into her now engorged and pulsing slit. He had absolute control of his entry, her hips immobile against the desk. He savoured the parting of her lips with his cockhead, the growing slippery heat that enveloped his member as he probed for the tiny, almost closed mouth of her passage. A little deeper into the heavenly grotto, feeling the resistance of her doomed maidenhead. Then it tore apart. Jemima gave a gasp of pain as his cock forced its way into the tightness of her virgin passage beyond; the first intruder to sample its delights.

He rode her with increasing vigour, each thrust driving a small gasp from her bent form pressed onto the desktop, each shaping her insides to accommodate their new occupier and serve its pleasure. Finally the pressure in his balls could be denied no longer and he came in lusty spurts, revelling in the privilege of being the first to spend within her.

With a half-stifled cry Jemima succumbed to her own orgasm, gasping brokenly : "Yes... yes!" then: "Ohh... thank you."

He slumped across her, feeling the wonder of the vibrant living thing under him. When he finally withdrew his flaccid penis from her it was perfectly ringed with virgin blood.

24: The Night of the Ball

It was just before seven o'clock that evening. Miss Newcombe stood by her bike in front of the main door of Cranborough House, giving last minute instructions to the boys.

"Now, you will be sure to lock up at eight and make a last round at ten?" she said to Jackson for the third time.

"I will, Miss," he assured her, desperately trying not to sound impatient. "And I won't forget the windows and side doors."

She looked at them sternly. "When I get back tomorrow I expect to find everything exactly as I left it."

"Don't worry, Miss Newcombe, you will," they assured her.

"Very well. Have a good night."

She climbed onto her bike and pedalled briskly off down the drive. The boys waved to her dutifully.

"Wait for it," Jackson warned them out of the corner of his mouth.

Miss Newcombe's figure vanished round a bend in the drive.

"Go!" Jackson said.

They dashed back inside the house.

The first guests were arriving at Markham Hall for the County Ball.

Cars and carriages rattled along a drive now lined by flambeaux burning within coloured glass shades. Assisted by brass-buttoned footmen, their occupants alighted under the Hall's imposing portico. Naked packgirls were chained with their backs to the supporting columns, their arms secured above their heads supporting baskets of flowers as though they were canephorae; caryatid-like statues brought to life. Lengths of ivy trailing from these baskets had been artfully twined about the girls' bodies, as though further binding them in place. Above the main door a third girl had been hung from chains so that it appeared she was frozen in the act of performing an aerial splits, with her arms stretched above her and legs drawn out sideways so they were almost perfectly opposed. The heads of early wild-flowers sprouted in profusion from her gaping sex and more ivy coiled about her gently swaying body, turning her into some exotic hanging floral basket. The guests passed under her wide-spread legs as though accepting their symbolic invitation to enter within.

Inside the Hall the guests were relieved of their topcoats and ushered through to the Ballroom, where an orchestra was already playing softly. Here the Major greeted them heartily and drinks were served. People began to mingle and chat. The buffet tables lining one wall were inspected and small treats were consumed. More substantial portions were reserved for later after the dancing.

Three large chandeliers hung from the ceiling. At the centre of each, suspended within the rings of bulbs by many silver chains, was a spread-eagled slave girl. They hung face down in graceful bows, their bodies dusted with glitter and bound with strings of glass beads. They turned slowly within their cages of light; sparkling ethereally and sending transient reflections dancing about the room.

At regular intervals around the walls scrolled mouldings supported small shelves, set a little above head height. On these were wedge blocks which supported the feet of slave girls who appeared to be frozen in the act of launching themselves into swan dives; their bodies hanging dramatically out over the floor at angles of forty-five degrees. Chains fastened to wall rings held their arms swept out and behind them. Their hair had been tied back into single ponytails which were plaited about metal rings linked to slender chains which fastened to the wall behind them. This tension kept their heads lifted proudly so their upper bodies formed graceful bows. Their legs were chained tightly together at the ankles and knees about metal bracing rods which ran up from the wedges under their feet. The upward-curving tips of the rods were embedded six inches into the girl's rectums, ensuring they held their position perfectly all evening. Strings of sparkling baubles had been clipped to the erect nipples of their outthrust breasts. Glitter dusted their pubic hair, while growing impudently from the furrow between their nether lips were the trumpet heads of daffodils. Each girl wore a crown of ivy, lengths of which were also coiled about their bodies and securing chains, merging with the garlands of ivy interlaced with strings of beads that hung in graceful loops between the mounted girls.

In this fashion Sue, Sally and Jemima were displayed as the Major had promised.

As the Ballroom filled, Jemima thrilled at the feeling of so many strange eyes looking up at her; and revelled in her sense of helpless shame. By reflex her anal sphincter contracted once again about the metal rod on which she was impaled. Nothing like that had ever been put up her bottom before. It didn't hurt if she remained still, its unyielding presence somehow complementing the lingering soreness in her front passage from her recent, and wonderful, deflowering. She wondered to what other uses her body could be put. She wanted to try them all. She was no longer an innocent virgin but a curious young woman surrendering herself to the delights of submission. She had broken through the painful barrier of denial and now everything seemed possible.

She glanced sideways as far as her restraints permitted and exchanged knowing, expectant glances with Sue and Sally. The best part of the night was still to come.

In the kennels' Costume Room, George Platt was putting the finishing touches to Gillian.

The packgirl was squatting in the middle of a silver platter over four feet across which rested on a sturdy trolley. She was resting on her haunches with her feet spread so that her pubic pouch was only a couple of inches from the gleaming metal. Her arms were strapped behind her back just above the elbows, which were connected by a short chain to the back of her gag strap, thereby keeping her head well up. Fine chains from her wrists to the back of her collar kept her forearms pulled back but also folded into her body. This arrangement had the effect of thrusting out her shapely breasts.

Her awkward posture was maintained with the help of a thick supporting dildo which penetrated her deeply, having its base riveted to the centre of the platter. From this mounting an unobtrusive rigid black metal brace also ran upwards following the contours of Gillian's stomach, between her breasts and slotted onto her collar.

Once secured in this position, Platt, with Alison's assistance, had transformed Gillian from a woman into an exotic and fantastical bird-like creature. A fan of feathers rose from her head, her arms had become folded wings and stiffly erect tailfeathers sprouted from between her buttocks. With glue, smaller feathers had been applied around her cheeks and brow. A little paint had given her nose the look of a beak. Even her pubic hair bore a covering of downy feathers. As a finishing touch, Platt arranged some moss and leaves about her feet, concealing the base of her dildo mount. Now Gillian had become what was a living celebration of the hunt ready for display; a reminder of the stalking season that would soon begin.

When he was satisfied with his work, Platt checked his watch. "I'd better be going inside now. I must see that those three special girls are bearing up."

"Who'd have thought they'd have volunteered like that," Alison exclaimed. "Jemima Moncrief always seemed such a shy girl from what I saw of her."

"You never know what fancy will take the shy ones," Platt said. "But it's that Potts girl I want to keep an eye on. A right piece of mischief she can be."

Alison giggled. "Well, she won't be giving you much trouble secured like she is, Mister Platt."

Platt smiled. "I suppose not. I'll be an hour or so. The Major wants me on hand to discuss the new hunting season with the guests." He frowned. "I'm sorry you won't be seeing anything of the Ball."

Alison shrugged. "Somebody has to stay here while Melanie's in the sick room."

Once again her dedication and good nature touched George Platt. He could never reveal what he truly thought of her, but he could at least bring one small reward into her life.

"Tell you what, I'll come back here at about eleven and take over so you can slip in and see everything in place, guests and all. The Major will understand."

Alison's face lit up. "Oh, thank you, Mister Platt!"

"That's all right, Alison." He patted her arm paternally and secretly thrilled at the contact. "Now, you give Gillian a little water in about half an hour and don't put on the cover until the boy comes for her. And don't forget to tighten up the elbow strap before you do. I want her to look fresh when she's revealed."

Arabella crept along the outside of the overgrown hedge of the Playhouse and peered cautiously over the gate. In her hand was a heavy poker she had taken from the set of fire irons in her room.

As she had thought, it had been easy to sneak out of the Hall. With a pencil she had poked the key of her room out of the door lock so that it fell onto the sheet of paper she had pushed underneath the door and which she had then drawn back inside. The backstairs had been deserted, with all the servants' attention on the Ball, and she had slipped unnoticed out through a side door. Once outside away from the party lights, and with full night having fallen, she had little fear of being seen by any of the legitimate occupants of the estate. Her only concern was now focused upon the unknown writers of the letter which had brought her here.

She saw that the playhouse sitting room was illuminated by the pallid yellow glow of candles. Every few seconds a shadowy form appeared to cross in front of them, though it was impossible to make out any details through the grimy windows. She watched for several minutes but the figure continued to move back and forth, sometimes gesticulating with its arms as though engaged in some heated argument, though she could hear no words spoken. Perhaps it was somebody pacing about waiting for her? But then why the odd gestures?

Taking a deep breath she eased open the gate and stole softly forward. She would take a closer look before revealing herself. She wanted to be sure Sue was there before trying to make any sort of exchange for the phallus.

Too late she heard the slight rustle of feet on grass.

She twisted about, but before she could raise her poker a

sack was thrown over her head. Even as she was wrestled to the ground, shrieking with fear and rage, she realised with bitter dismay that the pacing, gesturing figure had only been a distraction from the others waiting in the shadows of the hedge...

After checking on Melanie once again, Alison walked slowly out into the dark and deserted yard of the kennel block. The night air was still and drifting over the rooftops she could hear distant sounds of music and merrymaking. She sighed. She would have loved to go to the Ball. As a distant relation of the Major's she would have been entitled to dance - if somebody had asked her. She'd had a dress put aside for weeks...

But it wasn't to be.

Perhaps it was only right. If she'd stood up to Arabella then Melanie would not need somebody to stay with her now and she would have been free to go. And it was kind of Mister Platt to say he'd relieve her later so she could at least take a look at the party, even if she would have to stay in the background with the other servants.

She went back into the office and made herself a cup of tea. As she was sipping the sweet brew she gazed around the walls at the photographs and cuttings from newspapers that Platt had pinned up on them. They of course all featured bondslaves and packgirls, showing them running on the track or in harness pulling ploughs or carriages. Others were immaculately groomed and resting on all fours being examined by judges for a beauty show, or bound in the latest restraint harness.

Alison thought wistfully once again of what a unique occupation a keeper and trainer of such beautiful creatures was. How remarkable that girls, often from the very lowest origins, could become the favourites of the richest and oldest families in the land; sometimes being traded for large sums of money. Her own family of course hadn't much money anymore, and unless she made a good marriage she would have to make her way in the world unaided. Of course she had a marvellous opportunity here at the Hall to learn a valuable skill, one that could support her in later life. But would she ever be as good as Mister Platt? If only she could that bit more assured and masterful with the girls...

Her thoughts were interrupted by a scratching at the door. Was it a cat? The noise came again. She got up, opened the door and stepped out into the yard again, blinking for a moment in the transition from the brightly lit office to the darkness.

She had the fleeting impression of large shadowy figures rising up on either side of her. Before she could scream they had taken hold of her. A hand clamped over her mouth, forcing a ball gag between her teeth.

She kicked and twisted desperately as some sort of hood was pulled over her head, but could not break free.

"She's very strong," an indistinct male voice grunted.

"Stop struggling," another muffled, grating voice said in her ear. "We aren't going to hurt you, we just need to borrow something..."

Melanie blinked awake, staring up at the ceiling of her sickroom cell. Something had roused her, but what was it? Voices, she thought, but not Platt's or Alison's. She turned over gingerly, pleased to find the sting of her many cuts and scratches was fading. She saw the windows were dark. She must have been sleeping. What was the time?

The muffled voices came again. Who was out there?

She climbed out of her bed and tried to peer through the bars.

"Hallo... Miss Chalmers... Is everything all right?"

For a moment there was silence, then she heard footsteps. The yard door opened and a woman came in. She was wearing Alison Chalmers' boots, jodhpurs and coat - but she was not Alison.

Melanie gasped. "You!"

"Hi there," said Amber Jones cheerfully, stepping up to the bars and looking Melanie's naked body up and down with a grin. "I see you've picked up the local customs. The bondslave look suits you. Finding out how the other half lives, eh?"

By this time Melanie had recovered her voice. "What are you doing here - and how did you get Alison's clothes? Is she all right?"

"Don't worry. Some, er, friends of mine are talking care of her. Now, do you want to be rescued?"

"What?"

Amber's face took on a sterner set. She lowered her voice and spoke rapidly. "We haven't got much time, so make up your mind fast. I know pretty much what's happened around here, especially what that bitch Arabella did to you. If you don't want to risk that happening again, just say the word..." She held up Alison's key ring meaningfully. "Then maybe we can get back to where we belong."

"I don't understand. Why do you want to help me?"

"Long story - I'll tell you the rest later." Amber glanced quickly over her shoulder. "I'm not exactly my own master here - literally. But you'll have a better chance coming with me than staying here. Trust me."

"Trust you? Are you kidding?"

"So you want to wear a slave collar for the rest of your life?"

Melanie gave a little start, and reached up and touched her collar. It had become so familiar to her over the last week that she'd almost forgotten it was there.

"I... don't know," she said helplessly.

Amber's face softened in genuine sympathy. "Believe me I know how you feel. This slave-thing gets to you like a drug. But I don't think I'm ready to go all the way just yet. Are you?"

Melanie screwed up her eyes, suddenly feeling lost and uncertain. How could she leave the Major and the pack... but equally, how could she chance Arabella ever getting her hands on her again? And what about the duty she had left behind in her own world? She needed time to think... somewhere away from it all. Perhaps she could straighten herself out in a few days.

She took a deep breath and nodded to Amber.

"All right, let me out of here."

Amber began trying keys in the lock. "We'll need to collect your things. It'll look best if you leave nothing behind. Where are your clothes... and the phallus. You did use one, didn't you?"

Melanie found herself blushing at the memory. "Yes. It's all in a cupboard in Platt's office, I suppose.

"Right, we'll pick them up next..." The lock clicked and Amber threw the door open. "Just don't draw attention to the phallus if anybody asks, okay?"

"If who asks?"

"My, uh, backers. They're waiting outside. I said I wanted a few words alone with you first."

"They'll help us get away?"

"Not quite. It's complicated. You'll have to play along with them a bit. There's a little matter to take care of first. Something they'd like to see you do."

"What?"

Amber grinned maliciously. "How do you feel about good old fashioned revenge?"

For the first time in her life, Arabella knew real, stomach churning, fear.

She was gagged and hooded and bound to a pole, hanging face down as she was carried shoulder-high by her abductors across the fields. With sickening clarity she knew that all her position and influence counted for nothing right now. They knew who she was and had still dared to lay hands on her. They might do anything. Suddenly she was no better off than a common bondslave.

The footsteps of her captors sounded on some hard surface

and she realised she had been taken inside a building. The pole she was bound to was put on the floor. Hands loosened the ropes holding her and suddenly she was free. She rolled over, tearing frantically at her hood in an attempt to pull it off. But her desperate fingers found there was a padlock on the buckle at the back of her neck. And if she could not remove the hood she could not take off her gag.

Without warning she felt a sharp pain in her side.

She flinched away only to be jabbed from another direction. She twisted about in complete disorientation, scrabbling awkwardly on her hands and knees, only to receive a third painful poke in her buttocks. They were playing with her! She tried to scuttle away from her tormentors, only to have a stick lash across her back. She slumped to the floor, snivelling and moaning behind her hood.

"Strip!"

It was the first word she had heard her assailants utter. It was strangely muffled and guttural. In her current state of mind it sounded macabre. It was several seconds before she took in its meaning. She shook her head, making pleading noises. More unseen pointed objects jabbed her painfully in the thigh, shoulder and bottom.

"Strip!" the command came again, but more menacingly.

Sobbing, her fingers trembling, Arabella began blindly pulling at her clothes.

Numb disbelief settled on her more heavily with every garment she discarded. It couldn't be happening to her, not to Arabella Westlake! But it was. And in a minute she was huddled stark naked in a frightened ball; blind to the eyes upon her, but sensing their gaze with horrible clarity as they took in every inch of her exposed flesh.

Unseen hands grabbed her and hauled her upright, pulling her arms away from her body, handling her with casual disregard as though she was a rag doll.

She was doubled over so that the whip marks on her bottom could be traced and agonisingly pinched. She was fingered and pounded and pummelled. Her swaying breasts were clasped and squeezed unmercifully, then rolled around and yanked hard. Her nipples were pinched and stretched until she thought they would snap. She was pulled upright and bowed over backwards, thrusting her hips out. Her legs were wrenched apart and stiff fingers were rammed up into her slit, brutally probing the depths of her vagina. Her golden pubic bush was tugged, tearing tufts of hair out by the roots. Thumbnails dug into her labia and twisted the delicate petals of flesh. She squealed and shrieked and cried, all to no avail. The gag and muffling hood absorbed them all. Nobody would hear her. There would be no rescue. All she heard were the chuckles of her abusers as they enjoyed her distress.

In the depths of her misery she prayed that if they were going to rape her then they would get it over with quickly. But she was not to suffer any such crude fate.

Without warning her torment ceased. Distantly she seemed to hear a door bang followed by a murmur of conversation. Then the buckle of her hood was unlocked and stripped off and the gag was torn from between her aching jaws. A shove and she was standing unsupported.

Arabella blinked and rubbed the tears from her eyes, looking round fearfully. She was standing on the coconut matting in front of the tiers of kennels in the packgirls' sleeping quarters. A single ceiling light was on, the rest of the room fading into shadow. Her kidnappers were ringed about her; grotesque figures seen in the half-light. Masks of some dark material covered their faces and they were swathed in equally dark clothes. They were all tall, with broad shoulders, huge heads and strange lumpy bodies.

Struggling to master her ragged breathing, Arabella said: "Well... get it over with... go on, damn you!" She meant to sound defiant, but her voice cracked as she spoke.

A figure was pushed forward into the light. It was Melanie.

Unollared and naked, just as she was.

"Fight her!" one of the dark figures grated. "If you win, we just leave you. If you lose, you get punished as you deserve!"

"Fight... a bondslave!?" Arabella choked out in disbelief, an edge of scorn returning to her voice. "I don't fight slaves!"

A sharpened stick was thrust out of the shadows, stabbing into her buttock.

"You will!"

Arabella glanced wildly about her, but there was no escape. She turned back to Melanie and pointed a quivering finger. "You will submit to me, girl, do you understand? Down on your knees... tell them I've beaten you!"

"No," Melanie said simply.

"You said you'd do anything for me out on the thistle field!"

"That was then, this is now. You want to beat me, you have to do it without any help. Just you on your own. Well, are you up to it?"

With a scream of fear and hate, Arabella threw herself at Melanie, fingernails raked, clawing at her face.

Melanie stepped into the attack, catching hold of Arabella's wrist even as she twisted about, heaving and ducking forward. Arabella flew over her shoulder and landed with a thud on her back on the matting.

The masked onlookers clapped and cheered.

Before Arabella could recover her breath, Melanie hauled her to her feet by a fistful of hair and punched her very precisely in the stomach. As Arabella doubled over, Melanie grabbed her arm, whipped it around and threw Arabella onto her back again.

Melanie stood astride Arabella's prostrate body and sat down, straddling her chest. She lifted Arabella's head by the hair and slapped her hard on both cheeks. Arabella groaned and burbled incoherently.

"How do you like a taste of your own medicine?" Melanie asked.

She rose far enough to turn Arabella's limp body over onto her front, then twisted round so that she faced Arabella's buttocks. For a moment she examined the precise pattern of lash marks the Major had put there, nodding and smiling slightly to herself. Then she raised her hand and brought it down hard enough to leave a scarlet imprint on the creamy flesh and making the half-moon cheeks jump and shiver. She lifted her other hand and struck again... and again.

As the blazing pain from her rear suffused her body, Arabella knew she was beaten, crushed. Melanie was stronger, better, than her. Arabella felt the shame of fear and impotence as she never had before. Was this the taste of defeat?

"Do you submit?" Melanie said over her shoulder.

"Yes, yes!" Arabella choked.

"What are you?"

"I'm nothing... nothing!" And Arabella knew it was true.

The young footman sent to collect the packgirl for the table display strode briskly along the covered way connecting the main house with the Stable Court buildings. He had almost reached the door leading off to the Kennel Block when it opened in front of him.

He saw the silhouette of a woman's figure in cap and jodhpurs push the trolley with its covered platter out to him. He heard a voice, which he assumed to be Alison Chalmers', say simply: "Here she is."

"Thanks, Miss," he called back, but the door had already shut. He swung the trolley round by its handle and set off back along the corridor. As he went he thought he could hear muffled groans and whimpers from under the domed silver cover.

In the Ballroom there was a pause in the dancing. As more people drifted to the buffet tables and the tempo of the evening began to mellow, the Major had called for his guests' attention.

"Ladies and Gentlemen," he said. "As is traditional at these

201

occasions, I am proud to offer you the finest specimens of the Markham pack. Please welcome the dishes of the evening!"

Amid polite applause, four footmen came in bearing the first of the Hall chef's offerings shoulder high. They carried the long, covered silver platter round the room, then set it down on its reserved space on a table.

"First, the savoury dish!" the Major said.

A footman pulled the cover off to reveal Una lying on her back on the platter, secured in place with fine silver chains. She was surrounded by wafer thin cuts of rolled meat and tiny slices of herb bread. Her body itself served as a condiment stand. Her mouth was filled with the base of a pot of relish, which she clenched between her teeth to keep it upright. A figure-of-eight cut glass trough of sauces encircled her breasts and squeezed them into taut domes. Her navel was filled with a cone of salt. The handle of a long spoon protruded from between her legs, where her lovemouth stretched wide to accommodate a long silver pot of cheese dip, warmed by her body heat.

The guests applauded the novel display enthusiastically.

"And now the sweet dish," the Major announced.

Another platter was carried in and set down. When the cover was removed with a flourish it revealed Jill chained to the platter, with sliced fruit and tiny cakes of all descriptions carefully arranged about her. She held a pot of cream in her mouth. Stacks of pineapple segments encircled her breasts like twin pagodas, each topped by a half cherry. More cherries spilled out from her gaping vaginal lips to form a tiny scree between her thighs. She had been stuffed with cherries. Tongs and a long handled fine-tined fork lay between her legs for those who wished to probe for any of the fruits remaining within her after the more accessible samples had been removed.

"And no feast would be complete without the game bird," the Major said.

The last platter was brought in and set down. The cover was

removed.

The anticipatory applause faltered and died away. Somebody's half laugh turned into a choked gasp of disbelief.

Arabella was mounted on the brace intended for Gillian, but reversed, so her body was bowed outward for all to see; her arms bound tightly behind her, wrists tied to the crossed ankles of her folded and splayed legs. Her tearful eyes bulged over her gag with the strain of holding the dildo up her rear. Her jutting breasts were studded with the heads of drawing pins and a few trickles of blood. Her knees were held wide in a vain attempt at preventing the thick spray of holly that had been pushed up her front passage from scratching her inner thighs any further. From the wetness of her hair and a certain aroma it was apparent that she had been drenched in urine.

In the stupefied silence they all heard the Major say foolishly: "Good God, Arabella - what are you doing there?"

Then the spell was broken.

Platt burst out through the doors and pelted down the corridor beyond. He was not thinking of Arabella as he tore though the house to the kennels. Sprinting into the pack yard he was calling out: "Alison!" at the top of his voice.

There was no reply. But to his horror he saw her coat and britches lying on the brick cobbles as though they'd been discarded in haste.

With a cry of dismay he plunged into the office. It was empty. He threw open the door to the Sick Room. Lying on the cell bed where Melanie had been were Gillian and Alison. They were gagged and bound hand and foot.

Gasping with fear and relief, Platt unlocked the door and bent tenderly over Alison, prying the gag from her lips. For the first time her realised she was only wearing a thin slip and panties. He felt the heat of her body. He allowed his eyes to pass over her, telling himself that he was just checking for any signs of injury. She was... beautiful.

She gazed up at him in dismay.

"Oh... Mister Platt. I'm so sorry... I couldn't stop them... They've taken Melanie!"

Platt felt dizzy with shock as the full implications sank in. The Major's niece publicly humiliated and his prize packgirl stolen!

Then he saw Alison's stricken face. He drew in a deep breath and patted her bare arm reassuringly.

"As long as you're safe," he said simply.

25: School Orgy

"They've never had a black girl before," Amber called over to Melanie helpfully. "You'd better not disappoint them."

The boys had led them back to the school loft in triumph, grinning foolishly and obviously elated by the success of their daring clandestine raid. They had taken their revenge on Arabella at last and had obtained a new and exotic slave into the bargain. Now, still bubbling with excitement, they stripped of the padded masks and jumpers that had distorted their figures and pulled off the folded leather strips under their boot soles that had added deceptive inches to their height. Then they could take their first proper look at Melanie.

She squirmed uncertainly at their touch, still trying to come to terms with her changed circumstances. Her hands were bound behind her back and she had a rope collar and lead about her neck, so she could not prevent them crowding about her; stroking the silky smoothness of her brown skin, testing the weight of her breasts, patting the fullness of her buttocks. As they fingered her pubic mound Melanie gave a quick gasp of pain.

"Please... I'm still sore there!"

The boys just chuckled.

Amber, standing almost forgotten to one side, said: "Do go easy on her. Remember what she's been through."

Jackson snapped: "We didn't give her those scratches in

the first place. We made Arabella pay for it and now this one's got to please us. We're her masters now."

"That's right," said Gosset sharply, "don't you forget it, girl."

"Sorry, Masters," Amber said quickly, a little surprised by their change of mood.

"Maybe she needs another lesson to remind her," Harris suggested, his eyes not moving from Melanie's face as her kneaded her breasts experimentally.

With a cruel gleam in his eye, Gosset stepped towards Amber.

Amber backed away from him apprehensively. "No, Masters, please. Look what I've done for you. I helped bring you Sally... and Sue and Jemima. I got you your revenge on Arabella... I've given you Melanie."

"But only because we let you," Gosset said, catching hold of Amber's trailing leash and pulling her against him with a jerk. "You couldn't have done it without us. You're our slave, don't forget."

"I won't, I won't!" Amber said fearfully.

"Let's show them who's in charge!" Bickley suggested, his face flushed with pent-up excitement.

The others were nodding, clearly liking the idea.

"But we should have this one first," Parsons said, sliding his forefinger up into Melanie's slit and giving her a tickle.

"We can do both," Jackson said, a wild look in his eyes. "Don't you see? The School's empty, nobody's going to disturb us. Tonight we can do anything we like!"

The boys grinned as the possibilities of their situation dawned upon them.

Suddenly Amber understood with horrible clarity what was happening. The boys were on a high from their adventure. They had participated in Arabella's humiliation and it had filled them with a desire to taste more of the same. They wanted to flaunt their new self-confidence and exercise their power to the full. That latent sadistic streak she had briefly glimpsed in them

205

before had been stimulated. Now it demanded release. They boys would do exactly what they wanted and there was nothing she could do to stop them.

Amber flashed a last despairing glance at Melanie. "Sorry!" she mouthed.

Melanie lay spread-eagled on Amber's bed, her dark skin glistening, arms and legs roped to the sides of the pen and drawn taut. The boys were taking turns to sample the delights of her fleshy grotto, ramming their hard young cocks into her with brutal insistence and with no regard for her comfort, so that she grunted and moaned under the onslaught of their thrusts.

When each boy finished he went over to Amber, bound over the Training Horse, his drooping erection hanging from under his shirtfront. He caught hold of a double handful of her hair and rammed his genitals into her face.

"Lick me clean!" he commanded.

Amber obeyed without hesitation: she couldn't help herself. She sucked and licked furiously, tasting both male ejaculate and Melanie's juices as they melted into her mouth. At least it was the taste of sex, and in her desperation she couldn't be choosy. Perhaps that even added to her arousal. Under her ministrations the boy's penis swelled and stiffened once again, and its head began to probe the back of her throat.

The other boys looked on in fascination, dividing their attention between Amber and their friends' efforts between Melanie's legs. After a minute, the cock Amber had been tending was withdrawn glistening and freshly hardened from her mouth, ignoring her groan of dismay and still hungry lips.

With a grunt and a gasp, the next boy spent himself. He looked round with slightly glazed eyes, withdrew from Melanie, stood up, lurched over to Amber and stabbed his cock, still dripping semen from its head, between her gaping lips.

One by one the boys made the round of the two women; exiting Melanie's hot sticky cunt, only to plunge into Amber's warm, wet mouth...

The boys rested, briefly satiated, but there was to be no rest for the girls. Fired by their lust the boys' ingenuity was working overtime. Melanie was released from the bed, only to be positioned standing between Amber's splayed and doubled legs and have her hands bound behind her back. The boys had found a length of very old thick red rubber garden hose and cut off a length about fifteen inches long. Covering it in petroleum jelly, they thrust one end up Melanie's already sperm-rimmed and well-used vaginal passage and the other into Amber's gaping hole. A shove on Melanie's bottom pushed the two girls together so that their pubic bushes mingled.

"Now you keep pushing it into her," Melanie was told. A rubber paddle blade smacked her rear. "When she comes, we stop hitting you."

Melanie's broad hips jerked as her buttocks tightened, pushing the hose into Amber's soft interior. The boys watched in delight as their two slaves were forced to copulate for their amusement.

As the frequency of the smacks on her behind increased, Melanie was driven lower over Amber's rigidly bound body, thrusting faster and deeper. Melanie's full breasts in heaving fluid motion brushed across Amber's own fleshy cones. Taut rubbery nipples touched, folded over and sprang stiffly erect once more. Their eyes met, mutely acknowledging their shared helplessness and sense of degradation, yet knowing themselves unable to suppress that part of their natures which was untouched by shame or propriety, but which turned crude stimulation into pleasure.

They climaxed together with desperate cries of relief, and Melanie collapsed over Amber, their sweaty bodies coming to rest in perfect union. The boys cheered their unwilling performance, then began thinking up a new torment that would play pink flesh against brown...

Bound face to face, breasts flattened against breasts, hands tied to the smalls of their backs, Melanie and Amber hung by their ankles from a beam, twisting slowly this way then that as the boys lambasted their defenceless buttocks. Tight coils of rope encircled their bodies, allowing them only the freedom to squirm and wriggle against each other. Their sexes were still joined by the versatile hosepipe, bent now into a sharp 'V'. Each flinch of hips away from a stinging slap drove the hose into the other girl. Two slippery wet muscular tunnels squeezed with growing need on the rubber intruder.

"Kiss!" the boys commanded them again, and they obeyed; breath hot, tongues flicking, lips sucking; helpless in the grip of the passion that had been so forcefully roused within them. Their pubic deltas merged into one sticky tangled matt.

When they had been driven to a second orgasm they were left hanging where they were as the boys retired a little way to discus what they would do when the other girls returned. Eventually Amber recovered her breath enough to whisper brokenly in Melanie's ear:

"Sorry... about all this. The boys... usually better behaved. Tonight they're... full of themselves. We've just got to put up with it."

Melanie huskily panted back: "You really didn't plan this?"

"No way!"

"I suppose they're not as bad as Arabella," Melanie said. "At least you feel they're enjoying themselves... Oh God! I feel good that my rapists enjoyed having me. What a thing to say."

"We can't help it even though we hate it." The heat and intimate scent of Melanie's body was overwhelming. Amber looked into her eyes as they hung nose to nose. "Not you, I mean. You're fantastic, by the way."

Melanie gulped. "You too..."

They kissed passionately and ground their hips together. After a few seconds they pulled apart with an effort, blushing with embarrassment, heads pounding with blood from their inverted position.

"God, that was good!" Amber said. "Which is why we have to get away before we lose it completely. We've got three phalluses here now. Between the two of us we should be able to get our hands on them."

"That's why you wanted to get me here."

"One reason. The phalluses must be able to get us back."

"Are you sure?"

"No, but have you any better ideas? If it works, you can have my stash in the woods if you forget you caught me."

"You can't buy me off like that."

"What? You wouldn't turn me in, lover?"

"I'm not your lover..." She groaned. "I don't know what I am anymore."

"So, if you do get back, what are you going to tell your superiors? You'll need my help to put together a story they'll believe."

"What story?"

"I don't know, yet. Depends on how long we stay here. But I do know that if you try to tell the truth, the men in white coats will be coming for you. Think about it."

They heard excited voices coming up the loft stairs. The other girls had returned and were apparently telling the boys what they had seen of Arabella's humiliation in the Ballroom.

"...then everybody shouted at once," Jemima was saying. "Somebody tried to put the cover back over her at the same time as somebody else tried to untie her, so he got hit on the head and the cover fell on the floor. A few people were trying not to laugh. The Major was shouting for quiet and for the footmen to carry Arabella out again. All the time she did look so uncomfortable... Oh!" The girls had reached the loft and Jemima had seen Melanie and Amber. "What have you done with them?"

"They needed reminding who are the masters around here," Jackson said. "Now we're going to do the same to you."

Sue and Jemima looked surprised but did not resist as they

were stripped and bound. Sally struggled and cursed, so that it took three of the boys to remove her clothes. Then she appeared to shrug and submitted to the inevitable.

They took Amber and Melanie down and lined up all the girls so that they knelt on the floor in a row, hands tied behind them, rope leashes round their necks, knees spread wide to display their treasures to their masters. Their mouths were stopped with rope gags, not for fear of the noise they might make, but to add to their subjugation. The boys looked down in triumph at their five captives, seeing the fear and uncertainty in their eye, excited by their renewed sense of power over such pretty creatures.

"What do we do now?" Bickley wondered.

"Whatever we want," said Jackson. "We don't have to use them here. We can take them into the house. We can have them in our beds... Tonight we can do anything we like!"

The girls trembled at his words.

With a boy leading each girl, hurrying her along with smacks from his paddle stick, the slaves were taken out of the loft.

For some minutes they ran the girls round in circles like ponies on the lawn in front of the front entrance of the school, illuminated by the porch light which cast long shadows over the dew-wet grass. The girls were set trotting and prancing at the ends of their tethers, lifting their knees high on command. Breasts trembled and bounced prettily. The girls were run until they were panting and glistening with sweat, with saliva dribbling about their gags. Then they were led into the school.

The boys savoured the strange delight of dragging their slaves through the empty halls and classrooms, seeing their naked bodies posed in such studious surroundings. The idea of leaving some secret sign to commemorate their presence came to them. They made the rounds of the classrooms. Blackboard pegs were inserted in the girls' bottoms and then carefully replaced. Rulers and pointers from the teachers' desks were rubbed vigorously in the girl's slots and left with a film of female lubrication to dry on them. They laughed at the thought of what their teachers would say if they ever knew how they had so outrageously defiled academic sanctity, or what they would be handling next term.

They held an egg and spoon race in the kitchen, with the girls on their hands and knees and the handles of dessertspoons thrust up their bottom holes. The eggs wobbled precariously as they shuffled desperately along in laps round the big kitchen tables. Several eggs were broken and the offending girls were forced to sit in the mess and grind their pouting crotches into it before they cleaned it up.

It followed that they next took the girls along to the showers. The line of toilet cubicles suggested that they could watch the girls relieve themselves and note any differences between them. The girls were tied in position on the toilet seats with their ankles pulled back behind the toilet bowls so they were splayed wide open. With the boys crowding the cubicles and shining torches up into their clefts so that no detail should be missed, each girl was ordered to pee in turn. By pulling back their labia and pinning them wide with clothes pegs, they were at last able to see the hidden orifice from which it issued, and listen to the distinctive hiss it made leaving each girl's body.

It was while they were still conveniently placed that the boys decided they should all be cleaned out in case their bottoms were required for use later. Water was heated in the kitchen while water bottles and more hose was obtained. Methodically the hoses were inserted into the girls' rears, causing pretty expressions of distress to pass over their faces, and they were flushed out.

The idea of a peeing contest came up. Jugs of water were fetched and the girls were forced to drink until they were full and desperate to relieve themselves again. A line was marked on the tiled floor and old newspapers were laid down opposite it. The boys chose girls and laid them on their backs just behind the line, with their wrists tied to their ankles so they held themselves open, their gaping clefts facing the targets. The boys straddled them so they looked through the 'V's of their open legs, and at the signal pressed down on the girls' stomachs. Five streams of pee arched gracefully out over the tiles and splattered onto the newspapers. Sue won with an effort that reached over six feet.

Soiled and sweaty, the girls were put under the showers, their wrists tied above their heads to the pipework. By playing alternately hot and cold water over them, the boys found they could cause a lot of futile twisting and jerking about, accompanied by choked squeals and gasps of surprise. Eventually they relented and soaped down their slaves, working the lather into every fold and cleft, lifting every breast, until the showers gleamed with pliant glistening limbs. They found an amusing amount of lather could be created by working soap bars vigorously into the girls' split peaches. The resulting mass of foamy bubbles could be sculpted as required, so that soon each girl appeared to have a pelt of shining white pubic hair.

When the girls were finally rinsed and dried, they were dragged off to the boys' dormitory.

It was at this point that the boys recalled Jemima's virginity, which they had so far delighted in saving. They decided they would play a round robin of Scissors-Paper-Rock to decide who had her first, before they started on the rest of the girls. Parsons won, but found just as he was about to breach Jemima, tied conveniently over the end of his bed, that the tight little mouth of her passage had recently been breached.

The story of how she had lost her maidenhead to the Major was extracted from Jemima by smacks and slaps and repeated nipple pinching. The boys decided that though it had been done in a good cause, she had selfishly denied them their right to take her first. She was made to kiss each boy's feet and beg to be punished for her thoughtlessness. Her bottom was quite rosy by the time they had finished, and her eyes glistened with tears of pain and delight.

Finally the boys were ready for the main event. But how could they celebrate their triumph in suitable style?

After some debate and the preparations of a few more special restraints, five chairs were placed in a line down the middle of the room. A girl was bent over the back of each with her hands tied behind her, so that her head and shoulders hung over the seat and her rear was thrust out in counterbalance. Her ankles and knees were tied to the outside of the back chair legs, so that her legs were slightly splayed, and a rope went over the small of her back to hold her in place. Clothes pegs were clipped to the nipples of their dangling breasts to ensure the girls stayed alert. More jaw-spreading gags of rope and old washers were forced between their teeth, so that their mouths were held invitingly open. The pot of petroleum jelly they had used on Amber was produced and the boys dipped their fingers into it. Generous dollops were smeared around the crinkled puckers of their anuses and into the hot, elastic passages beyond; thereby ensuring ease of entry when the time came. As a final touch the girls were blindfolded so they could not tell what would be done to them next, nor who was using them.

The boys stepped back to admire their creation. It was a living work of art; a display of fifteen orifices waiting to be sampled at will. It was enough to make their mouths water.

The boys stripped off their own clothes, free to be totally naked with their captives for the first time. Their erections bobbed stiffly, plumb-tips already glistening with anticipation.

Each boy picked up a paddle-stick and flicked it sharply over a pair of smooth buttocks until each girl was jerking and twisting in her bonds.

"Now listen," Jackson said. "We're going to have you all together now. If any of you doesn't please us, you all get punished, do you understand?"

The row of blindfolded heads nodded desperately.

The grinning boys stepped up to their chosen girls and thrust, entering a mouth, a vagina or bottom hole as they pleased; grasping hips or hair or swaying breasts to steady themselves. After a few quick lunges they withdrew and moved round to the next girl and a new opening to be probed. And as they moved around the boys could pinch or fondle any available piece of breast or bottom flesh that happened to be free. One moment a girl would be serving cocks at both ends, the next she would be empty, but an unseen hand would be sliding stiff fingers into her slippery crotch or a leather paddle would smack down on some part of her exposed body.

Now the girls knew they had truly been put in their place; reduced to mere playthings to be used at their masters' pleasure, never knowing who was next or what orifice might be filled, nor whether this would be the moment that the boy spent inside her. The heavy scent of sex filled the air. Gradually the girls began to taste their sister slaves on every cock that was pushed into their mouths, as secretions from each of their orifices mingled.

Inevitably their own arousal grew, but they were being used too quickly to sustain the sensation. Frustration added to their torture, making them suck on every cock that penetrated them by whatever entrance in the hope that they would climax before it was snatched away from them.

Finally their desperate efforts brought forth reward. One by one, unable to hold back any longer, the boys discharged into whatever sheath of flesh they happened to be occupying at that moment, then sank over the helpless body under them in the afterglow of blissful release.

For what remained of that night the boys slept soundly indeed. Each bed in the dormitory had been supplement by the warm, scented, living mattress of a gagged and spread-eagled slave girl bound to its four corners.

Shortly before seven o'clock the next morning, when Jackson had prudently set his alarm to waken them, the dormitory curtains were drawn back allowing the fresh light of dawn to flood into the room. The boys stirred on their fleshy cushioned beds, blinking against the sudden illumination, looking about in annoyance to see which of their number had denied them their last few minutes of blissful rest.

"Well now! What have we here?" said Miss Newcombe.

26: The Morning After

Major Havercotte-Gore sat, tired and morose, in his study. He had had no sleep and the bright clear light of dawn had yet to lift his spirits, still numbed by the events of the previous night. It had been a bitter double blow, under which both his family pride and his property had suffered.

And yet, as he turned the incredible happenings over in his mind, it struck him that the strangest thing was how vague Arabella had been about it all. Surely it was not simple shame and embarrassment at her treatment that made her so uncertain how many intruders there had been (perhaps three or four, she could not say for sure), nor could it explain why she was so evasive about seeing anything of them taking Melanie away. For that matter, she would not explain what she had been doing out of the house against his express orders. It was as though she was hiding something from them. But she had been quite forthright in her assertion that, despite everything she had suffered, she had not actually been raped by the intruders. So what could have been worse than the humiliation they all knew she had been put through?

Perhaps, when the investigation team from the County Police Headquarters arrived in a few hours' time, they could make something of it. Bailey, called up from the village by telephone, had taken initial statements from all concerned and had made a cursory examination of the scene, but the Major knew a crime of this scope was beyond his powers. It looked like the work of the same gang who had removed Amber Jones from the police station. Had they some special interest in outsider girls? In any case they were getting bolder. But why had they stooped to such an elaborate personal attack on Arabella?

A maid brought in his morning tea and toast, and under its soothing influence he began to see one small positive aspect to the affair.

Arabella's public humiliation had at least won her some measure of sympathy to counteract the widespread distaste the news of her maltreatment of Melanie had generated. And with Melanie missing, no charges against her would be laid.

Spasms of remorse cut through him as he thought of Melanie. If truth be told, he would rather she was pressing charges against Arabella than have her taken from him like this. Surely her kidnappers would treat her well, knowing she was valuable? He might even expect a ransom note for her in a few days. Of course he could never submit to any such demand... or could he? He recalled Melanie's silky strong body surging under him on the riding machine, and a frisson of delight coursed through him. Well, that hurdle would have to be crossed in due course. Meanwhile, he would do everything he could to ensure her safe return.

Picking up a pen, he began drafting an advertisement offering a substantial reward for any information as to Melanie's whereabouts.

Nieces like Arabella were all too common, he reflected, but packgirls like Melanie were precious indeed.

"The girls are all eating breakfast now, Mister Platt," Alison reported as she returned to the office.

"That's good," Platt said. "How are they taking the news about Melanie?"

"They're still shocked, of course, but keeping to the routine is helping. Una seems to have taken charge again, but she's being very careful how she treats the others."

"Hmm, Melanie's influence, I think. She'll be a sad loss if we can't get her back."

Alison's normally bright face crumpled. "Oh, I do hope she'll be all right!"

"I'm sure it'll work itself out," Platt assured her. "The Major won't give up on finding her, you can be certain of that. You just be ready to tell the detectives everything you saw."

"I will, Mister Platt. But really, I didn't see anything. They blindfolded me and took my clothes, then put me on the Sick Room bed. A little later they brought in Gillian and we just lay there until you found us."

Platt was looking at her in concern. "You could go home if you like, Alison," he suggested gently. "The detectives can call on you there. You've been through quite an ordeal."

Alison forced a smile. "No, I'd rather keep busy, if you don't mind. I just wish I could have done something to stop it all."

"You said there were at least three large men," Platt reminded her. "You couldn't have done anything to stop them, believe me."

Alison smiled in gratitude at his words, but then her face took on a curious expression. "Actually, Mister Platt, there was one useful thing I learnt from last night."

"Oh, and what's that, Alison?"

"Well... while I was tied up and blindfolded and gagged like that, I realised it must be what packgirls feel like when they're in their restraints."

"I suppose so," Platt agreed. "Did that make you feel sorry for them?"

"Oh no. It wasn't a bad feeling, exactly, not once I got over my fright and realised the men weren't going to hurt me. It was just so unusual. But it did make me think..." she hesitated.

"Yes?"

Alison took a deep breath. "I know I'm not always firm

enough with the girls, and I think it's because I don't really understand what it's like to be restrained or punished..." she lowered her eyes, "...or trained like you did with Gillian over the trestle in the Harness Room."

Platt started, an unaccustomed blush rising to his cheeks. "You saw me?"

"It was an accident!" Alison said quickly, the words pouring out of her. "I know I shouldn't have kept looking, but you were being so kind and yet so masterful with her. You knew just how to handle her, and I thought I'd never be that good. But now I think I might learn if you treat me the same way."

Platt thought his ears were failing him. "Sorry... what do you mean, Alison?"

"When you aren't too busy and all the girls are out working... if you can spare the time... could you put me in harness and use the whip and do, well, everything you would to train a packgirl? Then I think I can learn to be a proper keeper one day."

Platt felt the room spinning round him and had to take a firm grip on his desk to steady himself. He looked into Alison's hopeful face, searching for some sign that he had misunderstood her words or that it was a huge joke. But he read only naive trust, admiration and serious intent. She was genuinely convinced this was the way for her to learn her profession.

He found his voice. "You... want to be treated just like a packgirl. You'd... be naked?"

"Oh, of course," Alison said earnestly. "It wouldn't be very real if I wasn't. If you don't mind?"

Platt looked at her wondering silence for a long time. Then he smiled. "No, Alison, I don't mind in the least," he said.

27: Miss Newcombe Takes a Hand

The dumbstruck tableau in the dormitory lasted for a good thirty seconds. The boys were frozen in various half-risen postures amid the tangled sheets of their beds, the gagged and spread-eagled girls under them lay rigid in the bonds, eyes wide in alarm.

Then Miss Newcombe spoke again: "Get up at once! Stand straight at the foot of your beds facing me. No talking!"

Her voice was like a whipcrack, penetrating to the obedient core of brains still reeling from shock and permitting no thought of disobedience. The boys threw back their covers and scrambled to stand as she had commanded; their faces still masks of utter dismay.

Miss Newcombe paced up and down the aisle between the feet of the beds, looking the naked, pink and trembling boys up and down as though she was reviewing a motley parade of troops. Her grey eyes glinted coldly like chips of flint. None of the boys could meet her gaze.

"So, this is how you repay a trust, is it?" she said. "You hold an orgy on school property. Not only that, but one of the girls involved is an outsider illegally removed from police custody, while another is Major Havercotte-Gore's prize bondslave abducted only last night from the Hall - during which time, as I understand it, Arabella Westlake suffered a peculiar and humiliating misfortune. Well, have you any explanation for this outrageous behaviour?"

But the boys were temporarily beyond speech and could only stare fixedly at nothing. Miss Newcombe shook her head sadly.

"No, I see you haven't. But then what else would I expect from boys who would clamber over roofs and look through skylights to watch a woman undressing."

There was a groan of dismay from the boys. Their haggard eyes widened further.

"Oh, yes, I knew what you were doing," Miss Newcombe said. "You often left sperm-trails on the glass for me to see the next morning. Do you think I'm so innocent or unobservant? Well?"

They shook their heads mechanically.

"Exactly. In the same way I did not fail to recognise the difference between a cucumber and five young men's cocks."

It did not seem possible that the boys' misery could deepen any further, but it did. Parsons gave a strangled wail of anguish and Harris looked as though he was going to faint. "Stand straight!" Miss Newcombe snapped at him. White as a sheet he obeyed, still swaying.

Her rapier-like gaze passed over them once again, quelling their stifled groans and whimpers.

"Have you any idea what the Headmaster will do if he finds out even a half of this?"

The boys nodded dumbly.

"You will be severely punished and then expelled in total disgrace. Even supposing that I, the Major and the police do not press charges against you variously for theft, trespass, breaking and entering, assault and other offences, I doubt if any other school in the country will take you. What action your respective parents will choose to take I could not say, but I assume it will not be pleasant. It will take years for you to live such a thing down... if you ever do." She glanced at the girls bound to their beds and shook her head sadly. "I just hope you think the pleasure was worth the price."

The boys were utterly crushed now, looking as though they wished the earth would swallow them so they might be put out of their anguish.

"As I said, that is what will certainly happen if the headmaster finds out about all this," Miss Newcombe continued. She paused, then added: "But perhaps he does not have to find out. Perhaps nobody need ever know..."

It took a moment for the meaning of her words to penetrate

their numbed senses. Slowly their eyes focused on her with the first faint glimmerings of hope. She smiled back at them; a cool, calculating, masterful smile.

"Well, would you like all this to remain our secret?"

"Y... yes... Miss Newcombe," they stammered.

"And what are you prepared to do to keep it that way?"

"Anything... Miss."

"Really?" She stood before Jackson, examining him intently. "Will you obey me without question, Anthony?"

"Yes, Miss."

Suddenly her hand shot out and clasped his genitals. He gulped in surprise and horror, but wisely resisted the urge to pull away from her touch. She squeezed his balls thoughtfully for a minute, as, to his blushing shame, his penis swelled and stood erect.

Then abruptly she left him and moved along to Harris. Taking hold of him in the same fashion, she said: "Will you obey me without question, Martin...?"

Soon there were five tumescent and horribly confused boys, wondering just what the consequence of their pledges would be. Miss Newcombe favoured them with a smile.

"Very good. You will now shower and dress. I wish to talk to the girls alone. Wait outside until I call you. Quickly now!"

The boys gathered their clothes and left the dormitory at a gallop. As the door banged behind them, Miss Newcombe moved over to Jemima's bed and smiled down reassuringly at the apprehensive young girl.

"Now, Jemima. I promise nothing bad's going to happen to you. All I'd like you to do is answer a question honestly. Will you do that for me?"

Wide-eyed, Jemima nodded.

Miss Newcombe removed Jemima's gag, then trailed her fingers over the upstanding cones of Jemima's breasts, brushing the bruises round her nipples left by the boys' clothes pegs. "Last night the boys tied you up, beat you and forced you to

221

have sex several times using every orifice of you body. Did you enjoy yourself?"

Jemima blinked. "I... yes, I did."

"Would you like to do that sort of thing again?"

"Yes... please."

Miss Newcombe smiled. "Then we must see what we can do. Come to my cottage this afternoon and we'll talk some more."

"Yes, Miss Newcombe."

Miss Newcombe patted her on the cheek, then turned to Sally, her manner becoming more severe as she removed her gag. "Well, Sally. What do you think the police would say if they knew what you'd been up to? Collusion with the escape of a prisoner from custody, involvement with the kidnapping of a bondslave. How many years servitude do you think you'd get for that?"

Sally gave a resigned shrug as far as her bonds allowed. "I know, you warned me. But you're going to say you might keep quiet if I volunteer to be your bondslave, right?"

"I'm glad to see we understand each other. Well?"

Sally's mouth pinched defiantly. "Make me an offer!"

Miss Newcombe raised an eyebrow. "You are hardly in a position to dictate terms, young lady."

"I said I might serve you if the money was right. I still got my pride. Go on, make me an offer."

Miss Newcombe looked at her searchingly for a moment, then reached inside a pocket and pulled out a copper coin. "A penny?"

"Sold," said Sally.

Miss Newcombe smiled broadly. "It's going to be such fun training you." She reached forward and pushed the coin into Sally's sticky cleft as far as it would go, making the girl gasp in surprise. "The boys can retrieve it later," Miss Newcombe said. "They'll enjoy that."

She turned to Sue, Amber and Melanie and looked at them

thoughtfully. "As for you three... I think it's time you went home." She raised her voice: "You can come in now, boys."

Freshly washed and still pulling on their clothes, the boys piled into the room and quickly formed a line, waiting expectantly.

"Jemima will be going home now," she told them. "Release her and find her clothes. Kiss her goodbye and thank her for the pleasure she has give you. If you are good I may allow you to enjoy her again." As the boys hurried to obey, Miss Newcombe added: "Sally has volunteered to be my bondslave. For the rest of the day you can secure her in the loft and use her as you like in between your work. You will bring her to my cottage this evening where we shall find some permanent quarters for her. Again, if you are good, I may allow you the continued use of her. Would you like that?"

"Yes, Miss," the boys chorused, hardly able to believe their ears.

"Bring Susan's bike and Melanie's bag from the loft with you. Oh, before I forget, you'd better take out Amber's bag and the other items you have hidden behind the panel over there."

Gosset exclaimed in a barely stifled whisper: "She knows everything!"

"Yes, Nigel," said Miss Newcombe gravely, "I think you can assume that I do."

Twenty minutes later Jemima had set off for home and Sally was secured in the loft. Melanie, Sue and Amber had been bound hand and foot, wrapped in blankets and carried by the boys to Miss Newcombe's cottage by the school gates, along with Sue's bike and the other items of the girls' property. At Miss Newcombe's direction, the girls were sat up in a row against the wall of her small but neat living room.

Jackson looked at them uncertainly, then at Miss Newcombe.

"What are you going to do with them?" he asked.

"They will have to go away for a while. It's for the best. One day I may explain why."

"Will we see them again?"

Miss Newcombe looked thoughtful. "I think so. Now, you must be going."

As Miss Newcombe was showing them out, Jackson paused. Something was troubling him. "Can I just ask - why did you come back so early from Boxley?"

Miss Newcombe raised her eyebrows. "Boxley? I've not been to Boxley. I never left the school grounds last night."

"But your patient..."

Miss Newcombe smiled indulgently. "And what patient would this be, Anthony? Now back to the school with you all and have breakfast. Then start the next job on your list. I'll be along to check on you later."

Their jaws dropped as comprehension dawned, and they walked away in silence; just beginning to realise what a very special lady the Matron of Cranborough House was.

Miss Newcombe returned to the living room and stood with her hands resting on her hips in a businesslike fashion, contemplating the three girls. With her toe she prodded their crossed and bound ankles until they pulled them in, splaying their thighs wider and so exposing the treasures of their clefts to her view.

"Three pretty maids all in a row," she mused aloud. "Well, I suppose I'd better get you back home."

The girls made such a protesting chorus of indignant grunts that Miss Newcombe tut-tutted and removed their gags.

"Just like that!" Melanie exclaimed, forcing her dry, stretched lips to shape the words. "No explanations?"

"Please tell us what's going on," said Sue.

"You know all you need to for now," Miss Newcombe said. "I will tell you more when the time is right."

"Hold on," Amber insisted. "You're from our version of England, right?"

"Yes," Miss Newcombe said patiently.

224

"And you got here using a phallus?"

"Yes."

"And using them again will get us back safely."

"You should return to your own world line - where, if you take my advice, you'll say nothing about what happened here. Nobody would believe you anyway."

"Well I don't know about these two," Melanie said, "but there'll be plenty of people looking for me by now. They'll need some sort of explanation."

"Nobody is looking for you, PC Kingston," Miss Newcombe said simply. "Your colleagues think you are with friends recovering from a touch of pneumonia brought on by too much running about Hoakam Woods in all weathers."

"What! Why do they think that?"

"Because I, in the guise of a friend, told them so. There are several get-well cards waiting for you, by the way. Also a suitable doctor's certificate - please don't ask how it was obtained. However the deception could not have been played out much longer. I was so pleased the boys took you away from the Major when they did. The whole thing was very well planned, Amber. Congratulations."

Amber ignored the compliment. "You've done this sort of thing before, haven't you?" she said.

"I've told you quite enough for now," Miss Newcombe said. "Time we were getting away."

"Wait!" Amber implored. "You couldn't have known we'd all arrive as we did, yet you knew everything that was going on and managed to make it work out exactly as you wanted. How?"

"I've had my eye on the boys for some time, for reasons I will not go into now. To keep abreast of their activities I planted miniature transmitting microphones in their dormitory, the old stables, the cricket pavilion and a few other places. The receiver, connected to a tape recorder, is upstairs. Common surveillance devices in our world, but unknown here. With them I was able to hear everything you and they said. I knew the boys were planning to take their revenge on Arabella and intended to use that to gain a measure of control over them. Your arrival was a surprise, but I adjusted my plans to suit. In fact, things have worked out better than expected." She checked her watch. "Now we really must be going."

She rummaged amongst their possessions and brought out the three phalluses. "It was a clever idea to get Arabella to bring you Susan's phallus as part of a ransom deal," she said to Amber. "I was wondering how I would recover that one."

"The phallus I used felt dead once it had done its thing," Amber said. "How do you make it work again?"

Miss Newcombe unscrewed the handle from the shaft of a phallus and held out the two halves. "You re-set by screwing them together again."

Amber groaned. "I didn't think to try anything as simple as that!"

"But what are they?" Melanie asked. "Is there some sort of mechanism inside them or are they...?"

"I don't know what they are," Miss Newcombe admitted, pushing furniture aside to leave a clear space on the floor. "Perhaps they're part of a science the world has forgotten. I do know the phalluses only transport people who truly belong here. You have all fitted in rather well, have you not?" She gave them a searching stare. "In fact, I suspect you are in two minds whether to go back or not. You have found excitement, challenge and satisfaction here. Home may seem rather dull by comparison."

It was the truth and the girls knew it. How easy to accept their bondage and submit to masterful people, such as the woman who even now looked down at them with her assured gaze. With an effort, Melanie said: "If we're going to go, let's do it quickly."

Tight lipped, Amber nodded in agreement.

"If I'm really a natural slave, then maybe I should stay," Sue asked hesitantly.

"Don't worry, I'll take care of you," Amber·reassured her. "You can be my secret slave back home. Would you like that?"

Sue gave a shy smile and nodded.

Miss Newcombe had taken several items from a locked cabinet. One in particular caught Amber's eye. "The phallus box! How did you get that?"

"I took the phallus from your bag the boys had hidden in their dormitory the first chance I had," Miss Newcombe explained. "I gambled that after only a couple of days, the box it came from would still be in Hoakam woods, and I was right. By default, a phallus will automatically take its user back to its parent box. I brought it with me and returned the phallus to your bag. Now it's here, I can adjust the settings to send you back..." She pressed on the hidden catches and opened the box, then tapped a combination into the keyboard built into the lid. "There. Now let's get you all arranged properly."

She laid Sue's bike on its side and dragged Sue over to it, tying her securely to the frame. "It's remarkable that you brought something as large as your bike and baggage with you," she told Sue. "You obviously have a talent for transporting inanimate materials, and that can be put to good use." Sue smiled uncertainly. Miss Newcombe dragged Amber and Melanie onto the open floor, laid them beside Sue and strapped their holdall and backpack onto them. "Usually the only inanimate objects that can be carried are the clothes one is wearing and small items such as your bags."

Miss Newcombe produced two lengths of stick and a reel of adhesive tape. She fastened the ends of the sticks to Sue and Amber's ankles, so that they pointed upwards between their thighs. More tape secured the handle sections of two phalluses to the upper ends of the sticks, so they they brushed their pubic lips. Miss Newcombe laid the heads of the matching phalluses on their stomachs.

Holding the last phallus in her hand she added: "Other living beings can be carried with you quite easily, provided there is plenty of skin contact."

She hitched up her skirt and pulled off her pants, then stood astride Melanie and squatted down so that she sat on Melanie's face. She squirmed her hips to settle herself in place, squeezing her thighs together. "I want to feel your tongue inside me, girl... that's better."

Reaching over she screwed the heads onto the handles of Sue and Amber's phalluses, pushing the carved heads into their clefts, then assembled the phallus she was holding.

The air warmed and thickened. Distant sounds faded away. Each girl felt a tingle spring into being in her loins. The blood surged through them and their nipples stood up, becoming rock hard in seconds. The tingle became an ache, then a sense of terrible emptiness. Their lovelips thickened and ran with lubrication as the need to be filled overwhelmed them.

Clasping a plump dark breast in one hand, Miss Newcombe plunged the phallus into the waiting tunnel of Melanie's vagina and began to work it back and forth. Sue and Amber instinctively, helplessly, bent their knees in a frantic effort to drive their stick-mounted phalluses deeper up into them.

Hard ivory parted soft flesh. The air filled with the intimate scent of sex. The girls rode a gathering wave of desire to its summit...

Everything blurred. There was a monstrous wrenching, twisting sensation. Something seemed to snap within them as they climaxed ecstatically...

Then the cottage living room was empty.

Epilogue: In Another Place

Sometime later in the kennels of Markham Hall...
The police team had come and gone. The packgirls were out at work. The yard gates were shut and bolted. The sun shone. Peace had returned... and George Platt was giving Alison her first practical lesson in bondslavery.

He fought to keep his voice steady, trying to sound businesslike and a little gruff.

"Now, being a new girl I want to see how well you move. Bitches must be graceful on two legs as well as four. Trot round in a circle for a minute. Lift your knees high..."

Alison was naked except for flat running shoes. A bridle harness was buckled about her head, her white teeth biting down on a rubber bit. Despite the stretching of the skin about her mouth she appeared to be smiling. Her shaggy mane of sun-bleached blonde hair was tied back in a ponytail to hold it clear of the unnumbered collar round her neck, clipped to which was the training rein George held. Her arms were confined high behind her back in a sheath binding that enclosed them from wrists to elbows, making her throw her chest out. Her breasts were pert and delightful...

Platt tried to assess her body critically, as he would any other girl.

Her breasts were small, firm, high-set mounds with light brown conical nipples, showing full in proportion to their setting. Her build was sturdy, arms strong, good shoulders and back, stomach well defined, hips not wide. Perhaps a good runner, she had strong thighs and very round bottom cheeks. Her pubic bush was neat and sparse, with dark pink inner lips already showing, a sign of eagerness, perhaps...?

Alison trotted round him, her breasts jiggling neatly, tiny shivers running over the roundness of her buttocks. Platt swallowed hard at the sight, then moistened his lips: "Knees a little higher!" he ordered, and flicked the tail of the whip across her bouncing bottom, perfectly catching the undercurve of the twin cheeks.

Alison flinched and gave a little gasp from behind her bit, but she held step and obediently lifted her knees an inch higher.

Platt thrilled within himself. He had put his whip mark on that lovely, sweet girl's body - and she had accepted it!

He ran her until she began to bead with sweat, then reined her in.

"That was quite good, girl. Now we'll try it with a tail in. That alters the posture. You'll have to learn how to show it off to the best advantage."

His pulse racing, he led Alison into cool leather-scented haven of the Harness Room, and bent her over the padded trestle he had placed ready. Spreading her legs wide he strapped her ankles to one pair of the trestle legs, then, freeing her arms from the sheath, he fastened her wrists to the other pair.

For a moment he feasted on the sight of her docile body doubled over and so perfectly presented to him.

Her neat tight cunt pouch glistened, the petals of her inner lips pouting as though about to bloom with the promise of treasures yet to be unlocked. Fighting to keep his hands steady, he pried apart her firm buttocks and examined the pink eye of her anus with its fine starburst of crinkles.

"Hmmm. Looks tight. Ever had a tail plug or a dildo inside you girl?" he asked, knowing perfectly well the answer.

Alison shook her head.

"Then you may need a little stretching before we put a tail in. Don't worry, girl, you'll get used to it..."

He dipped his finger into a pot of lubricant and slid it carefully inside her hot, tight bottomhole. Lovely! He could feel the elasticity of her secret passage and knew the delights it could give. He introduced a second finger, working her entrance hole wider.

"Let yourself relax," he told her. "A packgirl has to be easy to enter. Rears are naturally tight, no need to make it any harder.

230

Just work your hips back and forward on my fingers... yes, good rhythm. Keep it up..." He gulped. "Now we'll try something a little thicker..."

He unbuttoned his flies and released his straining cock. He took up position between her pale moon cheeks and pushed forward, his plum sliding between the greased cheeks, touching the tiny pothole that was the gateway to heaven. A quick lunge. Penetration! The muscular ring of her anus stretched wide then slid over his cockhead and he sank all the way into her. Alison gave a tiny yelp and moan of surprise at the sensation, but she did not struggle; accepting the unnatural but so very rewarding violation of her person without protest.

Platt closed his eyes and bit his lip in joy, easing gently in and out of her clinging tunnel. The moist heat of her! How he wished he could be the only man ever to use her like this! There would be no rushing Alison's training. He would try out every device in the Harness Room on her. She would perform every service expected of a packgirl - and all just for him.

He let the pressure grow slowly within him as he rode Alison to the climax, slapping her bottom to keep her working herself to and fro against him, ensuring every thrust penetrated her to the hilt. In time her rear passage would accommodate itself to him like a lock to a key.

Alison's breathing was rasping round her bit and she jerked at her straps as the stimulation she was receiving forced her to the inevitable. Her sphincter squeezed desperately tight round his shaft as though she wanted his cock plugging her for ever. He felt her go into spasm as his own need could no longer be contained, and he pumped his essence into her soft, welcoming entrails.

And in that moment George Platt knew perfection.

He had the best job anyone could wish for. He was master of the sweetest, most pliant kennelmaid ever known, and keeper of the Markham bitches, the finest girlpack in the south of England!

And now for the opening of next months title "ROYAL SLAVE: A Slaveworld Story" by Stephen Douglas

CHAPTER ONE

Laughter, light and occasional squeaks of female pain spilled out of the Summer Palace's open windows onto the moonlit lawn; a small but vocal hen-party finally winding down. The party had been going on for well over twenty four hours, the young Ladies who moved in Royal circles priding themselves on partying hard. On the wide gravel driveway in front of the grand house, having been waiting since noon to take the departing guests to the mag-lev station two miles away, were three identical four-wheeled carriages.

Naked but for tightly buckled and polished harnesses and bridles holding bits between teeth, pony-slaves waited with placid patience in the traces. A pair of powerful pony-boys were hitched to one carriage, the remaining two were pulled by teams of four pony-girls. At the head of the row beside the first team, idly stroking a pony-girl on the belly, fingers following a tight crotch-strap down into her pussy to the base of the fat dildo that impaled her, a bored groom waited to remove hobbles and assist the young aristocrats into the carriages. Strap-bound breasts, nipple-rings trailing reins, rose and fell faster as he petted the young slave. She was quite lovely, but of little real interest. As a private he was allowed to handle the slaves but no more. He was dreamily looking forward to the day when he'd be a corporal, allowed to tit-fuck the female slaves; or better yet, the day he was promoted to a sergeant, allowed to come in their mouths. He wiped juices off his fingers on a firm, velvet thigh.

Another squeal followed by gales of laughter came from the open windows above. Princess Alice had a taste for slender blonde girls and owned over a dozen at the last count, and no doubt several were providing the entertainment as well as serving.

The Summer Palace was the Royal Family's country retreat, available for parties, events, or just a place for individual members of the family to enjoy a weekend break or a couple of weeks away from the bustle of the city. It was mostly used by hunting parties on the nearby Royal Hunting Preserve. Compared to the City Palace, the three storey building in the style of Richard IV was quite modest. The structure had replaced the far grander building of the same name destroyed by fire some 400 years earlier. That had dated from the 10th century, when the entire Royal Family had transplanted itself to the country to escape a noxious city only just discovering drains. Prince Samuel's suite was on the second floor, the King and Queen occupying the third floor between them.

Half listening to the wall-muffled excesses of the party Cousin Alice was hosting; Prince Samuel, the Prince of Wales, lying naked on a large four-poster bed watching 3V, was alone in his suite apart from some slaves. A girl he'd brought down on the hunt was chained face-down across the top of the bed so that he could use the small of her back as a pillow; the slave-boy he'd shot at the same time was locked in a corner cage. Beside his bed on all fours was a naked girl with a large clear oval of glass strapped to her back, a leather band tight around her waist. His human table would obediently crawl to one side of the bed or the other to be within reach as he wished. The suite's two naked serving-slaves were standing neatly to attention in their chains and collars beside the buffet table.

Secured to a ceiling winch, some of his come in her ass and some now drying on her breasts, was the main course; a newly purchased sexual-plaything, appropriately called Treasure, and she was quite simply gorgeous. In the four days she'd been his legal property, he'd enjoyed her many times, but he wasn't anywhere near finished with her yet. He would of course get bored with her eventually, he always did, and a new sex-toy would catch his eye. But for the moment, he was madly in lust. The top-heavy brunette was a spectacularly satisfying screw!

She wasn't the most expensive slave he'd ever bought. He'd spent more on competition and racing slaves, but never half as much on a purely sexual toy. She wasn't even the most beautiful he'd ever owned. The delicate, olive-skinned, Arab slave-girl, with lustrous dark eyes he'd been given by his grandmother on his last birthday was stunning by comparison. But Treasure was the most sexually exciting animal he'd come across in many a season. To see Treasure was to want her! When he'd first come across her in harness and bridle, pulling the pony-trap of a fellow hunter, his first reaction had been lust, he wanted to train her to sit up and beg, and then lick every inch of her body.

Treasure was a tall girl, powerfully built, with long legs, a neatly tucked waist, and large, full breasts. She had golden skin, pink nipples, a sweet heart-shaped face, long dark hair and wide, appealing, light-hazel eyes. Pretty yes, but a photo or holograph gave no real hint of her sexual allure. The draw she had on him, and almost every Lord or Lady who encountered her, even leaving aside her love of sex and subservient nature, puzzled him. But certainly added to her attraction! She'd been worth every crown he paid for her.

Life was good! Happy in himself and more than satisfied so far with his new sex-toy's stamina, endurance and willingness to please, he contentedly reached up to pat one of his pillow's firm buttocks. The mark of his shot was gone, but it was still a shot to be proud of. A single shot to the ass at over a hundred yards! Tranquilliser rifles had to be low velocity or the dart acted like a bullet, and the standard hunting rifle was generally reckoned to be accurate in the fifty to seventy five yard range. A great hunt!

He really ought to give the girl, and the male prey-slave in the cage, a quick shafting as a reward for running so hard and providing him and his fellow hunters with such excellent sport. He usually thoroughly enjoyed sex with prey-slaves he'd personally brought down, but his new purchase, the delightfully top-heavy Treasure, was patently more deserving of his attention.

"Table!" he called, waving a hand off the edge of the bed.

The table-slave looked up through the glass and edged closer, the oval surface strapped to her back about four foot by three, held perfectly steady. Like many table-slaves she was a little heavy around the hindquarters, broad hips and shoulders and plump buttocks were needed to keep the glass surface steady as she crawled along on all fours; but she would be pleasant to whip along at a trot as a carriage-slave. And she'd undoubtedly be of interest to any devotees of the traditional art of spanking. Her buttocks were squashed quite attractively against the glass's underside, two white ovals squeezed together. He nibbled a pastry then washed it down with champagne, his glass clicking on the table just above the girl's head when he returned it. He brushed her from his mind.

Human furniture was commonplace in noble houses; using slaves as footstools, pillows, cushions, benches, tables, foodtrays, swings and hammocks, was unremarkable. It was actually the kind thing to do when a slave wasn't required for other use. Instead of sitting alone and bored in her little cell, the slave was provided with a little variety, stimulation and interest. Allowed the privilege of being in the presence of her betters, she got to watch and learn as other toys were enjoyed, and so improve her own performance when she was next used for sex.

There was laughter below his window, shrieks and protests, the hen-party which Cousin Alice had been hosting was finally breaking up and spilling out onto the driveway below. A pony-girl squealed as leather landed on flesh with a delicious crack. Levering himself upright on the bed, Prince Samuel was just in time to see two carriages, pony-slaves responding with delightful little squeaks and yelps as they were lashed, tear across the lawn. The two teams of pony-girls were neck-and-neck, the third carriage following closely, each with three or four young Ladies the worse for drink, hanging on. He chuckled, flopping back down onto his bed. Real racing slaves, singly or in pairs, pulled a single driver in a small two-wheeled pony-trap. Carriage slaves, not normally selected or trained for speed, whipped to a sprint, could easily overturn their much larger, less stable, four-wheeled burden. And his mother, the Queen, was going to go berserk when she saw the state of her lawn!

On the three-dimensional television, the consumer programme 'What Slave', was testing shock-batons. Normally the presenter of a 3V program would be a personable young soldier, perhaps a distinguished older NCO for a more serious programme. But occasionally, for fun, a hobby, to annoy parents or simply because they were stage-struck, a young aristocrat would face the camera. It was one of those supposedly menial tasks, like training circus-slaves, that parents were supposed to disapprove of, but had probably done themselves in their youth.

"Cattle-prods, shock-dildos, shock-batons," the presenter, young, female and bouncy, was saying. "Call them what you will. But the important question is, how safe is yours?"

The young aristocrat patted the rump of the bound, naked, girl beside her. The test-slave, a large breasted blonde, was bent forward over a horizontal pole, ankles chained wide, her body pulled forward and arched up by a chain from her wrist-cuffs. A high collar held her head up so that her ball-gagged face was visible to the camera.

"Time to find out. Now Goldie's already had a few shocks to the clitoris and nipples, so she's nicely wet. Let's see how she takes the 2000-SI."

The helpless blonde gasped behind her gag as the young presenter rammed the shock-dildo deep into her pouting sex, breasts quivering as she jerked to the limit of her bonds. A lingering close-up showed wide blue eyes, the test-slave drooling around the pink ball strapped into her mouth. Presenters

236

came and went, but the full-breasted blonde was a familiar and popular feature of the programme, and not for sale at any price. Bought as an eighteen year old virgin by the show, she looked about 25 now, but had had the youth-treatment and had to be coming up for fifty years old. Prince Samuel remembered watching whips, racks and restraints tested on her a good twenty years ago.

The rejuvenation treatment that had held twenty years at bay was usually the preserve of the aristocracy, slaves' sentences usually ending when they were about thirty and could be returned to families and communities. But occasionally, if a slave was in some way special, he or she could be kept young and the sentence increased. His new purchase, Treasure, had already been given the treatment.

Goldie squealed in pain as the young presenter triggered the shock-baton, delivering a jolt of agony deep inside her pussy, once, twice and then three times.

"Now as you can see if you look closely, on the cheaper copy the dildo will not screw flush onto the battery-pack, leaving a small gap. And if you have a wet girl, and push the dildo in up to the hilt, slave-juice inside the battery can produce a short-circuit; which can give the user a very nasty shock!"

The image pulled back to reveal the presenter's proper look of outraged horror.

"In fact, in some tests the user was getting almost as powerful a shock as the slave!" she whispered in tones of earnest and solemn disapproval.

Her irrepressible grin bounced back as she inserted the second shock-dildo into the helpless Goldie from behind.

To be continued...

The cover photograph for this book and many others are
available as limited edition prints.
Write to:-

Viewfinders Photography
PO Box 200,
Reepham
Norfolk
NR10 4SY

for details, or see,

www.viewfinders.org.uk

TITLES IN PRINT

Silver Mink

UK £4.99 except *£5.99 --USA $8.95 except *$9.95

All titles, both in print and out of print, are available as electronic downloads at:

http://www.adultbookshops.com

**e-mail submissions to:
Editor@electronicbookshops.com**

TITLES IN PRINT

Silver Moon

*UK £4.99 except *£5.99 --USA $8.95 except *$9.95*